Two men wearing ski mask
the passenger side of the ca
to side, attempting to flip it.

"Get down," yelled Zack. With one swift motion, he released my seatbelt and pushed me to the floor.

A moment later a shot rang out.

Acclaim for the Anastasia Pollack Crafting Mysteries

Assault with a Deadly Glue Gun

"Crafty cozies don't get any better than this hilarious confection...Anastasia is as deadpan droll as Tina Fey's Liz Lemon, and readers can't help cheering as she copes with caring for a host of colorful characters." – *Publishers Weekly* (starred review)

"Winston has hit a homerun with this hilarious, laugh-until-your-sides-hurt tale. Oddball characters, uproariously funny situations, and a heroine with a strong sense of irony." – *Booklist* (starred review)

"A comic tour de force...Lovers of funny mysteries, outrageous puns, self-deprecating humor, and light romance will all find something here." – *ForeWord Magazine* (Book-of-the-Year nominee)

"North Jersey's more mature answer to Stephanie Plum. Funny, gutsy, and determined, Anastasia has a bright future in the planned series." – *Kirkus Reviews*

"...a delightful romp through the halls of who-done-it." – *The Star-Ledger*

"Make way for Lois Winston's promising new series...I'll be eagerly awaiting the next installment in this thoroughly delightful series." – *Mystery Scene Magazine*

"...madcap but tough-as-nails, no holds barred plot and main character...a step above the usual crafty cozy." – *The Mystery Reader*

"...once you read the first few pages of Lois Winston's first-in-series whodunit, you're hooked for the duration..." – *Bookpage*

"...Anastasia is, above all, a JERSEY girl..., and never, ever mess with one of them. I can't wait 'til the next book in this series..." – *Suspense Magazine*

"Anastasia is as crafty as Martha Stewart, as feisty as Stephanie Plum, and as resourceful as Kinsey Millhone." – Mary Kennedy, author of the Talk Radio Mysteries

"Fans of Stephanie Plum will love Lois Winston's cast of quirky, laughable, and loveable characters. *Assault with a Deadly Glue Gun* is clever and thoroughly entertaining—a must read!" – Brenda Novak, *New York Times* best-selling author

"What a treat—I can't stop laughing! Witty, wise, and delightfully clever, Anastasia is going to be your new best friend. Her mysterious adventures are irresistible—you'll be glued to the page!" – Hank Phillippi Ryan, Agatha, Anthony, and Macavity award-winning author

"You think you've got trouble? Say hello to Anastasia Pollack, who also happens to be queen of the one-liners. Funny, funny, funny— this is a series you don't want to miss!" – Kasey Michaels, *USA Today* best-selling author

Death by Killer Mop Doll
"Anastasia is a crafting Stephanie Plum, surrounded by characters sure to bring chuckles as she careens through the narrative, crossing paths with the detectives assigned to the case and snooping around to solve it." – *Booklist*

"Several crafts projects, oodles of laughs and an older, more centered version of Stephanie Plum." – *Kirkus Reviews*

"In Winston's droll second cozy featuring crafts magazine editor Anastasia Pollack...readers who relish the offbeat will be rewarded." – *Publishers Weekly*

"...a *30 Rock* vibe...Winston turns out another lighthearted amateur sleuth investigation. Laden with one-liners, Anastasia's second outing (after *Assault With a Deadly Glue Gun*) points to another successful series in the works." – *Library Journal*

"Winston...plays for plenty of laughs...while letting Anastasia shine as a risk-taking investigator who doesn't always know when to quit." – *Alfred Hitchcock Mystery Magazine*

Revenge of the Crafty Corpse
"Winston peppers the twisty and slightly edgy plot with humor and plenty of craft patterns. Fans of craft mysteries will like this, of course, but so will those who enjoy the smart and snarky humor of Janet Evanovich...." – *Booklist*

"Winston's entertaining third cozy plunges Anastasia into a surprisingly fraught stew of jealousy, greed, and sex..." and a "Sopranos-worthy lineup of eccentric character..." – *Publishers Weekly*

"A fun addition to a series that keeps getting stronger." – *Romantic Times Magazine*

"Chuckles begin on page one and the steady humor sustains a comedic crafts cozy ... Recommend for Chris Grabenstein ("John Ceepak" series) and Jess Lourey readers." – *Library Journal*

"You'll be both surprised and entertained by this terrific mystery." – *Suspense Magazine*

"The book has what a mystery should...It moves along at a good pace...Like all good sleuths, Anastasia pieces together what others don't." – *Star-Ledger*

Decoupage Can Be Deadly
"*Decoupage Can Be Deadly* is the fourth in the Anastasia Pollock

Crafting Mysteries by Lois Winston. And it's the best one yet. More, please!" – *Suspense Magazine*

"What a great cozy mystery series...Every single character in these books is awesomely quirky and downright hilarious. This series is a true laugh out loud read!" – Books Are Life–Vita Libri

"This is one of these series that no matter what, I'm going to be laughing my way through a comedy of errors as our reluctant heroine sets a course of action to find a killer while contending with her eccentrically dysfunctional family. This adventure grabs you immediately delivering a fast-paced and action-filled drama that doesn't let up from the first page to the surprising conclusion." – Dru's Book Musings

A Stitch to Die For
"If you're a reader who enjoys a well-plotted mystery and loves to laugh, don't miss this one!" – *Suspense Magazine*

Scrapbook of Murder
"This is one of the best books in this delightfully entertaining whodunit and I hope there are more stories in the future." – Dru's Book Musings

"...a perfect example of what mysteries are all about—deft plotting, believable characters, well-written dialogue, and a satisfying, logical ending. I loved it!" – *Suspense Magazine*

"I read an amazing book recently, y'all — *Scrapbook of Murder* by Lois Winston, #6 in the Anastasia Pollack Crafting Mysteries. All six novels and three novellas in the series are Five Star reads." – Jane Reads

"...a quick read, with humour, a good mystery and very interesting characters!" – Verietats

Drop Dead Ornaments

"I always forget how much I love this series until I read the next one and I fall in love all over again..." – Dru's Book Musings

"...a delightful addition to the Anastasia Pollack Crafting Mystery series. More, please!" – *Suspense Magazine*

"I love protagonist Anastasia Pollack. She's witty and funny, and she can be sarcastic at times...A great whodunit, with riotous twists and turns, *Drop Dead Ornaments* was a fast, exciting read that really kept me on my toes." – Lisa Ks Book reviews

"*Drop Dead Ornaments* is such a fantastic book...I adore Anastasia! She's clever, likable, fun to read about, and easy to root for." – Jane Reads

"...readers will be laughing continually at the antics of Anastasia and clan in *Drop Dead Ornaments*." – The Avid Reader

"I love this series! Not only is Anastasia a 'crime magnet,' she is hilarious and snarky, a delight to read about and a dedicated friend." – Mallory Heart's Cozies

"It is always a nice surprise when something I am reading has a tie in to actual news or events that are happening in the present moment. I don't want to spoil a major plot secret, but the timing could not have been better...Be prepared for a dysfunctional cast of quirky characters." – Laura's Interests

"This is a Tour de Force of a Murder/Mystery." – A Wytch's Book Review

"Lois Winston's cozy craft mystery *Drop Dead Ornaments* is an enjoyable...roller-coaster ride, with secrets and clues tugging the reader this way and that, and gentle climbs and drops of suspense and revelation to keep them reading." – Here's How It Happened

"...a light-hearted cozy mystery with lots of energy and definitely lots of action and interaction between characters." – Curling Up By the Fire

Handmade Ho-Ho Homicide

"Handmade Ho-Ho Homicide" is a laugh-out-loud, well plotted mystery, from a real pro! A ho-ho hoot!" – *Suspense Magazine*

"Merry *Crises*! Lois Winston has brought back Anastasia's delightful first-person narrative of family, friends, dysfunction, and murder, and made it again very entertaining! Anastasia's clever quips, fun stories, and well-deserved digs kept me smiling, and reading the many funny parts to my husband...does that count as two thumbs up in one?" – *Kings River Life Magazine*

"Once again, the author knows how to tell a story that immediately grabbed my attention and I couldn't put this book down until the last page was read.... This was one of the best books in this delightfully lovable series and I can't wait to see what exciting adventures await Anastasia and her friends." – Dru's Book Musings

"The story had me on the edge of my seat the entire time." – 5 Stars, Baroness Book Trove

"Christmas, cozy mystery, craft, how can I not love this book? Humor, twists and turns, adorable characters make this story truly engaging from the first to the last page." – LibriAmoriMiei

"Take a murder mystery, add some light-hearted humor and weird characters, sprinkle some snow and what you get is *Handmade Ho-Ho Homicide*—a perfect Christmas Cozy read." –5 stars, The Book Decoder

A Sew Deadly Cruise

"*A Sew Deadly Cruise* is absolutely delightful, and I was sorry when it was over. I devoured every word!" – *Suspense* Magazine

"Engaging Drama! Brilliant! *A Sew Deadly Cruise* earns 5/5 Upgraded Cabins. Winston's witty first-person narrative and banter keeps me a fan. Loved it!" –*Kings River Life* Magazine

"The author knows how to tell a story with great aplomb and when all was said and done, this was one fantastic whodunit that left me craving for more thrilling adventures." – Dru's Book Musings

"The combo of investigating and fun makes for a great read. The author does a good job of keeping the killer a secret. Overall a fun read that cozy fans are sure to enjoy." – Books a Plenty Book Reviews

"Winston has a gift for writing complicated cozy mysteries while entertaining and educating." – Here's How it Happened

Stitch, Bake, Die!

"Lois Winston has crafted another clever tale...with a backdrop of cross stitching, buttercream, bribery, sabotage, rumors, and murder...with vivid descriptions, witty banter, and clever details leading to an exciting and shocking conclusion. All making for a page-turner experience to delight cozy fans." – *Kings River Life* magazine

"...a crème de la crème of a cozy read." – Brianne's Book Reviews

"...a well-plotted mystery that takes the term 'crafty old lady' to new heights." – Mysteries with Character

"...fast-paced with wacky characters, a fun resort setting, and a puzzling mystery to solve." – Nancy J. Cohen, author of the Bad Hair Day Mysteries

"Lots of action, a bevy of quirky characters, and a treasure trove of secrets add up to another fine read from Lois Winston." – mystery author Maggie Toussaint/Valona Jones

"The mystery was nicely executed, with bits and pieces of clues here and there as well as humorous interludes that enhanced the telling of this tale. This is another great addition to this engagingly entertaining series and I'm patiently waiting for the wedding of the century." – Dru's Book Musings

Guilty as Framed

"Engaging and clever!" – Kings River Life Magazine

"Check out *Guilty as Framed*, another outrageously funny mystery in (the Anastasia Pollack Crafting Mysteries)" – Suspense Magazine

"This is another great entry in the Anastasia Pollack series." – Dru's Book Musings

"Winston not only combines (New) Jersey, well-crafted characters, and tight plotting, but she adds her own interpretation and possible solution to a factual museum art crime." – Debra H. Goldstein, author of the Sarah Blair Mysteries

"Author Lois Winston deftly frames the fast-moving investigation...with a dollop of mother-in-law hijinks, mama drama, home renovation, and doggie intervention." – mystery author Maggie Toussaint/Valona Jones

"Reading a book in this series is like visiting an old friend." – Nancy J. Cohen, author of the Bad Hair Day Mysteries

Books by Lois Winston

Anastasia Pollack Crafting Mystery series
Assault with a Deadly Glue Gun
Death by Killer Mop Doll
Revenge of the Crafty Corpse
Decoupage Can Be Deadly
A Stitch to Die For
Scrapbook of Murder
Drop Dead Ornaments
Handmade Ho-Ho Homicide
A Sew Deadly Cruise
Stitch, Bake, Die!
Guilty as Framed
A Crafty Collage of Crime

Anastasia Pollack Crafting Mini-Mysteries
Crewel Intentions
Mosaic Mayhem
Patchwork Peril
Crafty Crimes (all 3 novellas in one volume)

Empty Nest Mystery Series
Definitely Dead
Literally Dead

Romantic Suspense
Love, Lies and a Double Shot of Deception
Lost in Manhattan (writing as Emma Carlyle)
Someone to Watch Over Me (writing as Emma Carlyle)

Romance and Chick Lit
Talk Gertie to Me
Four Uncles and a Wedding (writing as Emma Carlyle)
Hooking Mr. Right (writing as Emma Carlyle)
Finding Hope (Writing as Emma Carlyle)

Novellas and Novelettes
Elementary, My Dear Gertie
Moms in Black, A Mom Squad Caper
Once Upon a Romance
Finding Mr. Right

Children's Chapter Book
The Magic Paintbrush

Nonfiction
Top Ten Reasons Your Novel is Rejected
House Unauthorized
Bake, Love, Write
We'd Rather Be Writing

A Crafty
Collage
Of Crime

LOIS WINSTON

Cover design by L. Winston

ISBN:978-1-940795-72-0

DEDICATION

To the readers who have fallen in love with Anastasia and her wacky family. You're the reason I hole up in my writer's cave and continue pecking away at the keyboard.

ACKNOWLEDGMENTS

As I've often done in the past, once again I offered character naming rights to one of my newsletter subscribers. Mariah Clatterbuck won the honor this time. Really, how could I not choose her? What a great name! And perfect for one of the characters Anastasia meets when she and Zack travel to Tennessee.

I'm extremely grateful to the members at CrimeSceneWriters. They freely share their professional expertise and keep us authors from making boneheaded mistakes in our books. For this book, author James L'Etoile, who spent two decades working in the criminal justice system, took the time to answer my questions about prisons.

And finally, as always, special thanks to Donnell Bell and Irene Peterson for their superb editorial skills.

ONE

Food editor Cloris McWerther stared bug-eyed at me, nearly dropping the coffee cup she held as I entered the break room. "Aren't you supposed to be in Barcelona on your honeymoon?"

"Change of plans," I said, grabbing a chocolate and raspberry croissant from the bakery box on the table.

Her left eyebrow disappeared under her wispy pixie bangs. "Should I be worried?"

"Only for my waistline."

"Said the woman currently scarfing down a croissant." She resumed pouring coffee and handed me the cup. "Why is there a correlation between your weight and a postponed honeymoon?"

"Not postponed, just slightly altered." I settled into one of the four molded plastic chairs around the circular table that took up much of the small room. "We're leaving tomorrow."

Cloris poured a second cup and took the seat opposite me. "Why the change?"

Zachary Barnes, photojournalist and possible spy (although he vehemently denies the latter), and I had married nine days ago in an intimate backyard wedding attended by close family and friends. Originally Zack and I had planned to jet off to Barcelona this morning for a bicycle tour of the city and surrounding towns. It had the makings of the perfect trip. I could eat tapas and various local delicacies to my heart's content, knowing I'd bike off the calories between meals. Or at least some of the calories. Given my aversion to exercise, I'd opted for a multi-speed bike that promised no huffing or puffing as we tooled around the Catalan countryside.

Last year I'd accompanied Zack to Barcelona for a weekend photo assignment. However, shortly after we had arrived, a couple of clueless kidnappers put a crimp in our mini vacation. At least my abductors had released me once they realized they'd grabbed the wrong woman.

Unfortunately, I wasn't so lucky with my more recent run-in with kidnappers. As much as I tried to put the harrowing incident behind me, the trauma continued to replay every night in nightmarish episodes of REM sleep.

I added a generous splash of half-and-half to my coffee and took a swig before answering Cloris. "Given recent events, Zack and I decided to postpone Barcelona for something quieter and more secluded."

"Where are you going?"

"Middle Tennessee."

Cloris nearly snorted into her coffee. "Don't tell me you're going to Nashville."

When I nodded, she squinted as she eyed me. "Who are you, and what have you done with my best friend?"

"What do you mean?"

"The Anastasia Pollack I know is more Broadway Baby than Honky-Tonk Woman. Besides, I've been to Nashville. Quiet and secluded are hardly adjectives I'd use to describe the place."

"We're only flying into Nashville, and we're not going for the music."

"What else is there?"

"Wineries."

"Tennessee wine?" This time Cloris couldn't stifle the snort. "Are you sure you don't mean whiskey? Aren't Tennessee and Kentucky known for their distilleries?"

I shrugged. "Who knew, right?"

"Apparently, not me."

"Or me. But it turns out winemaking was a big industry in the area before Prohibition, and it's made a huge comeback."

"Good for them, but if you want to spend your honeymoon touring wineries, why not fly to Napa?"

"Because Zack accepted an assignment from *Vine* for a photo essay on the wineries of Middle Tennessee."

Her eyebrows knit together as she digested that nugget of information. "Isn't *Vine* one of the magazines that's part of our new acquisition?"

I nodded. Along with the other magazines headquartered with *American Woman* in an office building situated in a former cornfield in Morris County, New Jersey, Trimedia had recently acquired an Atlanta-based publisher of consumer food and beverage magazines.

"And they can afford to hire your Pulitzer prize-winning husband?" continued Cloris.

"Not only can they afford it, but they're also paying him a premium for squeezing them into his schedule."

3

"If Trimedia is so flush with cash, we should demand a raise."

"Yeah, I can just see the suits in the corner offices agreeing to that." I held my hands out in front of me, palms up, imitating a set of scales. "*Vine* revenues," I said moving my right hand above my head. Then I lowered my left hand below my waist. "*American Woman* revenues. I'll bet *Vine's* operating budget is at least five times what ours is."

"Or more," she grumbled before changing the subject. "So, Zack is going to work during your honeymoon?"

I nodded. "He was scheduled to do the shoot after we returned from Barcelona but moved it up when I suggested we change our plans. We're staying at one of the wineries that includes half a dozen guest cottages."

"Compliments of the magazine, I presume?"

"Presumption confirmed."

"Hmm...maybe I should see how Gregg feels about moving to Atlanta. I just might ask for a transfer to one of our new food magazines."

"Except that knowing Trimedia, they'll merge magazines, layoff personnel, and hire new, less experienced staff at much lower salaries."

"There is that." Cloris sighed. "Now is probably not the time to make waves."

"Now is never the time to make waves when it comes to Trimedia."

Cloris frowned. "True. Anyway, I suppose, minus Zack spending part of his time working, you'll have a romantic honeymoon."

I offered her a mischievous wink. "Count on it."

~*~

The next day found Zack and me in a rental car driving through the rolling verdant hills of Williamson County, Tennessee on our way to Three Sisters Winery. I was used to New Jersey, where, with few exceptions, most towns and cities abut one another, and the only way to tell you'd crossed from one community into another was either a change in street sign color or the occasional "Welcome to Insert-Name-of-Town-Here" roadside plaque.

That was hardly the case for the towns we passed once we headed out of Nashville. Forested acres, parks, and farmlands separated each community. Interspersed among these areas were newer subdivisions, ones under construction, and billboards announcing future subdivisions. Starting prices rivaling metro New York suggested the area's farms were quickly becoming a dying breed. At some point in the not-too-distant future, Middle Tennessee might look like North Jersey.

This made me wonder if Trimedia was really footing the bill for Zack's services. Perhaps the local wineries had cut a deal with *Vine* to hire a world-renowned photographer to best promote their businesses. A favorable spread in a widely circulated and well-respected wine magazine would draw wine connoisseurs from across the country to the region, boosting the bottom line of the wineries as well as local tourism, thus keeping land-grabbing developers at bay.

"Is this shoot editorial or advertorial?" I asked him.

"Beats me. Does it matter?"

"I suppose not, but it seems odd that Trimedia would hire you when they could send a staff photographer. Especially since they rattle off a litany of excuses every year when we complain about our annual raises. The last few years haven't even kept up with cost-of-living increases."

And I needed every penny I could scrounge.

When Karl Marx Pollack had dropped dead at a Las Vegas casino a year and a half ago, I'd learned both my happy marriage and my comfortable middle-class existence were both figments of my imagination. Rather than a sizable life insurance policy, I'd inherited my husband's gargantuan gambling debts, a Mount Everest of past-due bills, his mob-connected loan shark, *and* his communist mother.

You'd think I would have had a clue that something was rotten in Westfield, but I was ensconced in blissful ignorance throughout my entire marriage.

That's how Zack and I met. As one of my cost-cutting measures, I'd rented him the apartment above my garage, which I'd previously used as my home office and studio. Zack had needed a place to crash between assignments and wanted to move out of the city.

What a guy who looks like he shares DNA with the likes of Pierce Brosnan and George Clooney sees in a pear-shaped forty-something widow with two teenage sons is beyond me, but who am I to question fate? I figured the universe owed me bigtime after the lollapalooza of a whammy it had recently dumped on me.

Although Zack could wipe out my monetary woes with one swipe of his pen and had offered on countless occasions, I repeatedly refuse his generosity. It's not his responsibility to assume the debts of my deceased deadbeat louse of a spouse. Of course, if he'd like to buy me a winning Powerball or MegaMillions ticket, I wouldn't turn down his two-dollar investment in my bottom line.

"You're suggesting advertorial, then?" he asked.

"Makes sense. Did you receive any guidelines for the shoot?"

"None."

"Isn't that unusual?"

He took his eyes off the road to offer me a quick wink. "My work speaks for itself."

"And yet you remain ever so humble."

"Always."

An understatement. The guy personified humility. It's one of his many charms. With no pithy retort on the tip of my tongue, I chuckled, then returned my attention to the scenery.

Several minutes later the disembodied woman living within the rental car's GPS announced, "You've arrived. Your destination is on your right."

A carved and painted wooden sign, reminiscent of Tiffany stained glass windows, stood at the entrance of a narrow tree-lined road. A border of deep green and purple grape-laden vines surrounding fanciful gold script announced *Three Sisters Winery*. As Zack drove along the winding lane that climbed upward through gently rolling hills, I caught glimpses of acres of neatly spaced rows of grapevines peeking through the stately red maples. Every so often, hints of a creek glistened in the distance.

Eventually, the road led us to a circular driveway in front of a two-story Southern-style plantation home reminiscent of Tara from *Gone with the Wind*. The road then forked to the left of the building. One fork led to a parking lot while the other continued toward a series of out-buildings. A path to the right of the house disappeared into an expansive manicured garden.

Before Zack had a chance to kill the engine, three women, dressed in matching deep purple bib aprons sporting the winery logo, stepped through the double-door entrance and onto the porch. One look at them told me they were the eponymous three sisters of the winery.

As we stepped from the car, they greeted us in unison with, "Welcome to Three Sisters Winery," punctuating their words with identical smiles.

We left our luggage and Zack's camera equipment in the trunk and crossed the short distance to the porch steps as the three women descended to meet us. "Thank you," said Zack. "We have a reservation under Zachary Barnes."

"Yes, the photographer," said one of the women offering Zack her hand. "We're looking forward to working with you, as are the other local wineries. We were so excited when you accepted the magazine assignment," she continued, placing her other hand over his. "You were the first choice of all the owners."

Definitely advertorial. Part of me was happy knowing Trimedia wasn't playing favorites with the corporate purse strings, but another part of me quickly realized the information meant none of the *American Woman* staff could use Zack's huge freelance fee as leverage when it came time to negotiate salary increases.

Zack laced the fingers of his free hand through mine and gently squeezed, having either read my mind or heard the sigh that escaped my lips. Then he tilted his head toward me and said, "And this is my wife An—"

"Oh, we know who *you* are," said one of the other sisters, cutting him off. She offered me a wide grin. The three women, all appearing to be somewhere in their late-forties to early-fifties, nodded vigorously. Now that we stood face to face, I could read their individual names, embroidered under the winery logo of their aprons. Each was named for a type of wine. The woman who claimed to know me was Marsala.

"Anastasia Pollack," said her sister Roussanne, reaching out to grab my free hand. "We're huge fans."

Zack and I shared a quick glance. Usually, he's the one swarmed by admirers, not me. After all, he's graced the cover of *People* magazine more than once. I pinch myself every morning as I wake up next to a former Sexiest Man of the Year. "You ladies are crafters?" I asked.

"Oh, my, no," said Constantia, the third sister. "Our only crafting is the art of crafting delicious wine and assorted wine products."

"Our lives are far too busy running the winery and B&B to have time for other endeavors," added Marsala.

"I'm afraid I don't understand," I said. "Then how do you know me?"

"From the podcasts, of course," said Constantia.

Now I was really perplexed. "I've never appeared on a podcast."

American Woman had recently ventured into podcasts for some of our editors. The medium lent itself more to discussions about health issues, travel, and fashion trends. We'd even recently bandied about the idea of starting an online book club with the editors and other staff choosing a favorite book to discuss each month.

However, Cloris and I needed visuals for recipes and craft projects. We connected better with our readers by producing short video demonstrations that were posted on our website and the magazine's YouTube channel.

"Perhaps you're confusing me with another Anastasia Pollack," I added. "It's not that uncommon a name."

"But there's only one Anastasia Pollack from New Jersey who's an amateur sleuth," said Roussanne. "That is you, isn't it?"

9

My mouth dropped open. "Are you saying someone has created a podcast about *me*?"

All three nodded. "*The Sleuth Sayer*," said Marsala. "You were the first sleuth she featured."

"She's already devoted three episodes to you," said Roussanne. "You really haven't heard of it?"

~*~

"How did I not know about that podcast?" I asked Zack after the sisters had checked us in and shown us to our guest cottage.

Our accommodations consisted of one large room with a king-size bed, a sitting area with two overstuffed chairs with matching ottomans, and an attached bathroom, complete with clawfoot tub.

The décor was quintessential *Southern Living*. Comfortable, inviting, and inspired by nature in both its color palette and the decorative elements scattered around the room, many of which, according to a framed sign on the dresser, were for sale in the gift shop. A large collage that incorporated old wine labels, photographs, and newspaper articles hung over the bed. If I wasn't currently so annoyed, I would have enjoyed studying the collage rather than giving it little more than a cursory glance.

"Maybe I should Google myself more often, but you'd think someone would have known a true-crime podcaster was blabbing about me all over cyberspace."

Zack dropped an armful of T-shirts into a dresser drawer and turned to face me. "Such as?"

"I don't know." Frustrated, I threw my arms up, then slapped my thighs. "Someone had to know. Tino? Spader? Ledbetter? All of them?"

Tino Martinelli worked in cyber-security. I once thought he

was trying to kill me. I was dead wrong. Pun intended. The guy had had my back on more than one occasion and had become a dear friend.

Detective Samuel Spader worked Union County Homicide, and Agent Aloysius Ledbetter was with the FBI. My reluctant amateur sleuthing had brought me in close contact with both men far more times than any normal law-abiding citizen would have cause to interact with law enforcement.

"How is this not an invasion of my privacy?" I asked, pacing along the hardwood floor from one end of the room to the other and back again.

"I don't know. Maybe it is, but I'm not a lawyer."

I stopped short and stared at him. "You think I should call a lawyer?"

He placed his hands on my shoulders and in a soothing tone said, "Why don't we first listen to the podcast before jumping to any conclusions?"

Why hadn't I thought of that? I inhaled deeply, then slowly released the air in my lungs in an attempt at manifesting a calming breath. It didn't help much. I've never been very good at the Zen thing. But Zack was right. Maybe this was all a nothing burger. Although, I failed to conjure up any scenario where such a possibility seemed feasible.

"When we drove in, I noticed a dirt path with a sign indicating the creek and a walking trail," he said.

"So?"

He grabbed his camera and pulled a set of earbuds from his pocket. "Let's take a stroll and listen to what this Sleuth Sayer has to say about you."

Zack handed me one of the earbuds and placed the other in his ear. Then he found the podcast on his phone. As we headed toward the path, a few bars of music played before a woman began to speak.

An old African proverb states that it takes a village to raise a child. Sometimes, though, it takes one woman's courage and determination to protect the people of that village from those who would do them harm.

I tried to identify the narrator's voice, but I couldn't think of anyone I knew who spoke in a rich dulcet British accent.

Throughout our country and the world, unremarkable women are doing remarkable things—solving crimes and bringing the perpetrators to justice, often with little or no recognition of their accomplishments.

In fiction these women are called amateur sleuths, but there are many of them walking among us, unsung heroines with no law enforcement training who find themselves in unusual situations where they're spurred into action.

I've made it my mission to tell the world about these courageous modern-day Miss Marples. I am the Sleuth Sayer, and this is Season One of The Sleuth Sayer Podcast.

Another group of chords followed before the narrator continued.

The Crafty Sleuth, Episode One. Our story begins not quite two years ago in Westfield, New Jersey, a quiet suburban commuter town outside of New York City, where one woman's world is unexpectedly turned upside down when her husband suddenly dies, and she discovers the secrets he's hidden from her throughout their marriage. One day Anastasia Pollack is living a typical middle-class life as a mother and magazine editor; the next day she's not only a widow but the prime suspect in the murder of one of her coworkers. And what a murder it was!

When I stopped short and reached for Zack's arm, he paused the podcast. "Had enough already?"

I couldn't answer. I stood frozen in my tracks. Through a break in the trees and dense shrubbery, at the bottom of a steep slope, I saw a body sprawled along the edge of the creek.

TWO

Even without a medical degree, I knew I was staring at a corpse. As Ralph, my Shakespeare-quoting parrot would squawk, the body on the creekbank had shuffled off his mortal coil.

Zack pulled out his phone, took one look at the screen, and cursed under his breath.

"No signal?"

"Not even a single bar."

I checked my phone. "Same. We should head back to the winery to call the police."

He shook his head. "You go. I'll climb down to keep predators away."

"Predators?" I pivoted, executing a quick three-sixty of our surroundings. "What sort of predators?"

"Anything from vultures to cougars."

"Coyotes? Here?" My voice squeaked several octaves higher. "Seriously?"

Zack nodded. "Coyotes. Bears. Bobcats. They're all native to the area."

I stole a peek at the deceased. "No disrespect to the gentleman sprawled below, but he's obviously dead. The coyotes, bears, and bobcats can have him. You can't fend off wild animals with your bare hands."

He patted his hip bone. "I don't intend to."

That's when I noticed the slight bulge under his shirt. "You brought your gun on our honeymoon?"

"Aren't you the one who suggested I start wearing it?"

"That was when we were dealing with a notorious mob boss in New Jersey."

He raised an eyebrow. "Would you have preferred I left the gun at home?"

"Heck, no! Not if there are coyotes, bears, and bobcats lurking in the woods." I shuddered. Turning my attention back toward the body, I asked, "Do you think he fell prey to some wild animal?"

Zack's expression darkened. "The deadliest of all animals."

I knew he didn't mean a grizzly or rhino or crocodile. "You think he was murdered."

"Don't you?"

I turned my gaze back to the corpse. Upon a closer look, I realized that not only were his clothes dry, but the creek was also too shallow for the man to have washed up on shore. I'd seen enough dead bodies the last year and a half to know foul play when I saw it. No animal had beaten that poor man to a pulp, crushed his skull, and broken his neck. Once again, I'd stumbled upon a murder scene. "I had hoped I was wrong."

"That makes two of us," Zack said, "but those wounds are man-made. Even if he'd lost his balance and tumbled down this embankment, he wouldn't have wound up looking like that. The ground is too soft and cushioned with moss and dead leaves. Maybe he'd have broken his leg or even his neck, but nothing between here and where he landed would account for his crushed skull. That injury is deliberate and caused by a weapon of some sort."

I sighed. Even on my honeymoon, I couldn't escape the Jessica Fletcher curse that had descended on me ever since Karl's demise. Like Jessica, even when I ventured away from my home turf, the dead body count rose.

Zack began traversing the slope toward the creekbank. He'd tackled the rainforests of the Amazon and the jungles of Madagascar, but I still held my breath and waited until he'd successfully navigated the steep incline. Once he'd safely arrived at the bottom, I rushed as fast as my non-runner's legs would carry me, back down the path toward the winery.

When I spied the garden through the trees, I stopped running and gulped in air to catch my breath and slow my pounding heart. Even though my jog had lasted only a few minutes, my body reacted as though I'd run a marathon. Someday I really needed to get serious about exercising more.

Who was I kidding? I needed to *start* exercising before I could exercise *more*.

Once my breathing had returned to near-normal, I whipped out my phone, found I had cell service, and called 9-1-1. Most people go their entire lives without having to call emergency services more than a few times. I'd dialed 9-1-1 so frequently the last year and a half that not only was I on a first-name basis with the dispatchers, but I considered adding them to my Christmas card list.

When the operator answered with the customary, "9-1-1, state your emergency," I calmly explained the situation, told her where I was and that Zack had remained with the body, assuring her he knew not to touch anything. Surprisingly, she didn't ask me to stay on the line after she'd told me the sheriff was en route. Odd, but perhaps procedures differed in rural Tennessee from what I was used to in New Jersey. Or maybe she'd inadvertently disconnected me.

Since I'd already related what I knew, I opted not to call back. Instead, I went in search of the sisters. It had occurred to me that the deceased might be one of their other guests or someone they knew. After all, how likely was it that a total stranger would wind up dead on their property?

As I made my way toward the main house, I noticed a housekeeper pushing a cleaning cart into one of the cottages, a gardener deadheading the rose bushes in the garden, and two couples taking part in an outdoor wine tasting on the side patio. Off in the distance, several men worked in the vineyard. I wondered if any of these people had a connection to the dead man.

Inside the house, I first checked the public areas. Aside from a stylishly coifed silver-haired saleswoman waiting on several tourists shopping for wine and souvenirs in the gift shop, I saw no one else. I made my way through the empty sitting room and dining room toward the kitchen where I found the three sisters. They sat on stools, chatting and drinking coffee around a large marble island where a white Persian cat, a perfect clone of Catherine the Great, held court.

"Anastasia!" Roussanne beamed when she noticed me. "Come join us."

"Are your accommodations satisfactory?" asked Marsala, handing me a cup of coffee as Constantia passed me the sugar bowl and pitcher of cream.

The sisters looked so much alike, that I would have had trouble telling them apart if not for the names embroidered on their aprons. All three wore their gray-streaked light brown hair pulled back in loose buns at the base of their necks, but Constantia was grayer and had a few more wrinkles than her sisters. Marsala appeared to be the youngest with the least amount of gray and barely any wrinkles.

"More than satisfactory," I assured them, adding a splash of cream to my cup, "but there's something I need to tell you."

All three women went from smiling at me to knitting their brows. "Is something wrong?" asked Roussanne.

Constantia gasped. "Please tell me you haven't discovered bedbugs in your cottage."

"No, nothing like that," I said.

Roussanne placed a hand over her heart. "That's a relief."

"I assure you, we've never had a problem," said Marsala.

"But we've heard horror stories about other establishments," added Constantia. "Not around here, mind you, but it's an innkeeper's greatest fear."

I frowned into my coffee. "I'm afraid this is much worse than bedbugs."

"Other than locusts descending on our vineyard," said Marsala, "I can't imagine *anything* worse than bedbugs."

I wondered which would be less harmful to their business, locusts destroying this year's grape crop or the bad press they'd receive from a murder committed on the grounds of their winery. What I was about to tell these women could bankrupt them. I first took a fortifying sip of caffeine, then asked, "Do you know if anyone is missing? Any staff or guests?"

"I'm sure some of our guests are out sightseeing," said Marsala. "No one hangs around all day."

"It's not like we ask them to sign out when they leave the grounds," added Roussanne.

"Of course not," I said. "What about staff? Everyone accounted for?"

The three women squinted at me. "What's this about?" asked Constantia.

"I hate to be the bearer of bad news," I said, "but the sheriff is on his way."

"Whatever for?" asked Roussanne.

"We discovered a body down by the creek."

"Oh dear," said Constantia. "Someone must have had a heart attack or stroke while out walking. The creek path is a favorite of hikers."

"This wasn't a natural death," I said.

"Someone drowned and washed up onshore?" asked Marsala. "How could that be? We haven't had rain in more than a week. The creek isn't that high."

I shook my head. "I don't think so."

"A bear attack, then?" asked Roussanne. "There hasn't been one of those around here in years."

When I shook my head again, three pairs of eyes stared wide-eyed, and three mouths dropped open. "Are you suggesting the person was murdered?" asked Marsala.

"It appears so," I said.

"How wonderful!" Constantia clapped her hands together. "We'll be able to help you solve another case."

"Yes," agreed Roussanne. "Just think, a real-life crime to investigate right here at Three Sisters Winery.

"What marvelous publicity!" added Marsala.

Wow! I didn't see that coming. Not by a long shot. It was my turn to stare bug-eyed at them, but before the shock subsided enough for my brain to formulate a response, sirens heralded the approach of law enforcement.

The sisters and I scurried toward the front door. When we passed the gift shop, I noticed the previous customers had departed. The saleswoman was busy replenishing a display of wine-scented body products. Although hard for me to fathom, she appeared oblivious to the blaring sirens and flashing red lights reflected in the shop's bay window, as if such an event were a common occurrence at the winery.

Was it? The sisters had admitted their fascination with true crime. Perhaps they constantly pestered the local police with their suspicions of supposed nefarious shenanigans perpetrated by neighbors, guests, or even employees.

As we exited onto the porch to meet the sheriff, I cast a sideways glance at my companions. Why weren't they more upset? Why hadn't they asked me to describe the victim? After all, odds were good they knew him. Even though the sisters presented as such sweet Southern ladies, experience had taught me looks can be—and often were— deceiving.

We stepped onto the porch to find two county sheriff vehicles, a Chevy Suburban and a squad car, parked in front of the house. Like magpies, the women began chattering all at once as they bounded down the porch steps and surrounded the man who had stepped from the Suburban. Reminiscent of every stereotypical sheriff in every sitcom ever produced—middle aged, paunchy, but extremely friendly with his constituents—he appeared to humor the women as they continued jabbering nonstop.

Since the sisters knew nothing about the victim or even exactly where on their property Zack and I had found him, I couldn't imagine why they were bending the sheriff's ear. He continued to listen patiently, but I sensed from the expressions of the two officers standing behind him, that they expected to find they'd driven out to the winery for no good reason.

Your tax dollars at work. Perhaps the sheriff made a point of humoring the true crime junkies in exchange for a steady supply of cases of the fruits of their labor.

I silently stood off to the side and observed the two deputies. The man was average height with a lesser paunch than the sheriff. I pegged him somewhere in his late forties. Clean-shaven with a graying buzzcut and a bald eagle tattoo partially hidden under his rolled-up shirtsleeve, he kept stealing glances at his phone.

The woman, no more than thirty, fought to keep a straight face. She stood slightly shorter than her male counterpart with not an ounce of fat on her well-toned figure. Wispy red bangs peeked out from beneath the brim of her deputy's hat, which otherwise hid the rest of her hair.

Catching her eye, I nodded to my left. She dipped her chin in acknowledgment. As she headed toward me, I widened my distance from the group.

When we were out of whispering earshot, we turned our backs on the others, and I introduced myself.

"Deputy Gillie Norwood," she replied. "How do you know the sisters, ma'am?"

I cringed inwardly at the appellation, exerting extreme effort to hide my annoyance. I knew it was a term of respect, especially in the South, but I hate when people call me ma'am. It makes me feel so old. "We only met a few hours ago," I said. "My husband

and I are staying in one of the guest cottages. We discovered the body while walking along the path by the creek."

Her eyebrows shot up. "There really is a body?"

"I take it you often deal with false alarms from the sisters?"

She rolled her eyes. "Constantly. The sheriff humors them. He's up for reelection this year, and it's a tight race. He needs all the votes he can get." She lowered her voice even further. "Besides, there's a bit of quid pro quo involved, if you get my drift."

I smiled. Chalk one up for Anastasia Pollack and her keen sense of deductive reasoning. I glanced toward the yammering sisters, the indulgent sheriff, and his bored deputy. "I can't imagine what they're telling him."

"Probably their theory as to how the victim died."

"How could they possibly have a theory when they haven't seen the body?"

"I doubt that would stop them. The sisters have very fertile imaginations. I'm sure they've already decided it was murder."

"It was."

She executed a double-take and narrowed her gaze at me. "How could you possibly know that?"

"By the condition of the body. I know an unnatural death when I see one." I proceeded to enumerate the victim's wounds.

When I'd finished, she asked, "Are you in law enforcement?"

"Not officially."

"How unofficially?" Before I could answer, she added, "Don't tell me you're another one of those true crime junkies."

"Definitely not. I'd like nothing better than not to see another murder victim for the remainder of my life."

She studied me for a moment, then said, "I think I'd better get Sheriff Granger and have you guide us to the crime scene."

23

She jogged back to where the sheriff still listened patiently to the sisters and whispered in his ear. The sheriff shot me a quick look before turning his attention back to the sisters, insisting they remain at the house.

The sheriff then scowled at the other deputy. In a booming tone and with words that left no ambiguity as to his feelings toward the man, he ordered him to get off his phone and remain with the sisters.

Deputy Norwood sniggered as a deep scarlet suffused her partner's neck and face. He glared at her before shoving his phone into his pocket. I hadn't witnessed so much interpersonal drama since the last time my mother and mother-in-law occupied the same room.

Sheriff Granger lumbered toward me with Deputy Norwood close on his heels. When he stood inches from me, Deputy Norwood introduced me. "This is Anastasia Pollack. She and her husband are staying at the winery."

He nodded and tipped the brim of his hat as he introduced himself. "Sheriff Buck Granger, ma'am. I understand you and your husband discovered a deceased individual down by the creek?"

"That's correct, Sheriff. My husband is still there. He wanted to make certain no scavengers attacked the body."

When he frowned, I added, "He knows not to disturb the crime scene."

His eyebrows shot up under the brim of his hat. "What makes you think the deceased was a crime victim?"

"Because he was murdered."

He narrowed his gaze and looked down his nose at me. "And just how would you know that, little lady?"

Although my five-foot-two stature plants me firmly in the

petite section at Macy's, and I am of the female persuasion, as far as I'm concerned, the only thing worse than being called *ma'am* is being called *little lady*. I suppose the sheriff had realized he didn't need to suck up to me the way he did the sisters because I was neither a prospective voter nor a supplier of free cases of fermented grapes.

I refrained from telling the chauvinist exactly what I thought of his attitude and instead calmy said, "Why don't I show you the body, and you can judge for yourself?"

"An excellent idea." He swept his arm out in front of him. "After you, ma'am."

The sheriff and Deputy Norwood followed as I walked through the garden toward the path that led to the creek. Once we arrived above the site of the body, the sheriff took one look down the embankment and whistled under his breath.

"The plot thickens," murmured Deputy Norwood.

"You recognize him?" I asked.

"Oh, yeah."

The sheriff speared her with a look that kept her from divulging anything further. "Radio for the crime scene unit," he told her. He then headed farther down the path.

"Where is he going?" I whispered.

"There's a trail that leads down to the creek a few yards from here." She then began speaking into her radio.

A few moments later, I spied Sheriff Granger as he emerged from the hidden path onto the creekbank. Once he made his way to where Zack stood near the body, they engaged in a brief conversation. Too bad I'd never learned to read lips. I strained to hear what they said, but between the sounds of the burbling water, the chirping birds, and the crackling of Deputy Norwood's radio,

I couldn't even make out an occasional word before the sheriff indicated Zack should rejoin me on the path.

As soon as Zack walked away from the body toward the path the sheriff had used, the sheriff called up to his deputy. "How long?"

"About ten minutes," she said. "They're on their way."

The sheriff stood over the body, his hands shoved in his pockets, a scowl on his face, but his eyes continually darted around the area as if he suspected the killer still lurked nearby.

Zack returned, and I introduced him to Deputy Norwood. The three of us stood on the path, watching the sheriff continue his scan of the area. "What did he say to you?" I asked.

Before he could answer, I heard arguing coming from the direction of the winery and turned toward the path Zack and I had taken. The arguing grew louder by the second. Eventually, Constantia emerged from a bend in the path with Deputy Norwood's partner close on her heels. The two continued to snipe at each other as they approached us.

The sheriff pulled his attention from his visual search and called up to Deputy Norwood. "What's going on up there?"

Instead of answering, she stepped in front of Constantia, blocking her from getting any closer to the edge of the slope. Her partner stood behind Constantia, preventing her from scooting around Deputy Norwood.

Constantia stood on her tiptoes and craned her neck, trying without success to see beyond Deputy Norwood's shoulder. "Buck Maddox Granger," she shouted, "this is our property. We have every right to know what's going on."

Instead of answering her, the sheriff said, "Deputy Bates, did I or did I not give you a direct order?"

"You did, sir," said Bates.

"Then pray tell, why is Miss Constantia standing up there with you?"

Bates reddened again. "Because it's impossible to herd cats, sir. You want me to hold them at gunpoint?"

"If that's what it takes."

The deputy reached for his gun, but Constantia slapped his hand. "Lyle Paxton Bates, you pull that gun on me, and I'll have your badge." Then she shouted down to the sheriff, "And I'll see you don't get a single vote in the upcoming election, Buck Maddox Granger."

"Now, Miss Constantia, you know I didn't mean it literally, but you need to let us do our job to figure out what happened to this poor soul down here."

"Fine," she said, "just as soon as you tell me who that poor soul is."

But Sheriff Granger didn't have a chance to respond. Both deputies were too busy herding the main cat to notice her sisters had arrived. As soon as Marsala and Roussanne crept close enough to the edge of the slope to view the creek below, Roussanne let out a blood curdling scream. "Waylon!"

She then fainted dead away. Zack reached out and grabbed her a split second before she would have plummeted down the slope.

THREE

Marsala and Constantia crowded around Zack as he squatted to cradle their sister in his arms. Marsala reached for Roussanne's limp arm and began patting the top of her hand. Constantia took a more aggressive approach, smacking Roussanne, none too lightly, across her cheek and yelling, "Wake up, Rou! Drop the Antebellum Belle routine."

Roussanne's eyes fluttered open, registering confusion as she stared first at Zack, then the two sisters leaning over her. The confusion soon dissipated as her memory returned. She glanced toward the edge of the slope and moaned before whispering the name she'd previously wailed. Then her gaze settled on Deputy Norwood. "Is he...?"

The deputy nodded. "I'm afraid so, Miss Roussanne."

Still in Zack's arms, Roussanne buried her face in his shoulder and bawled, her entire body racked by grief.

Constantia huffed and stepped away from her sobbing sister. Marsala shot her a sideways glance before returning her attention to Roussanne and gently rubbing her back.

Some people are horrified by public displays of emotion, but I sensed there was more to Constantia's reaction. As everyone else focused on Roussanne, I walked over to the oldest sister. "Who's Waylon?" I asked.

"Rou's husband."

That certainly explained Roussanne's emotional breakdown but not Constantia's annoyance. I raised an eyebrow. "You don't seem very broken up by his death."

"I'm not. Whoever killed him did my sister a huge favor."

"Oh?"

"Waylon Oakley thinks—thought—being a bigshot university professor made him an expert on everything. He constantly butted heads with everyone. Or did."

He sounded like the Y chromosome counterpart of my mother-in-law. "About what?" I asked.

"You name it. But especially about grape cultivation and wine making, even though he's never spent a day getting dirt under his manicured nails or wine stains on his uncalloused fingers."

She waved her hand back in the direction of the vineyard. "This winery has been in our family for four generations."

And yet the winery was named for Constantia and her sisters? That made no sense to me.

My puzzlement must have shown on my face because Constantia then explained, "My great-grandparents started the winery when Prohibition ended. They named it after our grandmother and her two sisters, our great-aunts. My sisters and I grew up learning every aspect of the business. It's in our blood. Grammy Mead left us the winery because we were the only other set of three sisters in the family. We've been extremely successful carrying on the family tradition." She cast a scowl toward the embankment. "No thanks to that pompous blowhard."

She then crossed her arms over her chest and stared toward her still crying sister. "Besides that, he constantly cheated on Rou. One student after another for years. You'd think one of them would have complained to the university."

"No one ever did?"

"I have reason to believe Waylon paid them for their silence." She sniffed in disdain before adding, "Knowing him, NDAs were probably involved."

"Did your sister know?"

Constantia grimaced. "Rou has always refused to believe her Mr. Perfect was anything less than perfect. It's her one fault."

By the time Roussanne's sobs subsided to an occasional hiccup of sorrow, the Crime Scene Unit had arrived. As they set to work, the sheriff ordered his deputies to escort us back to the main house. "Miss Roussanne, you able to walk? I can order up a stretcher if need be."

Zack settled her onto her feet. In a voice that trembled only slightly, she called down to the sheriff. "Thank you for offering, Buck, but I'm quite capable of walking."

"Good to hear, ma'am." Then he directed his attention to all of us. "I'll need to speak with each of you individually. As well as all the employees and any other guests."

"The guests are all out for the day," said Constantia.

"Still need to question them when they return," said the sheriff.

"Why?" asked Marsala.

"They may have seen or heard something earlier. No one leaves until I say so. Understood?" He directed this last word squarely at

Deputy Bates.

Bates glared at Constantia as he answered the sheriff. "Yes, sir."

Marsala and Constantia bookended Roussanne, each taking hold of an arm as we set off for the main house. Deputy Norwood led the way. Zack and I followed behind the sisters with Deputy Bates bringing up the rear.

As we trudged along the path, Zack reached for my hand and whispered, "Are you okay?"

"Now that's a loaded question if I ever heard one."

"Out with it."

I sighed. "At least you weren't mauled by a coyote or bear."

"There is that."

Once again, fate had dropped me smack in the middle of a murder investigation. So much for the bucolic serenity of rural Tennessee. "In hindsight, maybe we should have flown to Barcelona. I'd much prefer dealing with another kidnapper than another killer."

"And you think there are no killers in Barcelona?"

I offered him a sheepish grin. "At least they have great tapas."

As we approached the house, I noted ours was the only car in the guest parking area. The wine-tasting on the patio had ended, and the gift shop was empty. The saleswoman had removed her winery apron and was in the process of locking the gift shop door. When Deputy Bates motioned for her to follow us, she speared him with a moue of annoyance. "I'm on my way home," she said. "My shift has ended."

"No one leaves," said Bates, ordering everyone into the dining room.

Once he'd herded us all into the dining room, he turned to Deputy Norwood. "I'll keep an eye on them. "You round up whoever else is working today."

"What's going on?" demanded the saleswoman.

"No talking!" ordered Deputy Bates.

"Excuse me?" said Constantia. "What right do you have to order us not to speak?"

"This gives me the right," he said, pointing to his badge. "This property is a crime scene, and you're all potential suspects. Until Sheriff Granger has a chance to question all of you, no one utters a word."

"And why is that?" asked Marsala.

"So y'all can't collaborate."

"On what?" asked Constantia.

"Your alibis."

"Alibis for what?" asked the saleswoman.

"Murder."

"Murder?" Her voice cracked. She placed one hand over her heart. "Who was murdered?"

"Waylon Oakley, and one of you could be the killer."

"For heaven's sake," said Constantia. "Don't be ridiculous, Lyle."

"You telling me how to do my job, Miss Constantia?"

"I'm telling you no one in this room killed Waylon."

With hands fisted on his hips, the deputy sauntered over to where Constantia stood, tilted his head, and narrowed his gaze. "Now how would you know that, Miss Constantia?"

Instead of answering him, she said, "The sheriff only told you to bring us back to the house until he could speak with each of us. He never said we weren't allowed to converse with one another."

"That's right," said Marsala. She turned to the saleswoman and began filling her in on what Zack and I had discovered. The woman gasped and reached for the back of a chair to steady herself. "Not Waylon!"

"I said no talking!" yelled the deputy. "You want me to handcuff you and stick you in the squad car, Miss Marsala?"

"You do," said Constantia, wagging a finger at him, "and I'll have you kicked off the force before you arrive back in town, Lyle. And you know I can do it."

Deputy Bates glared at her. "You wouldn't dare."

Constantia raised an eyebrow. "Wouldn't I?"

The deputy's jaw flapped, but no words came out. He threw his arms up and stomped out of the room. We all stared silently after him for a moment before Marsala turned back to the saleswoman who had sunk onto the chair and now tightly clasped her purse to her body as if she expected Waylon's killer to come swooping into the dining room and try to steal it.

Constantia headed for the kitchen. "Since we'll all probably be here a while, I'll make a fresh pot of coffee."

She returned a few minutes later, rolling a cart laden with a large urn, a sugar bowl, a pitcher of cream, a large pitcher of sweet tea, and a plate of assorted homemade cookies. As if by rote, Roussanne rose and began pulling cups and saucers from the china cabinet.

Marsala jumped to her feet. "I'll do that, Rou. You sit yourself down. You've had a shock."

"Leave her," said Constantia. "It will take her mind off her pain."

"She didn't stub her toe," said Marsala. "She just learned someone murdered her husband."

"She needs to keep busy," said Constantia.

Zack and I exchanged a sideways glance as an awkward silence settled over the room. Marsala meekly returned to her chair, while Roussanne placed cups, saucers, glasses, napkins, plates, and silverware on the sideboard next to the items Constantia transferred from the cart.

One by one, we helped ourselves to refreshments. Rather than one large table, the dining room held half a dozen tables for four. Zack and I settled at one, the sisters at another. The saleswoman chose a table by herself and stared blankly into her glass of tea.

A few minutes later, we were joined by Deputy Norwood, the chambermaid, the gardener, and the three men who'd been working in the vineyard. They all helped themselves to refreshments and headed for seats at the remaining tables.

Before she sat, Deputy Norwood scanned the room. "Where's Bates?"

"He stormed out in a snit," said Constantia.

"And went where?" asked the deputy.

"He's not on the porch?" asked Marsala.

The deputy shook her head and muttered a bit too gleefully under her breath, "Someone's in for it."

"'bout time someone gave him what for," said Constantia.

I itched to know the backstory of Deputy Lyle Paxton Bates, but before I had a chance to ask, we heard Sheriff Granger's booming voice echoing through the house. "I don't give a flying fig whose nephew you are. Disobey my orders again, Lyle, and you're fired!"

"Looks like someone just got it," said Marsala.

A moment later, Sheriff Granger lumbered into the dining room with a hangdog Deputy Bates shuffling several steps behind him. The sheriff removed his hat and turned to Constantia. "Miss Constantia, if you don't mind, I'd like the use of your office while

I question everyone."

"Not at all, Buck." Her voice held none of the anger from their earlier encounter. "Help yourself to some refreshments while I clear the paperwork off my desk."

He nodded. "Much obliged, ma'am."

When Constantia returned a few minutes later, Sheriff Granger tapped Zack for the first interview, which took less than five minutes. Afterwards, it was my turn.

The sheriff nodded and took notes as I related what I assumed was a reiteration of what Zack had told him. "And you left Mr. Barnes with the body?" he asked.

"To call 9-1-1. Neither of us had a cell signal where we had discovered the body."

"And you saw no one else?"

I rattled off the few people I'd noticed. "The saleswoman and some customers in the shop, a winetasting group on the patio, the chambermaid, the gardener, and a few men working in the vineyard. The shoppers and winetasting group were both gone by the time you sent us back to the house. Our car was the only one in the guest parking lot by then."

"What about the wine steward? Did you see him again after he finished serving the group at the tasting?"

I shook my head. "I only saw him from behind as he entered the building through the patio doors. Other than a tall, muscular man dressed in black slacks, matching vest, and white shirt, I wouldn't recognize him again. However, I didn't see anyone fitting that limited description a second time."

He jotted another line or two on a pad, then glanced up. "Thank you, Mrs. Barnes. You and your husband are free to leave. Please ask Miss Tilly to come see me."

I hadn't met anyone by that name. "I'm sorry?"

"Tilly Calhoun. The woman who works in the shop."

"Of course." I'm not sure why he thought I'd know her name. No one in the dining room had bothered to make introductions. No matter. We all had a more pressing issue on our minds. In my not-so-limited experience, I've learned murder will do that. I stood and made my way back to the group.

~*~

The sun was beginning to set behind the mountains by the time Zack and I returned to the guest cottage. On the short walk, I caught him up on what I'd learned from Constantia and asked about his interview with the sheriff. "Did he divulge anything to you?"

"Of course not. Did you expect he would?"

"Not really. But you never know. All my interactions have been with highly trained law enforcement in New York and New Jersey, not small town elected sheriffs. Do they even go through any sort of training before they step into the position?"

"Most states have training academies," he said. "The length of the course varies from state to state."

Why wasn't I surprised he knew this? Knowing where my question would lead, I decided not to ask. I'd promised I'd stop trying to get him to admit he worked for an alphabet agency, a government gig he swore only existed in my imagination.

"I got the sense Granger knows what he's doing," he added.

"Good to know."

The first day of our honeymoon had turned out less than stellar, but the scene nature had painted along the horizon nearly made up for it. I stood on the porch and soaked in the view. The sky, bathed in pastel shades of pinks, yellows, oranges, lilacs, and blues, reminded me of Monet's *Sunset on the Seine at Lavacourt*. Zack raised his camera and took a few shots before we stepped inside the guest cottage.

While we changed and freshened up for dinner, we resumed listening to the Sleuth Sayer podcast. Suddenly, I found myself thrust back in time, discovering my first murder victim, and dealing with a loan shark threatening my life and the lives of my family. I shuddered as the memories rushed back to the forefront of my brain.

I hit pause on the podcast and asked, "Where did she get all this information? It's as if she was right there, shadowing me at every step."

Or it was someone I knew and trusted, someone who had betrayed that trust and blabbed to this podcasting stranger who had now exposed intimate details of my life, like my humiliation at having been duped by Dead Louse of a Spouse, to countless crime junkies.

I plopped onto the bed and considered suspects. Lucille immediately came to mind. I wouldn't put it past her to stoop to something so low, given how she felt about me. However, the podcaster knew things that Lucille didn't. For that reason, I could also rule out the other members of the October Revolution. As well as Detective Spader and all the other law enforcement officers I'd encountered since Karl's death. Same for Tino Martinelli, and Ira Pollack.

Surely, it wasn't Cloris or Mama. Although...Mama did tend to run off at the mouth, especially when she found herself the center of attention. If she'd spilled my life to the Sleuth Sayer, under the circumstances, could matricide be considered justifiable homicide?

"There's probably quite a bit of information about the cases online," said Zack, pulling my thoughts back to the present. "Newspaper articles. Eyewitness accounts. Police reports. Court proceedings. Some of your coworkers may have given interviews and never told you. Have you thought to do a Google search of your name?"

I scowled. "Not my favorite rabbit hole to tumble down but maybe I should."

"Or not."

"You just suggested—"

"I asked. I didn't suggest. You might discover things that will only upset you more."

Which is why I refrain from searching myself online. "Do you ever Google yourself?"

"I leave that to my publicist."

"I don't have a publicist."

Zack didn't comment. He was busy tapping something into his phone. Finally, he looked up as a swoosh indicated he'd sent either a text or an email and said, "You do now. By proxy."

I quirked an eyebrow. "A perk of tying the knot?"

He wrapped his arms around me and planted a kiss on my lips. "One of many. I'll let you know if she discovers anything worth passing on to you."

I tilted my head back for an eye-to-eye. "Which means you plan to filter out anything you think might upset me?"

He grinned. "Consider it another perk of tying the knot."

~*~

Before flying to Nashville, Zack had researched restaurants and made dinner reservations for each night of our stay. Most were in various Williamson County towns close to the wineries, but for our first evening, he'd chosen a highly recommended farm-to-table restaurant in Nashville. It was after eleven o'clock by the time we returned to the winery.

We were walking from the guest parking lot toward our cottage when we heard Constantia call from the porch of the main house. "About time you got back."

"I didn't realize there was a curfew," I whispered to Zack. Did Constantia wait up until all her guests returned for the evening? It wasn't like we were staying in the main house. She didn't need us to return before she locked up for the night.

"Is something wrong?" asked Zack as we approached the porch steps.

"I'll say there is," said Constantia. She rose from the rocking chair where she'd been waiting for us and bounded down the porch steps. "The sheriff is suggesting Rou killed Waylon. We need Anastasia to help us find the real killer."

FOUR

The last thing I wanted to do on my honeymoon—or any other time, for that matter—was get involved in yet another murder investigation. I'd promised my sons. I'd promised Zack. I'd even promised myself. Besides, although I'd earned the respect of Union County Detective Samuel Spader, various other New Jersey law enforcement operatives, and FBI Special Agent Aloysius Ledbetter, I seriously doubted Sheriff Buck Granger would appreciate me sticking my nose into his investigation.

"I'm sorry, Constantia," I said, "but I don't see how I can help."

She grabbed both of my hands in hers and squeezed hard enough that I winced. "Please! I know my sister didn't kill Waylon. She worshipped that rotter."

"Has the sheriff arrested your sister?" asked Zack.

She shook her head. "Not yet."

"Does he have any evidence?" I asked, extricating my hands.

"Not that he's said."

"Then why does he think your sister killed her husband?"

asked Zack.

"She's the likeliest suspect."

"Why is that?" I asked.

"Because she was Waylon's wife." She spouted off some nonsense about spousal murder statistics, then said, "So that's where he'll concentrate his investigation unless he finds evidence proving otherwise."

I suspected those statistics applied more to men killing their wives than wives killing their husbands. Besides, I'd learned that women often resort to poison in a planned homicide. In crimes of passion, their weapon of choice is usually a gun or knife. They rarely bash in the victim's brains, especially when the accused is roughly half a foot shorter and at least fifty pounds lighter than her victim. However, I kept my thought to myself. No point letting Constantia think her arm twisting was succeeding.

She inhaled sharply before adding in a wave of panic, "He's going to pin Waylon's murder on Rou because he's too lazy to find the real killer. Meanwhile, someone will get away with murder. And for all we know, maybe kill again since we don't know why Waylon was murdered. That's why we need your help, Anastasia. According to the Sleuth Sayer, you've solved dozens of murders. Please, you have to help us!"

I needed to finish listening to that podcast. No guessing what fiction that British woman had spewed about me. Yes, I'd solved some murders. I'd also nearly gotten myself killed more than once. A cat may have nine lives, but I didn't, and I'd already tempted fate at least one time too often.

I searched for a diplomatic way to refuse Constantia, but between my exhaustion from the events of the day and the wine I'd consumed at dinner, all I could think to say was, "Where is

Roussanne now?"

"Upstairs. I gave her a sedative and put her to bed. I didn't want her staying in her home by herself tonight."

"Nothing is going to happen this evening," said Zack. "Let's all get a good night's sleep, and we'll discuss this tomorrow morning."

"Then you'll help us?" asked Constantia.

"I didn't say that," said Zack.

"But—"

I placed my hand on her arm. "Try to get some sleep, Constantia. We'll talk in the morning."

Zack reached for my other hand. "Good night, Constantia," he said as he nudged me toward our cottage.

Once inside, he closed the door, crossed his arms over his chest, and said, "Absolutely not."

"You don't need to convince me. I'm in full agreement."

"I'm glad we got that out of the way."

"But we can't sit back and let an innocent woman get railroaded."

He sighed. "I should have known that was too easy. May I remind you that we have no proof Roussanne is innocent."

"We also have no proof she's guilty. Why don't we at least listen to the sisters? Maybe we can help them generate a list of people who might have had a reason to want Waylon dead."

"Other than his sister-in-law? From what you told me earlier, I wouldn't rule out Constantia."

I frowned. "I was thinking the same thing. She certainly made no effort to keep her hatred of the man a secret. I'm surprised the sheriff didn't zero in on her."

"Granger didn't strike me as some country rube. If he suspects Roussanne, he must have good reason, other than stats about spousal murders."

"Like the fact her husband was a notorious womanizer?"

"For some, that would be enough motive for murder."

"But why now, after all these years? Constantia said Waylon has cheated on Roussanne for most of their marriage."

"Maybe she'd reached her limit and finally snapped."

I mulled that over for a moment, then suggested an alternate theory. "Or maybe he'd told her he was leaving her for someone else."

"Enough murder talk," said Zack. He wrapped his arms around me and nuzzled my neck. "Do I need to remind you, Mrs. Barnes, that we're on our honeymoon?"

I melted into him. "Absolutely not, Mr. Barnes."

~*~

Three hours later, I woke with a gasp. Zack rolled over and reached for me. "What's wrong?"

"*Murder on the Orient Express.*"

"What about it?"

"What if they *all* killed Waylon Oakley."

"All who?"

"All three sisters."

Zack rolled on top of me. "Exactly what do I have to do to take your mind off murder?"

I sighed. "I think you're doing it."

~*~

The next morning, Zack had an appointment to photograph on the grounds of one of the other area wineries. This gave us the perfect excuse not to get sucked into spending more than a few minutes with the sisters after breakfast.

We arrived in the dining room to find two of the tables

occupied by other guests. We settled into chairs at a table flanking the floor-to-ceiling windows that looked out onto the lush gardens.

Marsala wheeled over a cart holding a coffee pot, teapot, pitchers of assorted juices, and a basket of warm muffins and biscuits. "I hope you slept well," she said, placing the basket on the table. She then poured us both coffee and orange juice.

"Yes, thank you," I said. Probably better than she had, judging from the dark circles under her eyes.

She turned to Zack. After he nodded in agreement, she turned her attention to refilling the other guests' coffee cups.

A moment later, Constantia arrived with two steaming plates of vegetable quiche, a rasher of bacon, and assorted seasonal fruits. She also sported dark circles under her eyes. I suspected both sisters had stayed up talking late into the night.

"How is Roussanne this morning?" I asked.

"Still sleeping," said Constantia. "I didn't have the heart to wake her." She glanced at the two other couples in the dining room. Both having finished their meals, they stood to depart. "Thank you," she called to both groups. "I hope you enjoyed your stay."

Neither couple looked anywhere near happy. Both responded with almost imperceptible nods and hurried from the dining room. I suspected their skittishness had everything to do with arriving back at the winery late yesterday afternoon to find the place crawling with crime scene unit personnel.

Once both couples had departed, Constantia and Marsala planted themselves in the two remaining chairs at our table. "What's our first step?" asked Constantia.

"First step?" I asked.

"In finding Waylon's killer."

Zack and I both took a sip of coffee, locking eyes over the rims of our cups. He placed his cup back on the saucer and turned to both women, stating what we had agreed upon last night. "Ladies, we understand your desire to prove your sister's innocence, but there's really nothing my wife can do to help you other than listen to you."

"What good will that do?" asked Constantia. "We need someone to investigate."

"That's what the sheriff is doing," I said.

"No," said Marsala, her lower lip trembling. "Constantia says he's already made up his mind. Rou will go to prison for a crime she didn't commit."

"That won't happen," said Zack. "Not if she's innocent."

"And what makes you so sure?" asked Constantia. "Innocent people are convicted all the time. There are dozens of podcasts that have helped set them free. Haven't you ever followed any of them?"

Most days I couldn't squeeze everything I needed to accomplish in my daily life into twenty-four hours. If I had any free time, I wouldn't spend it listening to podcasts. Or scrolling through time-sucking social media sites. Or binge-watching YouTube videos. But I held my tongue and merely shook my head.

Zack, however, stared pointedly at Constantia as he answered her. "Because you've already told us your sister loved her husband, warts and all."

"There must be someone else who wanted Waylon dead," I said. "Do you know if he had any enemies?"

Constantia offered a derisive exhalation. "Plenty."

"Good," I said. "Let's start there." I pulled out my phone and checked the time. "Zack and I need to leave soon for an appointment. We can give you thirty minutes."

Constantia gasped. "That's hardly enough time!"

"It's a start." I turned to Marsala. "Would you bring us some paper and pens?"

She jumped up and scurried toward the kitchen, returning a moment later with a sheaf of copy paper and several ballpoints. Zack and I each took a sheet of paper and a pen. "Now," I said. "Tell me about these enemies."

Marsala and Constantia shared a glance before Constantia finally said, "I don't know the names of any of his jilted lovers."

"Do you know for a fact that he did have lovers?" asked Zack, narrowing his gaze at her.

Her features tightened. "The entire town knew Waylon was a serial philanderer."

"Including the sheriff?" I asked.

Constantia shrugged. "He's part of the town."

"Then he'd have the names of some of the women?" I asked.

"Hard to say. Waylon had a way of covering his tracks."

"Let me get this straight," I said. "Everyone knew Waylon cheated on Roussanne, but no one knew the names of any of the women?"

"Is that so hard to believe?" asked Constantia.

Frankly, yes. From what I'd observed so far, the area was more Mayberry than Manhattan. Everyone seemed to know everyone else's business. Before I could challenge her, though, Zack asked, "How did Waylon cover his tracks?"

She waved her hand. "He had frat boy connections throughout the country. You know how that is."

"Actually, I don't," said Zack. "Enlighten me."

"They cover for each other. I suspect he secured well-paying jobs for the women once they graduated."

"How do you know this?" I asked.

She knotted her hands and mumbled, "I'd rather not say. I just know it's true."

Her younger sister turned to her. "Were you spying on Waylon and Rou?"

Constantia glared at her. "Only Waylon. I may have overheard some phone conversations. Seen some hotel receipts."

"Constantia! How could you?"

"It was for Rou's own good. Someone had to protect her from that scoundrel."

While the two sisters fumed at each other, I drummed my pen on the still-empty page in front of me. When I was certain the women wouldn't come to blows, I turned to Constantia. "Forgive me for saying this, but you're presenting quite a bit of circumstantial evidence suggesting you killed Waylon."

"That's absurd!" she said.

"Is it?" asked Marsala. "Anastasia makes a valid point."

Constantia huffed. "Well, I'll be the first to admit I'm glad he's dead, but I didn't kill him. As much as I disliked the man, I wouldn't hurt Rou in that way."

"But you had no qualms about spying on her husband and presenting the evidence to her," said Marsala.

"That's different," said Constantia. "She needed to know the truth."

"And what did you expect would happen?" Zack asked.

Constantia slammed her hand on the table. "I expected her to wise up and divorce him, but she never did."

"How often did you show her evidence of his affairs?" asked

Marsala.

"Often enough."

"You never told me."

"I knew you'd disapprove."

"And rightly so. You had no business sticking your nose into what goes on in their marriage."

"I had every right. She's my sister. And yours. You should be sticking up for me!"

Marsala heaved a huge sigh. "Waylon and Rou loved each other."

"A man who loves his wife doesn't cheat on her," said Constantia.

"He wasn't cheating on her."

"I have proof."

"And Waylon had Rou's permission."

"What? That's ridiculous."

"Is it? Why not ask me, Constantia."

We all turned to find Roussanne standing in the dining room entrance. She'd dressed in a conservative black suit, wore her hair pulled back and secured at the nape with a large barrette, and had applied the barest amount of makeup. As she made her way toward us, Zack stood and offered her his chair.

"Not only was I aware of everything about my husband," she said, directing her comment to her older sister, "we agreed on everything."

"Why on earth would you do that?" asked Constantia.

Roussanne glanced toward Zack, then me. "That was between my husband and me and no one else's business."

"But—"

"Enough, Constantia. I will not discuss this with you now or ever. You're correct in that I didn't kill Waylon, but you're wrong about everything else that went on between us. Waylon loved me, and I loved him."

"He sure had a funny way of showing it," grumbled Constantia.

"That's not for you to decide," said Marsala, siding with Roussanne. "Waylon is still dead. Someone killed him. If we want Anastasia's help, we need to move on. There are other people who held grudges against Waylon. I suggest we concentrate on them."

"Such as?" I asked, my pen poised over the blank page in front of me.

Roussanne stared directly at Constantia. "Hart Kingston, for one."

Constantia gasped. "You can't possibly think my husband had anything to do with Waylon's death!"

FIVE

Roussanne arched an eyebrow. "Can't I?"

I glanced at my phone. Zack and I needed to extricate ourselves from this Real Housewives blowup before someone flipped the table. I scribbled Hart Kingston's name on the paper in front of me, added a question mark, and passed the paper and pen to Roussanne. "Zack and I need to leave. If you're so convinced the sheriff is incapable of finding the real killer, I suggest the three of you put aside your differences and come up with a list of people who might have wanted Waylon dead."

Roussanne passed the paper to Marsala. "I have an appointment with the funeral director."

"The medical examiner released Waylon's body already?" asked Marsala.

"No, I'm making arrangements for when they do."

Constantia stood. "I'll go with you."

Roussanne glared at her sister. "Under the circumstances, I'd rather go alone." She rose and with her head held high, marched out of the dining room.

Zack and I took this as our cue. "We can talk more later," I told Marsala and Constantia. Then we followed behind Roussanne. She made her way around the house to where I assumed the three sisters parked their cars. Zack and I headed toward the visitors parking lot.

I climbed into the passenger seat of the rental car, threw my head against the backrest, and sighed. "Talk about a drop the mic moment."

"Or two," said Zack.

"Indeed. I get the feeling Marsala has known about Waylon and Roussanne's unorthodox marriage for some time, but both women have kept the secret from Constantia."

"Understandable." Zack started the engine, backed out of the parking space, and drove down the tree-lined thoroughfare that led to the main road. "Constantia strikes me as a very controlling woman, extremely set in her ways."

"Unbending and self- righteous."

"That, too." He glanced over at me. "Remind you of anyone you know?"

I chuckled as Zack turned onto the main road. "A certain communist mother-in-law? Constantia doesn't even come close. But the two do have something else in common."

"What's that?"

"Missing husbands." Although we now knew what had happened to Karl's father, for years Lucille had insisted J. Edgar Hoover had ordered his kidnapping and murder. When Karl's half-brother Ira entered our lives last year, I learned Karl's parents had gone their separate ways before his father even knew about the bun in Lucille's oven.

"Where is Hart Kingston?" I asked. "The only other person I noticed yesterday was the wine steward running the wine tasting on the patio, and he seems to have disappeared. He wasn't among the employees Deputy Norwood rounded up for questioning."

"He may have simply finished his shift for the day and gone home after the last wine tasting before the sheriff arrived."

"Or maybe the wine steward is the elusive Hart Kingston. Which would mean only one person is missing, not two."

Zack slowed for a traffic light. "I'm sure the sheriff has tracked him down and questioned him. Or them. Since we don't know if the wine steward is Constantia's husband or not."

"Still, it seems odd that he's not here. I got the impression Constantia lives in the main house."

"Hart might work elsewhere." The light changed, and Zack accelerated. "Or maybe he and Constantia live apart from one another."

I considered that for a moment. "You think they're separated?"

"Anything is possible."

"Constantia strikes me as a 'til-death-and-only-death-we-do-part kind of person, especially given her animosity toward Waylon and his extracurricular activities."

He shrugged. "Short of chaining him to the bed, there's not much she could do if her husband decided to leave her."

"True, but if that were the case, would he continue to work at the winery, assuming he's the wine steward?"

"I suppose it depends on his finances and whether he had other job prospects. Maybe he's more than a wine steward. If he's a master sommelier, he'd probably have quite a few job prospects, especially at some of the finer hotels and restaurants in Nashville."

"If he is the wine steward or some level of sommelier, and they are separated, that would certainly make for a tense work environment," I said. "But from what I've observed of Constantia, I doubt she'd continue employing a husband who wanted out of their marriage."

"So maybe Hart isn't the wine steward," said Zack.

"Either way, though, what happened between him and Waylon that Roussanne suggested Hart as a suspect?"

"There's one way to find out," he said, turning left at a sign that indicated we had arrived at Winely Made Vineyards.

"Ask one of the sisters?"

"Exactly."

"Oh, I plan to."

When Zack shot me a warning glance, I held up my hand and added, "Talk only. My investigating days are over."

He chuckled. "I'll believe that when I see it."

"You must admit, though," I said, "there are all sorts of curious undercurrents to Three Sisters Winery."

"However, not every mystery requires solving. At least not by you." He placed his hand on my thigh and turned to face me. "Agreed?"

I rested my hand on top of his. "Agreed." No matter my curiosity, I'd maintain a safe distance from the drama unfolding among the three sisters.

I changed the subject. "Do you think Waylon's murder will impact your assignment?"

"I don't think so, but the winery owners will probably want to push back the publication date until after the killer is caught."

"Makes sense. They won't want to spend the money to promote their businesses with a killer on the loose in the area."

"Unless they only want to attract crime junkies. However,

once the killer is caught, they'll need as much good publicity as they can get to erase the incident from the public's mind."

I mentioned the sisters' reaction when they first learned of the murder. "They thought it would be a publicity bonanza. Of course, that was before they discovered the identity of the victim."

Zack nodded and in a serious tone said, "When murder becomes personal, it's no longer a game for armchair sleuths."

From personal experience, we both knew the truth of that statement, which put a damper on the conversation. The two of us remained silent for the balance of the drive down another tree-lined road until we arrived at our destination.

Unlike Three Sisters Winery, Winely Made Vineyards had no overnight guest accommodations. Instead, several outdoor stages hosted concerts throughout the year, including all-day events, like the Bluegrass and Blues Festival taking place today.

Zack parked the car in a gravel parking lot and removed his camera bag from the trunk of the rental before we hiked down a path leading to the entrance. Clusters of chatting people walked in front of us; others followed behind us. With a soft warm breeze and not a cloud in the sky, the weather was ideal for both Zack's photo shoot and an outdoor music festival.

After we arrived at the ticket booth and Zack had presented his Press Pass, we were directed toward a large barn off in the distance. Along the way we passed a queue of assorted food trucks serving everything from gourmet grilled cheese sandwiches to sushi to crepes and row upon row of picnic tables, some already staked out by early arriving attendees.

The enormous, weathered wood red barn with its stone foundation housed the winery office, sectioned off in one corner. The remainder of the interior consisted of a tasting bar, gift shop, and restaurant. All were already doing a brisk business. The space buzzed with the din of customers, accompanied by background banjo music emanating from multiple speakers strategically mounted on the overhead rafters.

While Zack met with the winery owner to discuss details of the shoot, I wandered around the gift shop. With so many people milling about, I couldn't help but overhear snatches of conversations. I soon became aware that yesterday's murder at Three Sisters Winery was the main topic of discussion for many of the employees and festival attendees. Not unexpected in a close-knit community where nearly everybody knew everyone else.

Speculation ran rampant as to who had murdered Waylon Oakley. As I wandered around the area, whenever possible, I inched closer to various knots of people to catch more of their gossipy exchanges. While I eavesdropped, I opened the Notes app on my phone and began tapping out the names being bandied about as people speculated on who may have wanted Waylon dead. To my surprise, the same few names kept cropping up.

I was pretending interest in a display of wine-themed kitchen linens while straining to hear another conversation when Zack came up behind me and whispered in my ear. "They don't match."

I spun around to face him. "Huh?"

He tilted his head toward the display. "The colors are all wrong for the new kitchen."

Zack had recently surprised me with a unique wedding gift— a complete overhaul of my dated nineteen-fifties era rancher. Gone were the chipped Formica countertops, the cracked kitchen linoleum, and the shag carpets throughout the house. In their place we now had newly finished hardwood floors and a brand-new kitchen and bathrooms.

"The colors," he said pointing to a dishtowel and matching oven mitts. "They clash with the color scheme of the kitchen."

I glanced back at the display. "Oh...uhm...yes, I was just thinking the same thing."

He chuckled. "Sure you were. What's that?" he asked, pointing to my phone, his eyes narrowing to read the upside-down list of names. "Who are they?"

I should know I can't pull anything over on Hawkeye Barnes, the maybe spy. I slipped my phone into my jeans pocket. "I'll tell you later."

He placed his hand on my elbow. "We need to go," he said as he guided me through various groups of shoppers toward the entrance. "The owner is waiting to escort us around the grounds."

A young woman, probably no older than thirty, met us at the entrance. She wore jeans, cowboy boots, and a short-sleeved lilac T-shirt with the deep purple Winely Made Vineyards logo emblazoned across the front. A thick blonde braid fell from beneath her tan cowboy hat and looped across one shoulder.

As we approached, she smiled and held out her hand to me. "Welcome, Mrs. Barnes, I'm Shasta Summers. My husband and I own Winely Made. I'll be escorting you and your husband around the grounds and pointing out the spots we think would make for the best photos."

After I shook her hand, she added, "If you'll both follow me, we'll get started."

We headed down a gravel path behind the barn and to our left as Shasta continued, "As I told your husband, we'd also like some candid shots of the festival afterwards. And of course, you're welcome to stay for as long as you'd like to enjoy the music once Mr. Barnes is finished taking pictures. We have some fabulous groups lined up, including a surprise big name or two." She winked and added, "After all, many of Nashville's finest musicians live right here in Williamson County."

"We're looking forward to it," said Zack, ever the diplomat. He squeezed my hand, "Aren't we, Sweetheart?"

"Absolutely," I said, pasting a huge smile on my face, even though my musical tastes ran more to show tunes than bluegrass and blues, while Zack preferred jazz.

"Wonderful," said Shasta. "The festival runs through the weekend. I'd be happy to give you free passes if you can squeeze in another visit during your stay."

"We'd love to," said Zack, "but I'm not sure our schedule will allow for it. We still have the other wineries to photograph after yours."

"Just in case," said Shasta, "I'll see that you get those passes before you leave today."

After walking a short distance, she led us through a copse of trees. "This is the best view on our property," she said, waving to the expanse of valley below us with row after row of perfectly aligned lush grapevines. In the background rose the Cumberland Mountains. "Spectacular, isn't it?"

Zack wasted no time capturing the scene from various angles. As he worked, Shasta motioned me toward a fallen log at the edge of the tree line where we sat, waiting for him to finish.

The breeze carried strains of the first bluegrass band as they began to play. "That's the Bluegrass Banjo Brothers," she said. "Ever hear of them?"

I shook my head. "I'm not even sure we have a country music station in the New York Metro area."

She laughed. "That's about all we have here. Country, Gospel, and Christian Rock. You're in for a treat. The Bluegrass Banjo Brothers recently signed a huge record deal. They're going on tour and will even be on all the late-night shows in New York. I'll introduce you. You can tell all your friends you knew them before they became famous."

"I'll check our local listings when I get home," I said, mustering up feigned enthusiasm. Ever since I saw *Deliverance* on television years ago, banjo music brings Ned Beatty to mind—in a not at all good way.

Shasta then changed the subject. "I understand you're staying at The Three Sisters. Such a shame about Waylon."

"Did you know him?"

"He was one of my professors. A brilliant man and the nicest person you'd ever meet. When my husband and I took over the vineyard after my uncle passed away, he offered us advice that proved quite helpful."

"Financial advice?"

"Some, but mostly on how to maximize the business to draw in more customers. The music festivals were his idea. We owe him big time." She frowned, and her eyes welled up. "Now we no longer have the chance to keep paying back his kindness."

I was having difficulty reconciling this version of Waylon Oakley with his sister-in-law's opinion of the man. Constantia certainly had an axe to grind. The question was, why?

"I just can't understand why anyone would want to harm Waylon," said Shasta.

What I'd overheard in the barn led me to believe otherwise. "He didn't have problems with anyone?"

She started to shake her head but stopped short and turned toward me, her eyes growing wide. "There was one person."

"Who?"

"Carter Hewitt."

That name had cropped up several times as I'd eavesdropped and was one of the names I'd jotted on my phone. "Who is he?"

"A huge land developer in the area. He constantly pressures the winery and vineyard owners to sell out to him. He won't be happy until he turns the entire county into one huge business park, megamall, and housing development."

"But Waylon didn't own Three Sisters," I said. "The business belongs to his wife and her two sisters."

Shasta nodded. "True, but he was passionate about keeping developers from gobbling up all our greenspace. Quite a few of the local farmers caved over the last couple of decades. They couldn't afford to maintain their farms. Too many were on the verge of bankruptcy, and the developers were offering premium prices for the land. Now they've set their sights on the local vineyards and wineries. Waylon organized all of us to stick together and fight Hewitt."

"How?"

"He coordinated petition drives and was our spokesperson at council meetings whenever Hewitt lobbied for zoning changes. Believe me, there was no love lost between those two. Hewitt hated Waylon's guts. Said he was standing in the way of progress."

"Sounds like a motive for murder," I said.

Shasta's mouth flapped open. "Of course! I can't think of anyone else who hated Waylon enough to kill him, but if anyone did, it would be Carter Hewitt."

I could think of someone else, but I didn't mention her name. Besides, Zack had finished his shots and was ambling toward us. I thought it best that he completed his shoot before I mentioned any of what I'd learned in the barn and from Shasta.

"Where to now?" he asked Shasta once he arrived at our log.

She jumped up. "The vineyard. Follow me."

Instead of backtracking along the path we'd taken to arrive at our current location, she led us onto another trail that wound down the mountain toward the vineyard.

As we walked, Zack peppered her with questions about the vineyard and winery, from cultivation of the grapes to production of the wine. Shasta appeared glad to leave our conversation about Waylon's death behind and eagerly expounded on the entwined topics.

Fine by me. I wanted to discuss what I'd learned when Zack and I were alone. "I hope you're asking for the purpose of your assignment and not thinking about a new hobby," I said at one point. "We neither have the room in our postage stamp of a suburban backyard or the time in our schedules."

"Not willing to give up any sleep?" he asked, a mischievous glint in his eyes.

"Sleep? Hmm...the concept sounds vaguely familiar, but maybe it was only a dream I had once upon a time."

He swung his free arm around my shoulders and let loose with a huge belly laugh. Then he turned to Shasta and said, "Unfortunately, my wife will tell you that she was born lacking a green thumb gene."

Shasta raised both eyebrows in an expression of incredulity. "You don't garden?"

"Trust me. I'm doing Mother Nature a favor. Most plants take one look at me and opt for harikari rather than submitting to my torturous attempts at gardening. I'm lucky if I can keep the grass and a few hardy shrubs and trees alive."

"You should take some classes," she suggested. "There's nothing as satisfying as plunging your hands into rich soil."

Maybe for her. Given my track record, I prefer to admire the fruits of someone else's landscaping labors. Rather than sounding too negative, though, I said, "Perhaps, some day. Right now, it's hard to find the time for everything on my daily to-do list, much less any extra-curricular activities."

We had arrived at the edge of the vineyard, and as we walked down one of the rows, Shasta continued educating us on her life's passion for all things grape. When we reached the opposite edge of the field, Zack took off on his own to capture images of the vines, the grapes, and the workers tending them.

Shasta led me to a cooler-laden picnic table nestled under a group of trees. "We have these picnic tables scattered around for the workers to take their breaks," she explained. She opened one cooler and pulled out two bottles of ice-cold water, offering one to me.

Hesitating, I asked, "Don't these belong to your employees?"

"We supply them with beverages, snacks, and lunch each day. It's one of the perks of working at Winely Made." She pressed the bottle into my hand. "There's more than enough for us."

While we sat waiting for Zack to finish in the field, Shasta pulled out her phone. Out of the corner of my eye I noted her scrolling through a social media site. I leaned back against the table and enjoyed the scenery until she suddenly said, "How come you didn't mention you and your husband found Waylon's body?"

I turned to face her. "How do you know that?"

"It's all over Facebook. Not to mention that you're a famous detective."

SIX

I groaned. "I'm not a detective, and I'm not famous."

Shasta stuck her phone in front of my face. "According to Constantia you are. She says there's a podcast all about you, that you've solved lots of murders, you're working Waylon's case, and you'll probably find the killer before Sheriff Granger unearths his first clue."

I grabbed the phone from her hand and scanned the post. Constantia Kingston was swiftly becoming one enormous thorn in my side. Whatever possessed her to post about me on social media?

I didn't want my life broadcast across a middle Tennessee county, let alone the entire world. However, judging from the swiftly multiplying likes and comments her post was racking up, that's exactly what was happening. Before my eyes, my life was veering into territory where privacy didn't exist.

I handed her the phone. "I am not working on finding Waylon's killer. I'm here with my husband for his photography assignment. Period."

And a honeymoon that was turning out to be anything but a honeymoon. However, Shasta didn't need to know that.

She spent the next few minutes peppering me with questions about my involvement in the investigation of Waylon's murder. I did my best to deflect and change the subject, but she was single-minded in her focus. Nothing dissuaded her. Maybe she thought she could worm some information from me that would upstage Constantia. I didn't know, and I didn't care.

Finally, I pulled out my own phone, turned my back to her, and began scrolling through a growing queue of emails and texts. Even though my only presence on Facebook was through *American Woman*, many of my friends, relatives, and colleagues were addicted to the site, as well as several other popular social media sites. Thanks to the wonders of cyberspace, Constantia's post had already reached many of them.

When I glimpsed Zack emerging from the vineyard and making his way toward us, I slipped my phone back in my pocket, turned to face Shasta, and said, "If you don't mind, I'd appreciate it if you didn't mention anything about the murder in front of my husband."

"Sure, but why?"

I inhaled a deep breath, then expelled it in a rush of frustration. "Because he's not happy that Constantia is trying to suck us into running a parallel investigation."

"Then you *are* a detective?"

"No, I'm not. I'm just an ordinary suburban working mom who's had the misfortune of occasionally winding up in the wrong place at the wrong time."

Her brows knit together. "I don't understand."

"It's a long story." One apparently spelled out in excruciating detail on the Sleuth Sayer's podcast, which I'm certain Shasta had already downloaded to her phone. She'd probably finish listening to all three current episodes before I got halfway through the first one.

I stood as Zack approached, putting an end—I hoped—to Shasta's inquisition.

I should be so lucky. Halfway to the building that housed the wine production and bottling facility, she blurted out, "I can't imagine how much I'd freak out if I found a dead body. Do you ever get used to it?"

Zack shot me a side-eye. "Sounds like you two ladies had an interesting conversation without me."

"Thanks to Constantia's Facebook post," I said, scowling at Shasta.

"Oops!" The blurter in question feigned embarrassment, covering her mouth with her hand. "Guess I shouldn't have said that, huh?" Then she winced and added, "Sorry?"

"More like, sorry, not sorry," I muttered.

"What Facebook post?" asked Zack.

"Take a wild guess," I said.

His features tightened. "She didn't."

"She did. And her post has gone viral." I'd once read a statistic that claimed half the world's population had Facebook accounts. How many people across the country, not to mention from Azerbaijan to Djibouti to Liechtenstein to Tuvalu, were at this very moment gossiping about my life?

"As soon as we finish up here," said Zack, "you and I are going to have a serious conversation with Constantia."

"A little late for that," I said. "My life isn't a Las Vegas advertising slogan."

What happens on the Internet stays on the Internet. Forever. Even without Constantia posting about me on Facebook, the Sleuth Sayer had already opened Pandora's Box, releasing who knew what throughout cyberspace? After all, what podcaster doesn't have accounts on all social media sites to promote herself and her podcasts?

I really needed to find time to listen to those podcasts. The sooner the better. I wondered if stressing about what I knew was more productive than second guessing what I didn't know. Or stress being stress, if it even mattered.

Instead of following Shasta and Zack into the wine production facility, I chose to remain outside. I'd toured enough wineries in my life. When you've seen one stainless steel wine vat, you've seen them all.

I found a spot off to the side of the building in the shade of a huge tree, unlike any I'd ever encountered in the northeast, but it provided ample protection from the steadily increasing heat. As the day had inched toward noon, the breeze had dissipated, and the sun had begun to beat down with enough strength to remind me I was no longer in New Jersey.

Leaning against the trunk's smooth bark, I pulled out my phone and responded to texts from Cloris and Mama, assuring them both that I was not involved in another murder investigation.

Even though neither Alex nor Nick had sent a similarly frantic text, I also shot off a proactive message to Shane Lambert. The boys were staying with him and Sophie. Knowing how gossip spreads at the speed of light over social media, I figured at some point before the end of the day, they'd hear something from someone, either about the Sleuth Sayer podcasts, the murder at the winery, or both.

I ignored the remainder of the texts and emails. After all, I was supposed to be on my honeymoon.

Zack and Shasta exited the production facility shortly after I'd finished texting. I suppose Zack had also decided that if you've seen one stainless steel wine vat, you've seen them all, and that the readers of *Vine* would also have a similar view. Photos of wine vats wouldn't become a deciding factor in enticing connoisseurs of the grape to travel to Middle Tennessee.

As Zack and Shasta approached, I noticed that the winery owner had lost her enthusiastic perkiness. Her megawatt smile had disappeared, and she stared at the ground, avoiding eye contact with me, while her fingers worried the end of her thick braid.

Had Zack said something to her? About me? Normally, he's far more diplomatic than I am, but he's also extremely protective of the people he cares most about in his life. Not only am I now his wife, but my recurring brushes with murder and mayhem have placed me at the top of his People in Need of Protection list.

However, Shasta and the other winery owners had hired him, and Zack was the consummate professional. Even had he wanted to say something to her, he would have kept silent and gotten on with the job.

Besides, Shasta was merely the messenger. Constantia was the real culprit in this drama. Maybe Shasta now suffered from a bout of guilt after ignoring my request, but if she wanted to apologize or explain her sudden change in demeanor, I'd graciously accept either. She didn't, though, instead remaining downcast and silent.

Zack reached for my hand and said, "Let's grab some lunch at one of the food trucks before I take shots of the performers and festival attendees. Then we'll head back to Three Sisters."

I nodded my agreement, and with Shasta leading the way, the three of us walked back toward the festival. I took the opportunity to shoot Zack a questioning glance behind Shasta's back. He responded with a *beats me* expression.

When we arrived at the festival area, Shasta shook off her glumness, pasted a smile on her face, and said, "It was lovely to meet the two of you. I have a meeting scheduled now, but I hope to see you both back here for more of the festival. If you stop into the office before you leave, they'll have those passes for you." She then shook our hands before scurrying off in the direction of the barn.

"I wonder what got into her," I said when Shasta was out of earshot.

"All I can tell you," Zack said, "is that while I wandered around taking photos, I noticed her frowning at her phone and texting frantically."

"She didn't say anything?"

"Not a word but something upset her. I didn't think it was my place to ask."

"No, of course not, but it is curious." If Shasta's sudden personality change resulted from a text she'd received, I doubted it had anything to do with our conversation about Waylon's murder.

Then again, maybe it had. Shasta was a cheerleader for Team Waylon. Had she shot Constantia a text and started a war of words with her? Before I could voice those thoughts, my stomach rumbled loud enough to be heard eight hundred miles away in New Jersey.

Zack responded with a shocked expression. "Looks like I'd better get you fed." He reached for my hand, and we hurried toward the food trucks.

We queued up at one offering gourmet tacos. After placing our order, we stood off to the side with others waiting for their meals. In no time at all, we realized much of the conversation around us centered not on the various musical groups playing at the festival but on the recent murder of Waylon Oakley.

"Who would do such a thing?" asked one woman in a small group standing behind us.

"Beats me," answered a second female voice.

"He did have his detractors," said a third woman.

"Don't we all?" asked a fourth.

"Small world," whispered Zack.

"Too small," I said.

He raised an eyebrow. "Oh?"

"Not here. Later."

He nodded. We stood in silence, continuing to listen to the conversations bouncing around us. I caught another name bandied about as a possible suspect and whipped out my phone to add it to my list.

Zack read over my shoulder. "Sherlocking again?"

"Information gathering. I'm quickly learning that things are not exactly as we've been led to believe." I glanced around the crowds on either side and behind us. No one seemed interested in our conversation, but that meant nothing. I knew how to eavesdrop without appearing to do so, and I certainly wasn't the only person with such a talent. "But that's a conversation that requires a more private setting," I added.

At that moment one of the food truck guys called out Zack's

name, and we returned to the truck to claim our lunch. We then began the search for a place to sit. After wandering around an acre of picnic tables, we finally spotted a table with room at one end for two more people.

"Mind if we join you?" asked Zack.

"Not at all," said an older man with a flowing white beard and nearly bald head.

The three others at the table, two older women and another elderly man, all nodded to us as we climbed over the stationary bench seats, Zack on one side, me opposite him.

"You folks from around here?" the man asked.

"Just visiting," said Zack.

"Lots of people come to visit and wind up staying," said the woman seated next to him. She waved her hand to encompass the valley and the mountains surrounding us. "You can see why."

"It is a beautiful area," I said, offering her a smile, unfortunately punctuated by another loud rumble from my stomach. Heat rose to my cheeks as the others at the table roared with laughter.

"Looks like we'd better let you feed the beast," said the man seated next to me.

"Probably a good idea." I picked up one of the chicken tacos I'd ordered and took a bite.

The two other couples went back to their conversation. My ears perked up as I chewed. Across from me, Zack paused from taking a bite of his own taco, and our eyes met.

It seemed everyone at the festival was consumed with news of the murder at Three Sisters Winery. Once again, Zack had an opportunity to hear something other than Constantia's venomous words regarding Waylon Oakley. His eyebrows raised in question, and I nodded.

I noticed, however, that the locals at our table cautiously skirted around any mention of murder. Perhaps, they didn't want to scare us off. Instead, their conversation centered around what a loss Waylon's death was to the community and how everyone would miss him. To the uninformed, the eulogizing sounded like he had died of natural causes.

I had finished one of my two tacos and was about to take my first bite out of the second when the man seated next to me asked, "Where you folks from?"

"New Jersey," I said. "Not too far from New York City."

"I suppose you're used to crime, then."

Was he trying to push my buttons? Why did so many people think the New York metro area was a crime infested den of iniquity? "I don't think anyone ever gets used to crime," I said. "However, contrary to what some in the media would lead you to believe, the area is much safer than many other parts of the country."

His features grew full of skepticism. "Is that so?"

"As a matter of fact," I continued, "neither New York nor New Jersey are in the top ten states with the highest murder rates per capita." And then, because I felt the need to defend my preferred stomping ground, I finished with a zinger. "You might be surprised to learn that seven of the top ten states are right here in the South."

He cocked his head and studied me closer. "And how would you know that, darlin'?"

Darlin'? In my book, that appellation ranked up there with *little lady* and *ma'am.* Especially when coming out of the mouth of a total stranger. I was one person's—and only one person's— *darlin',* and he currently sat across the picnic table from me.

But I tamped down my ire and calmly answered, "Research." Then I took that bite.

"My wife is an editor," said Zack, shooting me a warning look as he jumped into the conversation. He didn't bother to mention my area of expertise was neither crime nor demographics, but I suppose I had become an expert of sorts when it came to murder. Although hardly by choice.

"Huh," said the man. He turned back to me before I had finished chewing. "So where do New York and New Jersey rank in that list?"

I swallowed as I grabbed a napkin and wiped a dribble of sauce from the corner of my mouth before answering. "Thirty-fourth and thirty-seventh respectively."

The woman seated next to the bearded man had taken an interest in the conversation and asked, "And Tennessee?"

"Seventh." Out of curiosity, and given my recent history, I'd looked up the statistics after finding Waylon's body. The numbers had taken me by surprise, and as it turned out, even this bucolic community was not immune to crime, as evidenced by the murder of Waylon Oakley.

"Hard to believe." The bearded man shook his head. "But I'm guessing most of those murders occur in the big cities. Nashville. Memphis. Knoxville."

"Most likely," I assured him while mentally crossing my fingers. Some people only followed sports, or in the case of Tennesseans, perhaps sports and music. I suspected our tablemates fit into that category. Otherwise, they'd know that murders are never contained only to within city limits. Or perhaps they knew but didn't want to know.

I probably should have kept my mouth shut. Glancing over at

Zack, I could tell by his eyes that our thoughts were on the same wavelength. Mindreading is one of his many superpowers.

"Still…." said the woman. Her brows knit together as her voice trailed off without finishing her thought. I was certain, though, that her thoughts were centered around yesterday's murder. Even someone without Zack's superpower could harness a bit of mindreading now and then.

The conversation returned to small talk, mostly on the musical groups set to play in the afternoon. Thankfully, our tablemates were more interested in educating us on the various bands. No one seemed interested in learning anything further about us.

Once we had finished our lunch and took our leave, Zack said, "What made you poke the bear back there?"

I sighed. "Stupidity."

"On their part or yours?"

"A little of both."

He wrapped his arm across my shoulders and drew me into the side of his body. "We'll chalk it up to stress."

"Honeymoons are not supposed to be stressful."

"Except that most couples don't stumble upon dead bodies on their honeymoon."

"I do seem to have developed a knack for finding them, haven't I? Maybe I was a bloodhound in a former life."

He stopped walking and pivoted to face me. Cocking his head to one side, he squinted and eyed me from the top of my head to my sneaker-clad feet. "Doubtful," he said with a shake of his head. "Your ears are much too small. Nose, too."

"I suppose that's a relief, but it would have explained a lot. Guess I'll just have to go back to blaming it all on Karl."

"Works for me," he said.

"Why is that?"

"I don't have to worry you'll start sniffing the ground and barking the next time you find a dead body."

"Next time?"

He tilted his head and quirked his mouth. "Unfortunately, you do have a track record."

Unfortunately being the key word. Were dead bodies such a common occurrence in my life at this point that we'd resorted to joking about them? *Unfortunately,* Zack was probably right. The universe had decided to have a good laugh at my expense, and judging from the latest dead body, I didn't even get time off for my honeymoon. How fair was that?

We spent another hour wandering around the three performance stages as Zack took photos of the singers and musicians, as well as their enthusiastic fans. He concentrated on those attendees also enjoying bottles of Winely Made wines while they listened.

The temperatures had soared as the day progressed. Once we trudged back to the barn, I welcomed the reprieve of another visit to the airconditioned gift shop while Zack took a few shots of the jams and various other products produced at the winery. Afterwards, we stopped at the office for the guest passes Shasta had promised, then made our way toward the field that served as both a parking lot and car-baking oven.

Zack opened the driver's side door and leaned in to turn on the engine and switch the AC to full-blast mode. Once the interior had cooled down enough to prevent third-degree burns, we slipped inside the car.

As we drove away from Winely Made Vineyards, I filled him in on everything I'd learned from both my eavesdropping and my conversation with Shasta. "From what I gather, Waylon was one of the good guys, a champion of the vintners, not the evil Sith lord Constantia would have us believe."

"Makes you wonder about her motivation," he said.

"Judging from what we witnessed this morning, even Marsala doesn't share Constantia's assessment of their late brother-in-law."

"Someone had it in for Waylon Oakley, though," said Zack. "Those wounds weren't sustained from a fall, and he certainly didn't bludgeon himself to death."

"Shasta suggested Carter Hewitt as a possible suspect."

"What's his connection to Oakley?"

"He's a local land developer who's eager to buy up the remaining farms and wineries in the area." I detailed what Shasta had told me of Waylon's efforts to thwart Hewitt's dream of paving paradise. "Except Waylon's death wouldn't enable Hewitt to buy Three Sisters."

"Unless Constantia has lied to us about the ownership of the winery."

"There is that. But assuming she was truthful about the three sisters owning the winery, Waylon had no financial stake in it."

"Other than through his wife," said Zack.

"But if we're to believe what Shasta told me, even if Waylon owned the winery outright, he'd never sell to Hewitt. He's the driving mechanism behind preventing Hewitt's efforts."

"Hmm," said Zack. "I wonder if Tennessee is a community property state."

I whipped out my phone and consulted the Oracle of Google. "It isn't."

"That eliminates Constantia hiring a hit man."

"How do you figure that?"

"Suppose she feared Waylon and Roussanne might someday divorce. Without community property, he wouldn't be entitled to half her share of the winery. There'd be no need for a preemptive strike." He paused for a moment. "Unless—"

"Unless she wanted him dead for some other reason. Which doesn't eliminate her as a suspect."

We drove along deep in our own thoughts for a few minutes before Zack added, "Maybe Hewitt hoped that with Waylon gone, some of the owners would be more receptive to selling out to him."

I chewed on that thought for a moment before dismissing it. "Not a guarantee by any means. According to Shasta, the winery owners were united in their opposition to him. Waylon was only their spokesperson. They thought his standing as a professor of environmental sciences gave him gravitas."

"Anyone else on your list stand out?"

I read through the notes I'd jotted on my phone. "Apparently, Grammy Mead left more than the winery to Constantia, Roussanne, and Marsala."

Zack shot me a raised eyebrow. "Oh?"

"The three sisters inherited the bulk of her sizeable estate."

"What about their parents?"

"Grammy Mead had two children—a son and a daughter. The son was Constantia, Roussanne, and Marsala's father. Grammy Mead outlived both of her children, her husband, and her two sisters. Her daughter had a son, Lonnie, but Grammy Mead cut him out of her will. There's been bad blood between the three sisters and their cousin ever since. Lonnie even challenged the will in court but lost."

Zack whistled under his breath. "And you learned all of this from eavesdropping at the winery?"

"There was an amazing treasure trove of speculation floating around among the crowds at the gift shop."

"I wonder why Grammy Mead disinherited her grandson," said Zack. "Or do you know that as well?"

I grinned at him. "Of course, I do. According to one of the conversations I overheard while waiting for you in the barn, Grammy Mead objected to what one person called sinful and another categorized as reprehensible behavior."

"Strong words. Did you learn what he did to earn such black marks against his character?"

I shrugged. "Eavesdropping only goes so far. The gossipers all seemed to know, but it's not like I could butt into the conversation and ask questions. Could be anything from gambling to drugs or as benign as Grammy Mead not liking the woman he married. Or his taste in music."

Zack squinted at me. "His taste in music? Hardly worthy of earning a guy a sinful or reprehensible reputation."

"Hey, maybe she was a huge Loretta Lynn fan, and her grandson was into Hip Hop. Some people might categorize that as sinful and reprehensible, especially sweet churchgoing Southern ladies."

Zack emitted a dramatic sigh. "I'm so disappointed in you."

"Very funny coming from the guy who continually tells me to keep my nose out of murder investigations."

He chuckled. "I'm pulling your leg."

I knew that. "I will admit, though, my curiosity was piqued. I hung around hoping to learn more, but at that point, they finished paying for their purchases and left the building."

"It's hard, though, to see how killing Waylon would have benefited the cousin in any way."

"True."

We'd arrived back at Three Sisters Winery. As we stepped from the car, a blast furnace of heat hit me. Even during the short drive from Winely Made to Three Sisters, the temperature had risen another five or ten degrees. The soft breeze of this morning was a distant memory. Summer didn't officially begin for another week, but it felt like we'd leaped from spring right into the dog days of August in the span of six hours.

"I'd like to stop at the cottage for a quick shower and change of clothes before we confront Constantia," I said.

When Zack answered with a raised eyebrow and a quirk of his mouth, I mentally edited out *quick*.

~*~

Half an hour later as we donned fresh clothes, someone began pounding loudly against the cottage door.

SEVEN

Zack grabbed a T-shirt and yelled, "Hold on," as he yanked the shirt over his head. I gathered up my sundress and dashed into the bathroom to finish dressing. When I returned to the bedroom a moment later, I discovered Sheriff Granger, sporting a huge frown, standing inside the front door.

"The Sheriff wants to speak with us about Waylon Oakley's murder," said Zack, the corners of his own mouth in a decidedly downward slant.

"Of course. Have a seat, Sheriff." I waved to one of the two overstuffed chairs in the sitting area. With only one other chair in the room and the bed unmade and rumpled from recent use, Zack indicated I should settle into the remaining chair opposite the sheriff. He took up a sentry position beside me.

From the sheriff's body language, I seriously doubted this was a social call, but I plastered a smile on my face and asked, "What can we do for you, Sheriff?"

He hesitated. Hat in hand, he concentrated on his fingers as they worried the brim. His mouth set in a tight line, his brows arrowed to a point above his nose. If he had arrived with something to say, was he now having second thoughts, or was he simply searching for the right words?

With the sheriff buried deep in thought weeds, Zack and I exchanged a quick glance. He quirked an eyebrow and the corner of his mouth. I quirked back, lifting my shoulders slightly.

Finally, Sheriff Granger cleared his throat and focused on me. "It's been brought to my attention, ma'am, that you've embarked on your own investigation into Waylon Oakley's murder."

I let loose a lungful of exasperation. "Did Constantia tell you that?"

"She did, ma'am. Among other things."

"Such as?"

"That you're a famous detective."

I bristled. "I can assure you, Sheriff, I am not a detective, famous or otherwise."

"That podcast Miss Constantia told me about says different."

I really needed to find time to listen to that podcast. And read Constantia Kingston the riot act. Not necessarily in that order. Both the Sleuth Sayer and the winery owner were becoming huge pains in my patootie.

I took a deep breath, then said, "Sheriff, I wasn't even aware of that podcast until Constantia told me about it when we arrived yesterday afternoon. I have no idea who the podcaster is or what she's said about me. I doubt there's much truth to any of it. I never sat for interviews with her, nor did I give her permission to talk about me."

I stared pointedly at him for a beat before continuing. "Furthermore, I can assure you that no matter what Constantia has told you, I am not investigating the murder of Waylon Oakley. I'm not investigating anyone or anything anywhere. If you're worried that I'll compromise your investigation, put the thought out of your head. I have no desire to stick my nose in your business."

"I'm afraid I can't do that, ma'am."

A huge *uh-oh* boulder materialized in the pit of my stomach. "And why is that?"

"Well, after listening to some of that podcast, I did a little digging of my own. Then I had a nice chat with a good friend of yours."

The *uh-oh* boulder's twin joined his brother in my stomach. "Who?"

"Detective Samuel Spader. He said you're better at solving murders than half the detectives he's worked with over his long career. Said I'd be a fool not to ask for your help." His face broke out in a sheepish grin. "So, here I am. Asking."

My jaw dropped. Not what I had expected. Not by a long shot. "Why?"

"We have our share of violent crimes here, ma'am, but mostly assaults and the occasional rape or manslaughter. Homicides?" He shook his head. "Most years, we don't have so much as one. When we do, it's usually cut and dry and requires very little investigating. Either the perp is caught red-handed, or there's plenty of concrete evidence against him. Waylon's murder is anything but cut and dry. Frankly, I'm stumped. We have no clues, nothing pointing to a suspect. The one person with any animosity toward Waylon has an airtight alibi."

I could think of at least two people with plenty of animosity toward Waylon Oakley. I opted for the more likely suspect.

"Carter Hewitt?"

His face registered surprise. "You know about him?"

"Shasta Summers mentioned him earlier today. As did several other people at the music festival."

Sheriff Granger eyed me suspiciously. "I thought you said you weren't investigating."

"I'm not, but just about everyone at the festival is obsessed with the murder. Many were speculating about the killer. Hewitt's name kept popping up."

"So, you were investigating."

"No, I was eavesdropping while I waited for my husband to finish his photography assignment."

Granger waved away my answer. "Call it what you will. I'm not too proud to admit I can use all the help I can get."

Zack had remained silent during this exchange, his hand resting on my shoulder. Finally, he spoke. "Sheriff, did Detective Spader mention that my wife was nearly killed on several occasions?"

The sheriff grew as red as a ripe strawberry. "I guess he forgot to mention that."

Spader and I were going to have a heart-to-heart as soon as I returned to Westfield. Whatever could have possessed him to suggest I get involved in Sheriff Granger's case? Was he trying to get me killed? Maybe I shouldn't wait until I returned home to confront him. Or maybe, like Constantia, Sheriff Granger had interpreted Spader's comments to suit his own need.

The sheriff leaned forward, dangling his hat between his man-spread knees. "Look, I understand your reluctance to get involved. I'm not asking you to place yourself in danger, ma'am, but is there any chance I can convince you to help behind the scenes?"

"In what way?"

"Bounce ideas around? Offer suggestions?"

"What about your two deputies?" asked Zack.

"What about them?"

"Isn't that part of their jobs?"

Sheriff Granger grimaced. "Gillie's okay. She's got a good head on her shoulders, but she doesn't have much experience yet."

"And Bates?" I asked.

Granger dismissed him with the wave of his hat. "He's worthless. I never should've hired him."

"Then why did you?" I asked.

"My hands were tied."

"In what way?"

"He has family connections."

I raised an eyebrow. "There's family, and then there's *family*, Sheriff. Which kind do you mean?"

Granger stared blankly at me. "I don't—"

"My wife wants to know if your deputy is connected to any crime families."

"Oh! You mean like the Sopranos?" He chuckled as he shook his head. "We don't have any Mafia around here."

"But you do have gangs, don't you?" I asked, "and various crime syndicates?"

"Some, but it's not as sinister as that. Lyle is our local state representative's nephew. It's not a good idea to turn down a request from your representative when you want him to lobby for more police funding."

"Quid pro quo?"

He offered me another blank stare. "Huh?"

"It's Latin," said Zack. "Loosely translated, it means one hand washes the other."

Granger nodded. "So, can I count on your help?"

I'll admit, I felt sorry for the guy, but darn it, I was on my honeymoon. I came to Tennessee for a few peaceful days with my husband. The last thing I wanted was to get involved in another murder investigation. Why was the universe bound and determined to throw yet another monkey wrench into my life?

Before I could answer, Zack said, "We'll be in touch if we learn anything that might help you, Sheriff. That's all we can promise."

Sheriff Granger scowled at his hat, then stood. "If that's all, I suppose it's better than nothing." He held out his hand to Zack. After they shook, Granger placed his hat back on his head and tipped the brim toward me, "Ma'am, I appreciate you taking the time to speak with me."

"Before you leave," I said, "would you mind answering one question?"

"What would that be, ma'am?"

"Why do you think Roussanne killed her husband?"

He stared at me as though I'd just asked him why the sky is pink with purple polka dots. "I don't. Like I said, we have no suspects. Where'd you get that idea?"

"From the same person who told you I'm a detective."

Sheriff Granger shook his head as he muttered something undiscernible under his breath. Then he said, "Wish I could get Miss Constantia to stop reading all those murder mysteries and listening to all those true crime podcasts. My job would be a heck of a lot easier."

Not to mention that my honeymoon would be more honeymoon and less déjà vu. I wondered how many newlyweds encountered a dead body on their honeymoon and got sucked into a murder investigation. Of all the people in the world who had recently married, I suspected I could count the number on one hand—with fingers to spare.

"Then why would she suggest such a thing?" I asked.

The sheriff screwed up the side of his mouth and squinted, as if he were trying to pull some memory from the deep recesses of his brain. Finally, he said, "When I questioned Miss Constantia, she said I'd better not be concentrating my investigation on Miss Roussanne."

"Why did she think you might?"

"From all those true crime TV shows, books, and podcasts she's addicted to. In many of the cases, the murders are committed by the victim's spouse. I told her I'd go where the clues led."

"And are they leading you to Roussanne?" I asked.

Sheriff Granger barked out a loud laugh. "Aside from Miss Roussanne's alibi checking out, she and Waylon were devoted to each other. From the time those two where in diapers, crawling through the grass, they've been inseparable."

"Constantia didn't think very highly of Waylon. Why is that?"

The sheriff shrugged. "Beats me. With few exceptions, everyone else loved Waylon."

After Zack closed the door behind the sheriff, I said, "I suppose it's too late to book a flight to Barcelona?"

Zack placed his hands on my arms and drew me toward him. "With your track record? You'd stumble across half a dozen murders between here and Spain."

I raised my chin and frowned. "Hyperbole doesn't help."

He chuckled. "Who said it was hyperbole?"

"A girl can hope, can't she?"

"What do you suggest we do?" he asked. "Short of jumping on

the first flight to Europe. Which, I'd love to do," he added, "but as enticing a thought, I still have an assignment to finish."

"You and your work ethic."

"My work ethic doesn't hold a candle to all your dead bodies."

I sighed. "Point taken," then changed the subject. "I suppose it's time we had a heart-to-heart with Constantia."

Zack and I left the air-conditioned comfort of our guest cottage and in what had now become brutal heat, trudged across the short distance to the main house. By the time we stepped into the lobby, I needed another shower.

Silence greeted us. We wandered through the dining room and into the kitchen but found no one. I glanced out the back window. The staff parking area held a white Ford Escort and a battered older model black pickup sporting a mismatched burgundy fender. An odd assortment of used wood moldings and doors filled the truck bed.

Retracing our steps, we returned to the lobby and entered the giftshop. We found Tilly Calhoun cocooned behind the counter. Nearly hidden by the cash register, she sat curled up on a padded bench, the cat I'd noticed yesterday ensconced on her lap. So lost in the pages of a book, she never heard us enter, and when I cleared my throat to gain her attention, she yelped and dropped her book. The cat jumped from her lap, darted out of the giftshop, skittered across the lobby, and bounded up the stairs.

"Sorry," I said. "I didn't mean to startle you."

She bent to retrieve her book, then stood and smoothed out the wrinkles of her skirt as she said, "No need to apologize. I forgot where I was for a moment."

"That good a book?" I asked, nodded to the paperback she clutched to her chest.

She sighed as she flashed the cover of *Finding Hope*, a contemporary romance. "Emma Carlyle writes the best to-die-for heroes."

"I know."

Her eyes widened in surprise. "You've read it?"

"Several years ago." Before Dead Louse of a Spouse turned my world upside down. Would I ever again have enough leisure time to read a book for pleasure? I shook off that depressing thought and added, "The book is set in the town where we live."

"Really? How fascinating."

But we weren't here to discuss books. I changed the subject. "We're looking for Constantia. Do you know when she'll be back?"

"She didn't say, just that she and Hart had an appointment in town."

Since Tilly had dropped him into the conversation, I jumped at the chance to learn more about the elusive Hart Kingston. "Hart? That's her husband?"

She nodded.

I plowed on. "Does he also work here at the winery?"

"Not full-time. He owns an architectural salvage company but occasionally fills in at the winery, mostly handling the tastings."

"He's a sommelier?" asked Zack.

"He's not a certified sommelier," said Tilly. "But he's knowledgeable enough about the wines produced at Three Sisters to run the tastings when our wine steward is on vacation, like this week."

That cleared up both the mystery of the man I briefly saw handling the wine-tasting yesterday and the contents of the pickup truck parked out back. However, it raised an entirely new set of questions.

If Hart Kingston owned an architectural salvage business, he'd benefit greatly by striking deals with any developers who bought up properties in the area. The more he carted away, the less the developer had to pay to dispose of any buildings and their contents situated on the properties they bought.

That would certainly put Hart at odds with Waylon. Not only that, but a man in such a business would also most likely have the physical strength to pummel someone to death.

As I mulled over the best way to ask Tilly what she knew about the relationship between Waylon and Hart, Zack broached a question of his own. "Miss Calhoun, we couldn't help but notice how upset you were yesterday when you learned of Waylon's death. Were you close friends?"

Tilly shifted her body to glance toward the bank of windows that looked out onto the front porch but not before I caught her try to blink away the tears gathering in her eyes. She spoke in a near whisper. "He was my late husband's closest friend."

She inhaled a deep breath before turning back to face us. "I don't know how I would have coped with my husband's illness and subsequent death without Waylon's help. And Roussanne's, of course," she added after sniffing back some additional tears that threatened to appear. "But Waylon was my rock."

Zack and I broke the awkward silence that followed by both quickly mumbling our sympathies.

She offered up a weak smile, then changed the subject. "Is there anything else I can help you with? We have a new line of wine vinegars." She pointed across the room to a table displaying boxed sets.

"We'll stock up on various items before we leave," said Zack, "but if you see Constantia, would you let her know we'd like to speak with her?"

"Of course." She pursed her lips as she glanced at her watch. "I'm closing up, but I'll leave her a note."

~*~

"You're very quiet," said Zack a few minutes later as we drove to dinner, the AC blasting on us at full force but doing little to cool down the interior of the car. "Thinking about what we learned from Tilly?"

"I am. And I think I know why there was bad blood between Waylon and Hart."

Zack chuckled. "Doesn't take a super-sleuth to figure that one out, Sweetheart. Seems rather obvious that there's some sort of arrangement between Hart Kingston and Carter Hewitt. Maybe even between Kingston and every other land developer in the area. There's big money to be made in the architectural salvage business."

I shot a glance at Zack. He never ceased to amaze me with the amount of minutia packed away inside his brain. "You should go on *Jeopardy!*"

"Why is that?"

"Is there anything you don't know?"

"Plenty."

"Like?"

"Like how to keep you from stumbling across murder victims."

"Hey, I wasn't alone. You stumbled right along with me this time."

"But I didn't see the dead body until you pointed him out."

"I don't think that counts."

"It counts. Ignorance is bliss."

"Really? I have three words for you, Mr. Barnes."

"And what would they be, Mrs. Barnes?"

"Karl Marx Pollack."

He grimaced. "Point taken."

"Getting back on topic," I said, "do you think that's why Constantia had so much animosity toward Waylon? I would have thought she'd be opposed to any land developers, given the pride she's expressed in the winery."

"Unless she and Hart secretly cut a deal with Hewitt."

"What sort of deal?"

"That Three Sisters would be the last winery standing. It's one way of ridding yourself of all your competition."

"That doesn't make sense to me," I said. "If Three Sisters was the only winery in the county, there wouldn't be much of a wine tourist industry. Why would wine connoisseurs travel to Middle Tennessee for one lone winery?"

"It's a theory. I didn't say it was a good one."

"Here's another theory," I said. "What if the winery is mortgaged up the wazoo? We have no idea how successful Three Sisters is. Constantia and Hart might secretly want to sell to Hewitt."

"That would put them at odds with at least one of the other sisters," said Zack.

"Right." I nodded. "The one married to the man spearheading the movement to keep Hewitt from buying up all the remaining farms and wineries in the county. However, given what we witnessed at breakfast this morning, I think Marsala is firmly in Waylon and Roussanne's camp."

"Agreed," said Zack. "Maybe Sheriff Granger should investigate the winery's financials. That just might give him the lead he needs to solve his case. And keep your nose out of it."

"My nose and every other part of me would like nothing better than to concentrate on nothing but our honeymoon."

If only the universe would comply. However, given my crappy karma, another thought popped unbidden into my brain. What if the killer deliberately waited until Zack and I had arrived before sending Waylon to his grave? Was Zack's assignment to Tennessee a coincidence? Or were we dealing with someone who wanted to prove himself smarter than a certain reluctant amateur sleuth admired by the sisters? Worse yet, knowing the sisters' obsession with true crime, was the killer someone who wanted to lure them into an investigation that would turn deadly for them?

I shuddered.

Zack noticed. He reached for the AC button. "Too cold?"

"More like frozen with fear." I offered up my newest theories.

I watched as his features grew dark—and not from the setting sun. Zack drew his hand away from the dashboard and settled it on my thigh. "As much as I hate to say it, I think we'd better step up our side of this investigation."

~*~

We had arrived in downtown Franklin. Zack found a parking spot down the street from the restaurant, a cozy Italian bistro that reminded me of many such restaurants in New Jersey, complete with red and white checkered tablecloths, bentwood bistro chairs, and empty Chianti bottles used as candle holders in the center of each table.

As we were led to a table off to the side, I thought I recognized Marsala at the opposite end of the room. I couldn't be certain, though. The lighting was subdued, and the woman was seated in such a way that I only caught a glimpse of a partial profile. She sat engrossed in conversation with a man I assumed was her husband, but I really had no basis for that assumption.

I turned my attention to the menu. The waiter arrived a few minutes later to take our wine and entrée orders. Several minutes later, I had just taken my first sip of wine when I noticed the woman who might be Marsala rise from her chair and make her way toward the ladies' room.

"Be right back," I told Zack and hurried after her.

The lavatory held two stalls, only one of which was occupied. I waited in front of the sink, hoping Marsala would emerge from behind the closed door.

After a few seconds, the toilet flushed, and luck shined on me for once. Marsala didn't appear the least bit surprised to see me. She noted my own surprise over her lack of surprise by saying, "I saw you and your husband approaching the restaurant. I assume you're standing there waiting for me because you have questions you want answered?"

"Bingo."

She stepped over to the sink and as she washed her hands, asked, "What would you like to know?"

"Everyone we've encountered, including random people at the festival as they gossiped about the murder, sing Waylon's praises. Why does Constantia feel differently?"

Marsala pulled some paper towels from the dispenser and concentrated on drying her hands. Finally, she spoke. "She blames him for our parents' death."

"Was he responsible?"

"He was driving the car, but the accident wasn't his fault."

"What happened?"

"A truck ran a red light and broadsided them. Mama and

Daddy were killed instantly. Roussanne sustained major injuries. Waylon walked away with nary a scratch on him."

"Why does Constantia blame Waylon?"

Marsala sighed. "There was no one else to blame. Not even the truck driver. He'd suffered a fatal stroke. The medical examiner said he was probably dead before he entered the intersection. This all happened decades ago, shortly after Waylon and Rou married, but Constantia continues to hold a grudge."

"What does that have to do with her thinking the sheriff wants to pin Waylon's murder on Roussanne? According to the sheriff, your sister is not a suspect."

Marsala dropped her gaze to the floor and fixated on the black and white penny tiles. "I think that was Constantia's way of drawing you into investigating. I think she'd like nothing better than to help solve a murder. She's obsessive when it comes to watching, reading, and listening to crime shows."

"Yes, I figured that out."

She glanced up, a look of chagrin on her face. "I'm sorry."

"Well, whether I like it or not, I seem to have been wrangled into helping figure out who killed Waylon, thanks to your sister strongarming the sheriff."

Marsala muttered another, "I'm sorry."

"One final question," I said.

"Yes?"

"Was Waylon a serial philanderer or not? I'm getting the sense that, too, is all in Constantia's head, but I'm not sure why. And it goes counter to what you and Roussanne said this morning. You both indicated that your sister had given Waylon permission to have affairs."

"That's a more complicated part of the story."

EIGHT

Marsala chewed on her lower lip for a moment before continuing. "If you're going to help solve Waylon's murder, I suppose you have the right to know. However, you must promise me you won't tell Constantia what I'm about to tell you. She doesn't know the full story. Rou has kept it from her all these years, and that's her right, whether I agree with her decision or not."

"But you know?"

"Rou and I have a much closer relationship. I'm far less judgmental and set in my ways than our older sister."

"You have my word."

Marsala began her tale. "Rou nearly died as a result of the accident. She sustained massive internal injuries that required a series of surgeries, including..."

She hesitated, and I saw in her features how much it pained her to relive the episode. Finally, she continued. "Including all her lady parts."

"She had a hysterectomy?"

"It went far beyond that. The surgeons had to reconstruct her pelvic region. Under the circumstances, they said they did the best they could. Rou was alive, and she recovered, but she was left with the inability to...to..."

"Perform?"

Marsala nodded. "That's a delicate way of putting it, I suppose."

"And that's when she gave Waylon permission to have affairs?"

"But he didn't. Not at first. And not for a long time. He said he didn't mind that there were limitations to their physical relationship. He'd married her in sickness and in health. He loved her. But Rou felt she wasn't being fair to him. She finally threatened to divorce him if he didn't look elsewhere for what she couldn't give him."

"And Constantia found out about the affairs?"

"There were only a few, more one-night-stands than affairs, and they all happened many years ago. Waylon had finally given in to Rou's demand. He said if that was the only way they could remain together, he'd bow to her wishes. But from the start, he was consumed with guilt. He considered it a betrayal of his wedding vows. Rou thought her unselfish gesture would fill a void in Waylon, but it only caused him greater pain."

Marsala left me speechless. Talk about a modern twist on *The Gift of the Magi*!

"Those two were truly soul mates," she added. "I've never seen such sacrifice in the name of love."

"And no one else knows about this?"

Marsala shook her head. "I've told no one. Not even my own husband."

"But surely, Constantia would have known something, given

the extent of your sister's injuries and her lengthy hospital stay."

"Grammy Mead sent Constantia off to Europe for a year-long immersive program in oenology shortly after our parents' funeral."

"Oenology?"

"It's the science and study of wine and winemaking. With our parents gone, Grammy Mead knew the survival of the winery depended on the three of us. Constantia had already graduated college, I was still in high school, and obviously, Rou wasn't a candidate."

"And Constantia went willingly, even knowing how seriously Rou was injured?"

"Grammy and Waylon kept the full extent of Rou's injuries from both of us. We were only told she'd recover, but that it would take some time."

"How did you find out?"

"Rou eventually confided in me after I overheard snatches of a conversation between her and Waylon. I was living with them for a time after Grammy Mead died."

When Marsala finished speaking, I had a far greater understanding of Roussanne and Waylon's relationship, but I was no closer to figuring out who had wanted him dead or why.

We were also at risk of having both our husbands send out a search party to find us. "Thank you for confiding in me," I said. "I'll do my best to help solve Waylon's murder, and I promise I won't divulge any of what you've told me to Constantia, but I will have to share this information with my husband."

"I understand." She reached out and pulled me into a hug before exiting the ladies' room. I waited a beat before returning to Zack.

His face filled with concern as he rose to hold out my chair.

"Are you feeling okay?"

"I'm fine."

"Then I can only assume you spent the last ten minutes in the ladies' room engrossed in an extremely interesting conversation with Marsala."

Zack was seated with his back to the table where Marsala and her husband sat. "Do you now have eyes in the back of your head? Or have you developed yet another superpower?"

He raised both eyebrows. "Another? I didn't know I had any superpowers."

"Well, feigned modesty certainly isn't one of them." Even if it was, but I wasn't going to admit that. Instead, I said, "I've suspected for some time now that you can read my mind. It can't be super-hearing. If so, you'd already know exactly what happened in the ladies' room."

He broke off a piece of bread from the basket that had arrived at our table while I was gone. I noticed he'd already made a sizeable dent in the small loaf. After dipping the bread in a saucer of seasoned olive oil, he offered the piece to me and said, "I do love the idea of being a superhero, especially your superhero. However, I'm afraid your vivid imagination has once again run amok."

"So, you're not a spy *or* a superhero?"

Zack winked. "Sorry to burst your bubble, Sweetheart. All I did was glance toward the ladies' room a minute ago and saw Marsala exiting."

I sighed. "How utterly disappointing. I was really hoping you'd sweep me into your arms and fly us to the moon."

"Now, that can be arranged."

At that moment our entrees arrived, ending the verbal foreplay. "What did you learn?" asked Zack after he'd taken a bite of his shrimp and scallop fettucine with asparagus.

I'd opted for pan seared scallops in a mushroom wine sauce served over angel hair pasta with a side of bacon Brussels sprouts. I glanced around the restaurant as I chewed. Everyone else was either engrossed in their own conversations, their meals, their phones, or all three at once. Still, you never know who might be listening. "Not here. This can't go any further than us. I don't want to run the risk of someone overhearing what I need to tell you."

"That explosive?"

"In a way but not in the way you're thinking."

He chuckled. "Now who's the mind reader?"

I lifted my fork in salute. "Touché!"

I'd made a considerable dent in my entrée and was sipping my second glass of wine when I noticed Marsala and her husband exiting the restaurant. "Odd," I said.

"What's odd?" asked Zack.

"That Marsala didn't introduce us to her husband before they left."

~*~

On our drive back from the restaurant, I told Zack what I'd learned from Marsala. He remained mostly silent throughout. When I finished, he clasped my hand in his and said, "I feel as though I've just sat through a Shakespearian tragedy."

"I know. The Karma gods sure screwed with those two. Marsala fought back tears throughout. If she had started bawling, I wouldn't have been able to keep from joining in. It's such a sad story."

As we pulled into the Three Sisters parking lot, I finished by saying, "I wonder if Constantia would have had a different opinion of Waylon had she known the true story."

He cut the engine and removed the key before saying, "I'm not sure it would have mattered if she continued to blame him for the deaths of her parents."

"Which could be a motive for murder. Someone who holds a decades-long grudge might eventually snap."

"Except, even with excess adrenalin coursing through her veins, I don't think she's physically capable of inflicting the wounds that killed Waylon."

"Besides," he added, "would a woman who had just committed murder beg you to help solve the crime?"

"Highly unlikely unless she's completely off her rocker, which I don't believe."

"Unless she's crazy like a fox."

"Now you're making my head spin."

"That's the wine, Sweetheart. As you've so often mentioned, you're a cheap drunk."

"Does that mean you plan to take advantage of me?"

"Absolutely."

"We still have to contend with Constantia," I reminded him. "She's probably sitting on the porch, waiting for us."

But as we made our way toward the main house, unlike the previous night, no one called out to us. The house appeared locked up for the night, dark except for the glow of one porch light above the front door and one in the foyer. If Constantia had seen the message that I'd asked Tilly to leave for her, she'd given up waiting for us and gone to bed. Fine by me. I was happy to put off the confrontation with her until tomorrow. Especially knowing what Zack had in mind for the remainder of the evening.

You'd think that with the wine I'd consumed at dinner and

our post-meal mattress mambo, I'd sleep like a baby—one not prone to colic or teething, of course. No such luck. Zack had succumbed to Dreamsville within minutes of kissing me goodnight, but hours later, I continued to plead with Mr. Sandman to pay me a visit.

I grabbed my phone from the nightstand and groaned at the time that popped up on the screen. In another few hours, the early birds would begin chirping away in the tree outside the bedroom window.

I gave up. Slipping out of bed, I silently rooted around in my handbag for my earbuds, then cocooned under an extra quilt on one of the overstuffed easy chairs. Time to find out more of what the Sleuth Sayer had to say about me.

~*~

Hours later, I woke to the aroma of freshly brewed coffee.

"Was it something I said?" asked Zack, handing me a steaming cup.

I held the cup under my nose and inhaled the welcoming scent of caffeine before taking a sip. "I couldn't sleep, and I didn't want to wake you with my tossing and turning."

Zack reached down and removed one of the earbuds from my ear and held it out to me. "Let me guess. You decided to listen to the Sleuth Sayer podcasts."

I nodded as I removed the other earbud.

He settled into the chair opposite me. "Learn anything?"

Had I? I tried to sift through the muddle of my sleep-deprived brain. "I'm not sure."

He offered me a quizzical look over the rim of his coffee cup.

"Right now," I said, "a lot of information is careening around in my brain. But is it from listening to the podcast? My own memories? A dream?" I shrugged. "Everything is fuzzy, and I can't even remember how many of the podcasts I listened to before I fell asleep. Or if I even finished listening to the first one."

"Which means you're going to have to listen to them again."

I yawned. "At least at some point The Sleuth Sayer put me to sleep. I'll give her credit for that."

"If you were able to fall asleep while listening, I'm guessing you were neither impressed nor upset by what you heard."

"Or my exhausted body won the battle against my over-stimulated brain." I glanced at my phone. "I climbed out of bed at four a.m. If I fell asleep immediately after beginning to listen, I managed to get a whopping four hours of sleep."

"Go back to bed," said Zack. He held his hand out to help me off the chair.

I winced as I started to unwind from under the quilt. Every muscle in my body was punishing me for spending half the night curled up in a chair. "At this point, I'd rather opt for a hot, pulsating shower."

"With company, I hope."

"Absolutely. I need someone to hold me up."

~*~

Forty minutes later we entered the dining room to find nearly every table occupied. As I glanced around the room, I wondered if all these new guests had booked their stays prior to the murder, or if they were true crime junkies who had descended upon Three Sisters Winery in the hopes of solving the case.

A more concerning thought popped into my head. Constantia had posted about me on Facebook. Where else had she posted? Assuming all the crime junkie podcasters were active on social media (and why wouldn't they be?), did Constantia follow all of them? Had she posted about me on their various social media accounts? And had she done so specifically to drum up business for the winery and B&B at my expense? I didn't want to jump to any conclusions, but given how few guests she'd had yesterday morning, this morning's crowd certainly raised my suspicions a few notches.

Zack and I settled in at one of the remaining tables. Marsala appeared from the kitchen and wheeled over the cart laden with juice, coffee, hot water for tea, and an assortment of biscuits and muffins. "I hope you slept well," she said as she filled our juice glasses and coffee cups.

I forced a smile. It wasn't her fault I couldn't fall asleep until close to daybreak. Instead of answering her, I whispered, "How is Roussanne this morning?"

"Harnessing her ancestral stiff upper lip English genes in public, crying her eyes out in private. We convinced her to take a few days off. Unlike what your previous husband did to you, Waylon worshipped Rou."

I fought to keep my features from betraying my shock, but my jaw dropped on its own accord. Obviously, I hadn't listened to the Sleuth Sayer for very long before falling asleep. I certainly would have remembered any comments she'd made regarding how Dead Louse of a Spouse had betrayed me and our sons.

Before I'd recovered, Zack grabbed Marsala's attention by asking her, "Do you know if Constantia will be available later today?"

"As far as I know," she said.

"We should be back by four o'clock," said Zack. "Would you let her know we'd like to speak with her?"

She nodded and headed off to refill coffee cups around the

crowded dining room before returning to the kitchen.

A few minutes later she returned with our breakfasts, stuffed French toast, scrambled eggs, and sausage patties. My waistline expanded two sizes at the sight of the plate she set in front of me. Not for the first time, I lamented that the calorie gods hadn't seen fit to bless me with Cloris's metabolism.

"Constantia said she'll be available to speak with both of you later," said Marsala, setting the second plate in front of Zack.

We thanked her before beginning to tackle the mountain of food in front of us. "Where are we off to this morning?" I asked.

"Vin de la Terre."

"Wine of the Earth? Rather literal but I suppose it does sound sexier in French than in English."

"It's a boutique operation, much smaller than either Three Sisters or Winely Made. They have a small shop and do wine tastings, nothing more, but apparently their wine has won several awards. I don't expect we'll be there long. Afterwards, we'll find a place for lunch, then head over to Clatterbuck Vineyards in Bedford County."

I stared at the food on my plate. "Lunch? After this breakfast? Maybe a yogurt. Anything special about Clatterbuck Vineyards besides the unusual name?"

"It's a guest farm."

"What does that mean?"

"It's called agricultural tourism. People book stays at working farms. They dig in the dirt, bale hay, pick crops, milk the cows, till the soil. All sorts of fun stuff."

I wrinkled my nose. "Most people go on vacation to get away from work and have a chance to relax. Shoveling manure is not exactly my idea of a fun vacation."

He winked. "To each his own. Some people scale mountains. Others want to leave the rat race behind for a week and experience what it was like to live in an agrarian society. I hear the Amish farms up north are cashing in big time with this new trend."

"The Amish don't have indoor plumbing. I wonder if people realize that when they book their stay."

"It would certainly make for a realistic experience."

"Count me out." Although, on second thought, I'd gladly trade shoveling manure for dead bodies. If I had a clothespin for my nose.

As I ate, I thought back to my conversation yesterday with Shasta. "I wonder if Waylon proposed the agricultural tourism idea to the owners of Clatterbuck Vineyards."

"One way to find out," said Zack.

We continued eating our breakfast as many of the other guests finished theirs and departed. Zack consumed every morsel on his plate. I ate my eggs but limited myself to half the French toast and passed on the sausage after only one bite, finding it too spicy for my taste. With any luck, I'd only consumed a thousand calories instead of the two thousand I'd guesstimated from my unscientific calculation.

We were in the foyer, about to leave the main house when we heard an ear-piercing scream coming from upstairs.

NINE

Zack raced up the stairs, taking them two at a time. I followed but not as swiftly and without skipping every other step. By the time I'd arrived on the second floor, the screaming had ceased. When Zack had reached the top of the staircase, he'd turned left. I watched for a moment as he systematically opened a door, scoped out the room, then went on to the next.

I turned in the opposite direction bent on covering the other wing of the second floor but immediately collided with the housekeeper. We lost our balance and wound up sprawled on the hardwood floor. Before I'd had a chance to catch my breath, she scampered to her feet. Without saying a word, she made a beeline for the staircase.

Zack raced down the hall toward us. "Whoa." He grabbed hold of her before she flew down the stairs. "What's the rush?"

She opened her mouth to speak, but no sound came out other than a plaintive keening. Her entire body trembled.

I pulled myself to my feet as Zack held onto the housekeeper's arm. He began to lead her back toward me, but at first, she dug in her heels, shaking her head, and refusing to move. After Zack whispered something in her ear, she nodded, then allowed him to escort her along the hallway.

As they drew closer, I got my first good look at her, late teens or early twenties with jet black hair pulled into a tight ponytail and curves in all the right places. The color had drained from her face, and her wide-set dark brown eyes bulged with fear. When they stopped in front of me, she raised a shaky hand and pointed behind me.

"Lead the way," said Zack.

Reluctantly, she led us to the last room on the left. "In there," she said, refusing to enter the room.

By this point we heard a loud commotion ascending the staircase. "Stay here," said Zack. "Don't let anyone in." He stepped into the room and closed the door behind him just as a phalanx of curiosity seekers turned down the hall toward us.

"What's going on?" asked one of the women at the front of the group.

"We heard a scream," said another.

Before I had a chance to come up with an answer that would get them to leave, Zack opened the door and stepped into the hallway, closing the door behind him. "Just a very large spider," he said. "You should all go back to your breakfasts before they get cold."

I noted a few skeptical expressions among the half-dozen or so guests and heard several grumbles, but the group turned and reluctantly retreated toward the staircase. As they left, I heard one of them say, "I was hoping for another murder."

Her companion huffed out a sigh of disappointment and

responded, "Me, too."

Definitely crime junkies. If any of them had ever had the misfortune of stumbling upon a real murder victim, they'd quickly change their tune, but I doubted they'd take my word for it.

Once the horde had descended, I turned to Zack. "Spider?" Unless the housekeeper had walked in on a mutant six-foot tarantula, my money—what little I had—was on another dead body.

Zack shrugged. "First thing that came to my mind. It worked, didn't it?"

"For the moment but I suspect there's a dead body on the other side of that door."

"There is."

"I'm hoping you're going to tell me the deceased died a natural death."

"Not unless he bashed himself in the head with a brass lamp."

I turned to the housekeeper. "Who is he?"

"M...M...Mr. Hart."

"Constantia's husband?"

She nodded.

"I've notified the sheriff," said Zack. "He asked us to keep everyone out of the room and tell no one what happened."

"I...I...have work to do," said the housekeeper, looking like she was about to make a run for it.

"The sheriff is on his way," said Zack. "You need to remain with us until he gets here. He's going to want to speak with you."

"But I didn't do it!" she wailed as she twisted her fingers into knots. "I don't know anything."

"You discovered the body."

She slumped to the floor, buried her head in her hands, and

began to sob softly.

As we waited, my mind raced. Could we eliminate Hart Kingston as a suspect in Waylon Oakley's murder? Or did Hart, along with someone else, kill Waylon? What if that someone had decided it was now in his best interest to eliminate his partner in crime?

Or was Hart Kingston killed for some other reason? For a county with an extremely low murder rate, two unrelated back-to-back murders at Three Sisters Winery seemed highly coincidental.

I glanced down at the sobbing housekeeper and wondered if there was more to her reaction than the shock of finding a dead body. Were she and Hart lovers? Did they have a regularly scheduled morning rendezvous while Constantia, unaware of the hanky-panky taking place upstairs, toiled away cooking breakfast for the B&B guests?

And how had someone snuck into the house and smashed Hart Kingston's skull without anyone hearing anything? Where was Constantia while a killer ended her husband's life? Or had she figured out he was cheating on her and taken matters into her own hands?

I sidled closer to Zack and whispered in his ear, "Where was Hart hit?"

"Back of the skull," he whispered back.

"Meaning someone sneaked up behind him."

"Or Hart had no reason to feel threatened and turned his back on his killer."

I leaned over and tapped the housekeeper on her shoulder. When she looked up, I asked, "What's your name?"

"Jolene."

"I'm Anastasia, Jolene. I know you're frightened, but there

have now been two murders here at Three Sisters. The sheriff needs to catch the killer before he strikes again. You can see that, can't you?"

She nodded.

"Good. It's possible you saw or heard something that you're not even aware of having seen or heard. That's why the sheriff will want to speak with you. Not because you're a suspect. Do you understand?"

"Y...yes. I guess so."

I nodded to the closed bedroom door. "Is this Constantia and Waylon's bedroom?"

She shook her head. With a shaky finger, she pointed toward the rooms situated on the other side of the staircase. "D...d...down th...the...hall. The room at th...the far end."

If the housekeeper and Hart were carrying on an affair, it was unlikely Constantia would have walked in on them in a spare bedroom at the opposite end of the large house. Had Hart awakened shortly after Constantia headed for the kitchen this morning and made his way down the hall to await his mistress? Or had he met his death sometime last night?

"Any idea when Hart was killed?" I again whispered to Zack.

"At least a few hours ago. Rigor mortis had already begun setting in."

Three Sisters served breakfast beginning at seven-thirty in the morning. Constantia would have awakened before six to dress and head downstairs to begin preparing the morning meal. Assuming she'd prepped the French toast last night, she'd still need an hour to pre-heat the oven and bake it before the earliest guests arrived. When she woke this morning, she would have discovered her husband absent from their bed. Why hadn't this alarmed her?

Had she thought Hart Kingston had gone off on a hunting or business trip, and she didn't expect him home for a few days? Or was it because she already knew he was dead? Had Constantia killed her husband and planned for his mistress to find him? Was she that cold-blooded and calculating?

I'll admit, my judgment concerning Constantia was clouded by some of her recent actions. Although I couldn't blame her for her fascination with true crime or her enthusiastic praise of the Sleuth Sayer podcasts, I did blame her for blabbing all over social media about my involvement in finding Waylon's body.

Besides that, her animosity toward Waylon seemed based on revisionist history and the twisting of events to cast him as the villain in her life. None of it jived with Marsala's account of the accident that had taken the lives of their parents decades ago, not to mention Constantia's obsession with Waylon's supposed philandering. Both seemed to have sprung entirely from her imagination, festering and growing for years. Had it finally resulted in the elimination of her brother-in-law?

The logical side of my brain leaned toward Constantia's complete innocence in Waylon's murder as well as Hart's murder. Although she could have snuck up behind Hart and bashed him over the head with a lamp, I failed to see how she could have inflicted the wounds sustained by Waylon.

Someone had killed Hart Kingston, though, and if not Constantia, then who? And why? And how had the killer gotten into the house undetected so early in the morning?

As I mulled over these thoughts, I heard sirens growing closer with every passing second. A minute later, the front door squeaked open.

Sheriff Granger's booming voice drifted up the staircase.

"Bates, you round up everyone on the property and bring them to the dining room. Don't let anyone leave. Norwood, you're with me."

When Sheriff Granger and Deputy Norwood joined us in front of the room containing Hart Kingston's body, the sheriff first spoke to Jolene. "Miss Jolene, did you touch anything in the room after finding Mr. Kingston?"

She glanced fearfully toward me before nodding. "I...I bent down to try to help him."

"In what way?"

"I shook his shoulder, but he didn't move. Th...then I held my hand under his nose to see if he was breathing, but he wasn't."

He scrutinized her for a moment. I couldn't tell if he believed her or not. Finally, he asked, "You sure you didn't touch anything else?"

She shook her head vigorously. Tears once again streamed down her cheeks. "N...no. I screamed and ran from the room. M...may I go now, please?"

"Only to the dining room," he said. "I may have more questions for you later."

Her eyes grew wide with fear. "But I don't know anything else. I...I only came in to clean the room, and there he was."

Zack had remained silent throughout the exchange. Until now. "You came to clean the room?" he repeated.

She hung her head and stared down at her hands, clenched around the twisted hem of her T-shirt. "Y...yes."

"Where are your cleaning supplies?" he asked. "I didn't see any in the room."

Jolene's cheeks grew beet red. She stumbled over several syllables until she finally said, "I...I always check to see what I'll need before I bring everything upstairs."

"Surely, you'd know you need certain items, no matter how clean or dirty a room is," he continued. "Vacuum? Dust cloth? Glass cleaner?"

Her head shot up, and she glared at Zack. "Who are you? If you think I'd ever hurt Hart, you know nothing."

Hart, not *Mr. Hart*? Had Jolene's anger accidentally allowed a vital clue to spew forth from her lips? Maybe I wasn't too far out in left field wondering about an affair between the two of them, even if Hart was probably closer in age to Jolene's father than Jolene.

Jolene's entire body tightened with tension as she leaned her back against the wall and continued to stare at Zack, her hands now fisted at her sides, her eyes narrowed. I decided to test my theory. With nearly a hundred percent certainty of the answer, I asked, "Is that because you were in love with him, Jolene?"

The bluster drained from her as quickly as it had appeared. She inhaled a ragged breath and nodded as her legs gave way, and she slid to the floor. Wrapping her arms around her legs, she lowered her head to her knees. In a near whisper, she said, "We...we were going to get married." She glanced up at me and added, "As soon as Hart divorced Miss Constantia."

Sheriff Granger muttered an expletive under his breath, then turned to Deputy Norwood. "Escort Miss Jolene to the dining room, then come back upstairs."

"Yes, sir."

Deputy Norwood reached down and offered Jolene her hand, but Jolene ignored the gesture, opting to push herself up on her own accord. Once she was on her feet, Deputy Norwood took hold of Jolene's upper arm and began to lead her toward the staircase.

The sheriff stopped them. "One more thing, Miss Jolene."

Deputy Norwood stopped and turned Jolene around. Once she faced us, he said, "You're not to say anything to anyone about what has happened. Not a word. I don't care who asks you. Understand?"

After she nodded, the deputy resumed escorting Jolene toward the staircase.

Once we heard them making their way downstairs, the sheriff scratched his chin and said, "Well, I'll be darned. Just when you think you know someone."

"Which someone is that?" asked Zack.

"All of them, I suppose," said Granger. "But little Jolene there?" He shook his head. "I've known her all her life. She's studying accounting at the local community college. Only works here part-time. I guess there's no accounting for some people's taste."

"That sounds like you weren't much of a fan of Hart Kingston," I said.

"Not many around here are, Miss Anastasia. Never could understand what Miss Constantia saw in that loser."

Zack and I exchanged a quick look, but neither of us commented.

The sheriff turned and opened the bedroom door. "The crime scene unit should be here soon. Let's poke our heads in and check out what we're dealing with."

The three of us crowded around the entrance to the room. The scene was much as Zack had described. Hart was sprawled on his stomach, his head turned to the side. He faced away from us, the gash at the base of his head evident. Blood had seeped from the wound, traveling down his neck and over his shoulder to collect on an antique-looking latch hook rug that covered much of the hardwood floor.

A large brass table lamp, minus its shade and with the remains of a shattered lightbulb screwed into the socket, lay on the floor next to him. Minute shards of glass glittered across the rug in the morning light streaming in from the window.

I glanced around the room and spied the crushed lampshade a few feet from the body and partially hidden under the bed. I wondered if the killer had stepped on it in his haste to flee the scene and kicked it—either deliberately or inadvertently—out of his way. From my vantage point, I made out what looked like a partial footprint. However, the gray shape might be nothing more than a shadow or the pattern of the lampshade fabric.

"Hmm," said Granger. "I wonder which one of Hart's many enemies finally got their revenge?"

Once again, Zack and I exchanged a quick look before I pointed to the smashed lampshade. "Looks like you may have your first clue, Sheriff. Is that a footprint on the lampshade?"

Granger took a single step into the room, remaining on the hardwood, but repositioning himself for a better view of where I'd pointed. He pulled out his phone, turned on the flashlight, and squatted to look under the bed. "That's definitely a man's boot print," he said.

TEN

As the sheriff stood, we heard footsteps running up the stairs and the unmistakable voice of Constantia Kingston. "I don't care what you say. This is my home, and I demand to know what's going on." she said. Then she yelled, "Buck Maddox Granger! Where are you?"

The three of us stepped back into the hall, and the sheriff quickly closed the bedroom door as Constantia barreled down the hall, swatting at Deputy Norwood's attempts to restrain her. Once they were upon us, Constantia threw her hands onto her hips and demanded, "What's going on, Buck? Why are you here? And why is that sniveling idiot Bates keeping my guests from leaving?"

Granger ignored her, instead scorching his deputy with an angry look. "I'm sorry, sir," said Deputy Norwood. "She gave me the slip."

"You telling me you let an unarmed fifty-year-old woman get the better of you, Deputy?"

"In my defense, sir, there's a near riot going on downstairs, and Bates is less than useless. Besides, she wasn't exactly unarmed. She threatened me with a rolling pin."

Granger turned his attention back to Constantia. "You realize I could lock you up for that, Miss Constantia?"

"Do what you have to do, Buck, but first you're going to tell me what's going on here."

"I think it's best we go somewhere you can sit down, Miss Constantia."

"Why?" She looked furtively from Granger to Deputy Norwood to Zack before she settled a questioning gaze on me.

I reached out and touched her arm. "Do as the sheriff requests, Constantia. It's important."

"Does this have anything to do with Waylon's murder?" she asked me.

"I don't know."

"Even in death that man is a thorn in my side," she muttered. "All right. There's a sitting room down the hall."

She began to lead the way. With her back turned to us, Sheriff Granger pulled Deputy Norwood aside and whispered that she should stand vigil in front of the bedroom until the Crime Scene Unit arrived. Then Zack, the sheriff, and I followed Constantia.

The sitting room consisted of a small leather upholstered sofa and matching recliner positioned opposite a wall of built-ins with book-lined shelves and a flatscreen TV. An end table with a brass lamp, the twin to the murder weapon, was positioned between the sofa and recliner. A walnut butler's tray coffee table sat in front of the sofa.

Constantia took a seat in the recliner, crossed her arms over her chest, and scowled. "I'm sitting, Buck. Now tell me what this is all about."

Zack indicated with his chin that he and I should move to the sofa. Knowing the bomb about to drop, I took the seat closest to Constantia, the better to offer support once she learned the truth.

The sheriff remained standing. He cleared his throat. "Miss Constantia, do you know where your husband is?"

"Hart?" She wrinkled her brow, then glanced at her watch. "He'd be in Birmingham by now. He left around five this morning. Why?" At first, she looked confused, but suddenly her eyes widened, and panic crept into her voice. She leaped out of the recliner and flung herself at the sheriff, grabbing hold of his shoulders. "Is he all right? Was there an accident?"

The sheriff led her back to the recliner. "I'm afraid not, ma'am."

"He's not...?" Her voice trailed off as she looked at each of us, and our grim expressions told her what she didn't want to hear. She gasped once, then buried her head in her hands and began to sob uncontrollably.

The worst was yet to come.

The sheriff continued with the bad news. "I'm afraid Hart never left the house this morning, Miss Constantia."

Constantia sniffed back her tears and lifted her head to stare at the sheriff. "What do you mean? Of course, he did. I heard him shower and leave the bedroom. He was already gone when I got up at six."

The sheriff cast a pleading look in my direction. He seemed incapable of imparting the bad news to her. Constantia's hands were balled together in her lap. I reached over and rested a hand on top of hers. "Hart is down the hall in one of the other rooms, Constantia. Jolene found him a little while ago."

Her eyes grew wide as she choked back a sob. "He had a heart attack?"

I shook my head. "Someone killed him."

She stared at me as if she hadn't comprehended my words. Finally, she said, "I don't understand. Everyone loves Hart."

I locked eyes with the sheriff. Constantia's statement directly contradicted his own earlier comment about Hart Kingston. Couple that with Constantia's animosity toward Waylon Oakley, a man praised by many, and it became apparent that she was either a poor judge of character or lived in a complete state of denial.

Constantia stared off into space. Focusing on no one, she whispered almost to herself, "Why would anyone kill Hart?"

The sheriff pulled out a small spiral-bound notepad and stub of a pencil from his shirt pocket. He flipped open the cover and said, "That's what we need to find out, ma'am."

She swiped the tears from her cheeks, set her jaw, and stiffened her spine, transforming before our eyes into a steel magnolia. "You find him, Buck. You find who did this to my Hart."

"I plan to, ma'am, but first I need to ask you a few questions."

I stood to leave. Constantia reached up and grabbed my hand, pulling me back. "Please stay."

"Zack and I have an appointment at one of the other wineries. Besides, this is the sheriff's investigation."

She turned to Granger. "I want her here, Buck."

I couldn't tell from his closed expression if the sheriff was grateful or annoyed by Constantia's demand. Given his acknowledged lack of experience investigating homicides, I suspected it was a combination of both with the annoyance part stemming from male pride.

"Do you mind staying?" he asked.

I looked to Zack for guidance. "I can head over to Vin de la Terre by myself if you want to stay. It shouldn't take me more than a few hours roundtrip, given the distance and the size of the winery. If I'm back here to pick you up by one o'clock, we'll arrive at Clatterbuck Vineyards with plenty of daylight left for shooting."

I was torn. Spending even a few hours away from Zack wasn't my idea of a honeymoon. Besides, I knew he didn't want me getting any more involved in yet another murder investigation, let alone two. But at the same time, I was confronted by a grieving widow needing answers and a sheriff desperate for my help in providing them. Not to mention catching the killer—or killers—before a third murder occurred.

Both Granger and Constantia stared at me, awaiting my decision. I looked from them to Zack and said, "If you don't mind..."

He tilted his head and quirked his mouth as he studied me. Of course, he minded, but his expression also told me he understood my dilemma and that I should stay to offer my support.

"Moral support only," I assured him. I had no intention of winding up in a killer's crosshairs.

"All right," said Zack. "I'll see you in a few hours." He paused, his hand on the sitting room doorknob, and turned back to face me. "Stay out of trouble."

"Always my goal." I winced. Just not always achievable.

He shook his head, sighed, and left the room.

I pulled Sheriff Granger aside for a private conversation. When he nodded, I resettled on the sofa and turned to speak to Constantia. "If I'm to help you, Constantia, I need a few things clarified."

"Of course," she said between sniffles. "What do you want to know?"

"For starters, your animosity toward Waylon Oakley appears contrary to everything else I've learned about the man, including your belief that he was responsible for your parents' deaths and that he's cheated on your sister for years. Both Roussanne and Marsala claim otherwise."

Scarlet creeped up her neck and suffused her cheeks. Her lower lip trembled, and her eyes welled with tears. "Waylon drove the car that night."

"But he was broadsided by a truck that ran a stop sign."

"He should have seen it coming. As for his cheating, I saw him with another woman."

"When was this?"

"Years ago."

"One other woman? Once?"

"Once a cheater, always a cheater. And don't try to peddle that poppycock about Rou giving him permission. Why would she do something so crazy?"

"Have you ever spoken to her about the injuries she sustained from the accident?"

Constantia dismissed the idea with a wave of her hand. "That has nothing to do with this."

"Maybe it's time you had a conversation with Roussanne."

"Why? What do you know?"

"That's not for me to say."

"This is ridiculous." She huffed. "What does it have to do with Hart's murder?"

"Maybe nothing. Or everything."

"There's no way the two are connected. Hart and Waylon

traveled in different circles. They're only connection to each other was Sunday family dinners, and even then, they rarely said more than two words to each other."

"All right," I said. "Let's put Waylon's murder aside for the moment and talk about Hart. Would you say the two of you had a good marriage?"

She glanced at the sheriff, who stood off to the side of the room, then back at me. "You're not saying I killed my husband, are you? Why would I do such a thing? Hart and I had our differences over the years, like any long-married couple, but we loved each other."

I decided to go out on a limb and call her bluff. "Then the meeting the two of you had yesterday wasn't with a divorce attorney?"

She gasped. "Who told you that?"

Bingo! Sometimes when I mix hypothetical apples and oranges, I wind up with a perfect fruit salad of the truth. "His girlfriend."

"You can't be serious. Hart would never cheat on me."

"Then why are you divorcing?"

"We weren't divorcing. We were going for counseling. We'd hit a rough patch and were working things out."

"His girlfriend said she and Hart were getting married as soon as he divorced you.

"Whoever she is, she's lying."

"Perhaps she is," I said. "People lie all the time." I stared at her, letting my last words sink in for a moment before I continued. "Who would want Hart dead?"

"No one. I already told you. Everyone likes Hart."

"Really? I've heard otherwise."

Constantia jumped to her feet. "I don't know who you've been talking to, Anastasia, but you're being fed a load of bull. Hart has no enemies."

I decided to punt. "Sheriff?"

Granger pulled away from the wall where he'd been leaning and walked over to Constantia. "Now you and I both know that's not true, Miss Constantia."

"I know no such thing. What's going on here? Why are the two of you trying to smear my husband's memory when you should be out looking for his killer?"

"Ma'am, are you aware that Hart had bilked investors all over the county?"

"Investors?" She jumped to her feet again. "You know very well Hart runs an architectural salvage company. He goes around the south removing windows, doors, trim, shutters, fireplace mantles and all sorts of things from old homes scheduled for demolition. Builders save steep county disposal fees by paying him to remove what otherwise would wind up in landfills. He works out of an old barn on our property. Why on earth would he need investors?"

"For his other business."

"What other business?"

"The one the district attorney is currently investigating."

I certainly didn't see that mic drop coming.

Constantia's legs gave way. She collapsed into the recliner and stared blankly at Buck.

Before anyone spoke further, we heard footsteps tramping up the staircase. "That's the crime scene unit," said Buck. He turned to me. "Miss Anastasia, would you mind escorting Miss Constantia to the dining room? I'll be down there shortly to begin interviewing everyone."

After Sheriff Granger closed the door behind himself, Constantia said, "I've been a damn fool, haven't I?"

"Welcome to the club," I said.

"Yes, I suppose you know exactly how I'm feeling right now."

Not exactly. No one murdered Dead Louse of a Spouse. Still, Constantia and I now shared a bond. We'd both been deceived by the men we'd married. "We should get back downstairs," I said.

"In a moment. There's something I need to do first." She rose and exited the room, striding across the hall to the opposite room. I followed her. "Shut the door," she said after we'd crossed the threshold. "And lock it."

We had entered a small room set up as a home office, most likely belonging to Hart Kingston. I knew Constantia's office was situated off the kitchen because two days ago, Sheriff Granger had commandeered it to question everyone in his investigation of Waylon Oakley's murder.

Floor to ceiling bookcases flanked a double window on the far wall. Instead of books, the shelves contained mostly sports memorabilia, including dozens of trophies and an equal number of faded and framed high school and college team photos. Football. Baseball. Basketball. Wrestling. Hart Kingston was quite the jock back in the day.

A desk stood in front of the windows. A large wall-mounted flat screen television hung on the wall to the left. A large gray and black houndstooth upholstered sofa took up much of the wall to the right.

Constantia marched straight to the desk, sat down, and switched on the computer. "What are you looking for?" I asked.

"I want to know if my husband screwed me the way yours screwed you."

Ouch! I'd worked so hard to keep Karl's betrayal a secret. I wanted to protect my sons from the embarrassment of their classmates whispering behind their backs. Only a handful of people I thought I could trust knew the truth. That is, until the Sleuth Sayer broadcast my life to the world.

Once the computer had booted up, Constantia pulled out her phone. "Calling someone?"

"Pulling up Hart's username and password." She typed in the information she'd found and hit the Enter key. From a pulldown menu, she then clicked on the name of a bank and entered the username and password for that site. Before hitting the Enter key again, she paused, closed her eyes, and inhaled a deep breath. Her lips moved silently as she exhaled what I assumed was a prayer.

After opening her eyes, she stared at the hefty balance on the screen. "Our joint account," she said, her voice filled with relief. "Everything looks intact."

She exited the account, then repeated her actions for a second account.

I stared at the low five-figure balance for Hart's business account. If he'd orchestrated a fraudulent investment scheme, he'd parked the money where both his wife's prying eyes and the district attorney wouldn't find it.

"What about your business account?" I asked.

"I was on it this morning. Nothing's missing. Besides, Hart doesn't have access to that account, just my sisters and me."

Somehow, I doubted that. With what I'd learned today, it was crystal clear that the Kingston marriage was not built on a very solid foundation of trust. If Constantia had Hart's usernames and passwords, with or without his knowledge, chances were good he also had hers.

"Now that you know your money is safe," I said, "we need to head down to the dining room. Sheriff Granger isn't going to be happy if he doesn't find you there."

"Too bad. I need to learn why Hart is under investigation."

I noted how she continued to speak of him in the present. She also hadn't asked to see his body, which I thought odd. But maybe after witnessing what had happened to Waylon, she didn't want to risk the possibility of seeing her husband in much the same state.

As I pondered this, I suddenly realized she'd also never asked the sheriff how Hart had died. Was that because she already knew?

I studied Constantia as she began poking around various folders on the computer, opening one file after another, then closing each in turn as they produced nothing suspicious. I still wasn't sure I trusted her. How much was genuine, and how much was a well-orchestrated act? I nearly asked if she'd ever starred in any school drama productions but bit my tongue. How on earth would I explain such a non sequitur?

She'd suddenly stopped her frantic clicking and now stared slack-jawed at the screen. "Find something?" I asked, peering closer. She'd moved on from files, had opened the Messages app, and was slowly scrolling through Hart's texts.

Constantia muttered something far from ladylike, then leaned over and yanked open the bottom file drawer of the desk. She spent the next several minutes rifling through the various file folders until she grabbed an unlabeled one buried in the back and slammed it onto the desk.

When she flipped open the manilla cover, the folder only held a single sheet of paper with a handwritten, three-column spreadsheet. The first column listed names, the second contained dollar amounts. Various one- and two-digit numbers were written in each of the boxes in the third column. No headings indicated what the three columns represented. My guess? Hart's investors and the funds they'd each ponied up, but the last column puzzled me. A code of some sort? If so, for what?

"Do you think those are Hart's investors?" I asked.

Constantia emitted a snort. "More like his marks."

Each had invested thousands of dollars in whatever scheme Hart had cooked up. The sums varied from a low of ten thousand dollars to a high of fifty grand for a total of nearly a quarter of a million dollars.

Unless architectural salvage held a hidden potential that escaped me, it made no sense that more than a dozen men had handed over huge sums of money to own shares of Hart's business. What was the money for, and where had it gone?

At that moment, someone rattled the doorknob, then pounded the door. "You two better get your butts into the dining room right now," yelled Deputy Bates, "or I'm kicking this door in and dragging you downstairs."

ELEVEN

"We have to go," I told Constantia.

"I need to get to the truth. What were these men investing in? I don't even recognize all the names. None of this makes any sense." She clicked frantically, opening one file after another, her fingers pounding harder and harder on the keys in what was quickly becoming an exercise in futility. Her voice filled with shrill panic. "Why can't I find anything else?"

Probably because Hart wasn't dumb enough to leave the evidence of his criminal activity on a computer his wife could access. Unfortunately, Constantia wasn't in a state of mind to hear such an obvious truth.

If the district attorney was investigating Hart for financial fraud, chances were also good that Hart hadn't deposited the funds with the local savings and loan. Given the huge sum, any swindler worthy of the title would use an offshore account, one in a country without an extradition treaty with the U.S.

What if someone had tipped Hart off to the D.A.'s

investigation, and he was in the process of planning his escape? Had he told Jolene he was leaving and wasn't taking her with him? Had she retaliated by walloping him with the lamp when he'd turned his back? Had she then faked her horror and grief at finding his corpse?

I kept these thoughts to myself, instead telling Constantia, "You can search more later." I wouldn't put it past Bates to shoot out the door's lock, and I didn't want either of us pierced by a bullet.

Constantia ignored me and continued pounding the keyboard. I crossed the room and unlocked the door. Before I had a chance to swing it open, Bates barged inside, ripping the doorknob from my hand and slamming the door against the wall. "Get downstairs now," he seethed.

I avoided eye contact with the deputy and stepped around him into the hall. Behind me Constantia ignored Bates and continued typing. Coward that I am, I didn't want to bear witness to whatever was about to go down between the stubborn winery owner and the belligerent deputy.

Since Sheriff Granger was looking for any excuse to fire Bates, one way or another, I suspected Constantia would make sure the deputy wound up on the losing end of their encounter. With the animosity I'd observed between them, I wouldn't put it past her to employ a bit of creative embellishing to do so.

When I entered the dining room, Deputy Norwood raised an eyebrow. I shrugged.

All but two of the seats in the dining room were filled, either with guests or winery staff. I recognized the group of disgruntled crime junkies and many of the same employees from two days ago. After taking one of the remaining chairs, I pulled out my phone and began texting Zack, but I paused as Constantia's potty-mouthed shrieks spilled down the staircase and filled the house.

A moment later, Bates appeared, carrying a handcuffed Constantia fireman-style, and dropped her with a thud onto the only other unoccupied chair, the one opposite me.

Deputy Norwood pounced on him. "Are you out of your freaking mind?"

He puffed out his chest. Standing with his feet apart, he placed his hand on the hilt of his service weapon. "She refused to do as she was told," he said. "I did what I had to do."

"You just signed your termination papers," said Norwood. She strode over to Constantia and unlocked the handcuffs.

Red rings circled Constantia's wrists. She rubbed them as she glared at Bates.

He glared back.

At that moment, Sheriff Granger appeared, his face scarlet with anger and a throbbing purple vein bulging from the side of his head. "What in blue blazes is going on here?"

"He manhandled me," said Constantia pointing to Bates. She held up her wrists to show Granger her injuries. "Either you fire him, or I'm pressing charges, Buck. Against him and the entire Sheriff's Department."

Granger turned on Bates and held out an amazingly steady hand, given the anger emanating from the sheriff. "Your gun and badge. Now."

Bates stared bug-eyed at the sheriff and roared, "You can't be serious."

"I'm dead serious," said Granger, his hand still extended.

A staring contest lasted only a few seconds before Bates reluctantly complied, ripping the badge from his shirt and yanking the gun from his holster. He slammed them both into Granger's hand.

The sheriff wrapped his fingers around the gun and badge, then extended his other hand. "And the cruiser keys."

The deputy's eyes narrowed. "How am I supposed to get back to town without wheels?"

"Not my problem. You've got a phone. Call someone for a ride."

Bates shoved a hand into his pants pocket and yanked out a set of keys. Instead of depositing them into the sheriff's free hand, he slammed them onto the nearest table.

Granger pointed in the direction of the front door. Between gritted teeth, he said, "Now. Get. Out."

"My uncle's gonna hear about this," said Bates.

"Damn right," said Granger. "From me."

Once we heard the front door slam, the sheriff turned to Constantia. "You all right, Miss Constantia?"

She scowled as she rubbed her wrists. "I'll survive."

Granger handed Deputy Norwood the items he'd taken from Bates. "Secure the gun and badge, then see that Miss Constantia gets some salve on her wrists."

"Yes, sir." Deputy Norwood helped Constantia to her feet and led her from the room.

"Sheriff," called a man sitting off to the side of the room. "When are you planning to let us leave? We had nothing to do with this, and we need to get on the road."

Others in the room grumbled their own complaints, until everyone was shouting at once.

Granger stood with his hands on his hips and glared at the restless mob. He said nothing until he'd stared them all into silence. "I've got a dead body upstairs. Right now, you're all either witnesses to a crime, whether you know it or not, or persons of interest. The sooner you all cooperate, the sooner you get to leave."

"And when will that be?" shouted another man.

"When I finish," said Granger. "The longer you pester me with questions, the longer it's going to take."

An undercurrent of hostile muttering rippled through the room. Granger ignored it. Instead, he directed his attention to a table of four ladies, the ones who earlier had led the pack that tromped upstairs, hoping to learn that another murder had occurred. They'd gotten their wish. Granger pointed to one of them and said, "Ma'am, if you'll accompany me, we'll get on with the interviews."

As she walked past the table where I sat, she shot me a dirty look and sneered, "Spider?" She punctuated the comment with a Lucille-style harrumph.

I glanced across to where her companions sat. All three narrowed daggers at me, obviously blaming me for depriving them of the opportunity to view a murder scene. Not that I had lied about the spider or barred them from the room. However, with Zack gone for the morning, I became the surrogate scapegoat by default.

I scanned the room and noticed neither Jolene nor Marsala seated with us. Granger had most likely already questioned both while I was with Constantia in Hart's office. I heard some puttering coming from the direction of the kitchen and figured Marsala was cleaning up the dishes from breakfast.

I suspected Sheriff Granger planned to speak with me last. Part of me was surprised he hadn't asked me to sit in on the interviews. It would have saved us both time. But that might jeopardize a conviction down the road.

My legal expertise, for what it was worth, was limited to episodes of *Law & Order*, and I knew how crime dramas often had little in common with reality. A person being questioned had the right to have an attorney present, but I had no idea if law enforcement could invite a reluctant amateur sleuth to sit in on the questioning of possible witnesses or suspects.

Muttering and grumbling continued to fill the room, peppered with the sound effects from various game apps played mostly by staff and a few guests neither muttering nor grumbling. A coffee station was set up at one end of the room. I rose from my chair and crossed the room to fill a cup and grab a mini muffin.

Out of the corner of my eye, I noticed one of the three remaining crime junkies making her way toward me. Hopefully, she only wanted a cup of coffee and not a confrontation, but I wasn't taking any chances. I quickly pivoted and returned to my seat. Before I buried my face in my phone, my peripheral vision caught her scowling at me, but instead of following me, she helped herself to a muffin and rejoined her companions.

With at least an hour or more before Zack returned from his photo shoot, I popped my earbuds in and opened the Sleuth Sayer podcast. Once again, I began with the first episode.

This time, I remained awake.

It really is true what they say about near-death experiences. At various times since Karl's death, my life had passed before me, thanks to killers bent on making me their next victim. Listening to a total stranger recount those episodes, created an angry mix of déjà vu garnished with a sprinkling of PTSD, as I once again was forced to relive my unfortunate encounter with Riccardo Ferrera, the mob loan shark and hitman. It was almost as if the Sleuth Sayer had a direct line into the part of my brain that housed my memories. Listening without becoming emotional took Herculean effort, but somehow, I managed to maintain a passive expression.

After a few minutes, Deputy Norwood returned with Constantia. I forced myself to continue focusing on the podcast. While I listened, the room continued to thin out as Sheriff Granger interviewed the remaining guests and staff, then allowed them to leave. By the time I'd finished the episode, the coroner had removed Hart's body, and the sheriff had wrapped up his interviews. Since he never spent more than a few minutes with each guest or staff member, I suspected none of the interviewees had offered anything worth noting.

Constantia had been Granger's last interview. I don't know if she'd admitted to searching through Hart's computer and files. After ushering her into her office, he'd spent about ten minutes with her, then returned alone to the dining room. After sending Deputy Norwood off on an errand, he poured himself a cup of coffee and filled a plate with several mini muffins before settling into the chair opposite me. We were now alone in the dining room.

"Learn anything useful?" I asked.

He shook his head. "No one heard anything. No one saw anything."

That didn't surprise me. None of the B&B guests would have been in the main house that early in the morning. Nor would the staff. "When did Marsala arrive?"

"Not until about six. According to the coroner's preliminary assessment, Hart was already dead by then."

"And she didn't pass anyone on the road on her way in?"

"Not that she remembers."

I told him about Constantia's search. He nodded. "She told me. I've got a copy of the spreadsheet she found."

"What about the text messages?"

"They confirmed Hart was having an affair with Jolene."

"I suspected as much. Do you have any idea why Hart was wooing investors? And for what?"

He drew his brows together. "Hart was the county golden boy with a bright future. He made a name for himself in multiple sports in high school and college."

"I noticed the trophies."

"Trouble is, he was a big fish swimming in various little ponds. There were hundreds of kids, as good or better throughout the country. It came as quite a blow to his ego when he wasn't picked up by any national team in any of the sports he'd played. On top of that, Constantia and her sisters had inherited a thriving business that grew more successful with each passing year."

"Another blow to Hart's ego?"

"Exactly. Some men just can't handle playing second fiddle to their wives' success. Hart was one of them. He pursued one pot of gold after another to prove himself. The architectural salvage business was the only thing he's ever done that didn't go bust. Thanks to all those TV decorating and real estate shows, for once in his life, he was in the right place at the right time with the right idea. It's been a huge success."

"Why would he need investors?"

The sheriff popped a muffin in his mouth, then took a sip of coffee before answering. "He wouldn't. Not for that kind of business."

"And the district attorney hasn't mentioned any details of his investigation?"

"Not a word. At least not to me."

"How did you find out?"

"A reliable source. I can't say more."

"If Hart was under investigation for fraud, why didn't the district attorney get a warrant for his computer?"

"I can't answer that, ma'am. He'd need probable cause for a search warrant. Maybe the investigation hasn't progressed that far yet. My source led me to believe it's in the very early stages. Other than that, no one's talking."

"Really? Not even the investors who lost their money?"

Granger thought for a moment. "Maybe they're too embarrassed over falling for a con."

"Or afraid their wives will find out they gambled away their nest eggs on some crazy get-rich-quick scheme?"

"Could be. You have any ideas?"

"A few," I said. "Given how little we know, I can think of three possibilities, but none seem quite right to me."

"Go on."

I held up a finger. "One, Constantia found out Hart was leaving her and killed him in a fit of rage."

"She does have a temper," he admitted, "but her grief sure seemed real."

"Unless she was channeling Sarah Bernhardt."

"Huh?"

I guess Sarah Bernhardt never played The Grand Ole Opry. "Famous French stage actress from the late nineteenth and early twentieth century," I explained.

"A little before my time." Then he quickly added, "And yours."

I shrugged. "I'm a theater buff. Anyway, Constantia may have been putting on a performance for our benefit. I never heard her ask how Hart was killed. Nor did she express a desire to see his body. However, both can be explained away by shock, and neither proves she killed him."

He torqued his mouth as he scratched at his chin. "True. What's your second scenario?"

"Jolene killed him."

"Why?"

"What if Hart got wind of the investigation and decided to make a run without her?"

He mulled that over for a minute. "Figuring he'd have a better chance of avoiding capture without a teenager tagging along."

"Especially since he'd have to leave the country. My guess is he'd head somewhere that doesn't have an extradition treaty with the U.S."

Granger shook his head. "I know Jolene's family. No way that little girl has a passport. The farthest her family has ever traveled is Orlando."

"If she and Hart were having an affair under Constantia's nose, which the texts prove, Hart probably gave Jolene a key to the main house to let herself in early in the morning."

Granger shook his head again, this time adding a deep scowl. "I hope you're wrong. I'd hate to think Jolene is capable of murder. I've known her since she was crawling around in diapers, but I suppose anything is possible."

"Also, neither that scenario nor the first accounts for the boot print on the lampshade, which would indicate a male assailant. Too bad Three Sisters doesn't have security cameras."

"Would've been helpful," he said, "but most folks around here don't even lock their doors, let alone have cameras around their property."

"Including Constantia and Hart?"

"Especially them. Jolene wouldn't have needed a key. With Three Sisters so far from town and the nearest neighbors a mile away, Miss Constantia kept the house open in case guests wanted a late-night snack. She always left a selection of beverages and baked goods on the dining room sideboard. There've been times when I've worked the late shift and stopped by in the middle of the night to help myself to a cup of coffee and a muffin or donut."

Southern hospitality at its finest. Still, given the recent break-ins at Casa Pollack, the idea of leaving my home unlocked and available to any Tom, Dick, or Vito made no sense to me.

Then again, I wasn't running a B&B. However, I didn't recall anyone mentioning the availability of late-night munchies. Maybe it's one of the perks listed in the Three Sisters brochure in our cottage. Not that I've looked at it, given my current dual obsessions with the Sleuth Sayer and now, not one, but two murders.

Granger changed the subject. "What's your third scenario?"

"One of Hart's investors killed him."

"You're suggesting someone entered the house before daybreak and snuck up behind Hart in an upstairs bedroom without him seeing or hearing anything?"

"Seems unlikely, doesn't it?"

"More like near impossible. Besides, none of these three possibilities tie into Waylon's death. I can't wrap my head around two unconnected murders. We're missing a huge piece of the puzzle."

"I did have one other thought," I said. "What if Hart killed Waylon?"

"Why?"

"Beats me. But I agree with you. Somehow these two murders are connected." The million-dollar question, though, was how? And for that, I had no answer.

Granger stood. "Given where Hart was killed, it's more likely he invited his killer upstairs. For the life of me, though, I can't figure out why he'd have such an early morning visitor and bring him up to a spare bedroom."

"Unless the killer entered the house earlier and was lying in wait for Hart."

"But how would he have known Hart would enter that bedroom this morning?" He shook his head. "Makes no sense. I'll sleep on it. Maybe something will come to me. Meanwhile, I've got a pile of paperwork to tackle, thanks to this latest case."

Once Sheriff Granger departed, Constantia cautiously entered the dining room. "He's gone?"

"The sheriff? He just left. If you hurry, you may be able to catch him."

"Why would I do that?"

"I thought—"

She dismissed the rest of my words with a wave of her hand. "I just wanted to make sure he was gone. I didn't kill Hart. You can scratch that possibility off your list."

"You were eavesdropping on us?"

She poured herself a cup of coffee and joined me at the table. "Of course, I was. You'd do the same if you were in my shoes. Come to think of it, you probably have been in my shoes, and I'll find out in some future episode from the Sleuth Sayer."

The difference being, I knew I hadn't killed anyone. I wasn't taking Constantia's word for her own innocence. As Ralph would squawk, *"The lady doth protest too much, methinks."*

"I also didn't know Hart was having an affair with Jolene. Not until I read those texts."

I wasn't going to challenge her. Maybe she did, and maybe she didn't. Instead, I said, "They say the wife is always the last to know." I certainly was when it came to Karl's secret life.

"Apparently, about many things." Constantia rose. "I'm going back upstairs to continue searching through Hart's computer. So far, I haven't found anything. I'm beginning to think Buck is full of cow patties. Maybe I should pay the district attorney a visit."

"I don't see why the sheriff would lie about something like that."

"I'm not accusing him of lying. Not exactly. But maybe he's mistaken."

That seemed like a huge mistake for a sheriff to make. Although Granger came across as a good ol' boy on the outside, I'd come to agree with Zack's assessment of him. I also appreciated that Granger admitted to his lack of homicide investigative experience. Not everyone in law enforcement would show such honesty and humility.

And how many of them, other than Detective Samuel Spader, would consider my opinions valid? All of this led me to believe that Sheriff Buck Granger wouldn't claim a dead man was under investigation for fraud if that weren't the case.

Rather than argue with Constantia, I asked, "Did Hart have an office in the barn he used for his architectural salvage business?"

"Yes, he needed one nearby to keep track of inventory."

"So, there's a computer in the barn?"

"Yes. Why?"

"You tell me."

She smacked her forehead. "Of course! Why didn't I think of that." She jumped up and raced out of the dining room, passing Zack on his way in.

"She seems excited about something," he said, the two of us watching Constantia fly through the lobby and out the front door.

"Not necessarily in a good way. I'll tell you all about it on our way to your next shoot. But first you need to feed me."

Zack cocked his head and studied me. "Hmm...seems I remember someone taking one look at the breakfast set before her this morning and swearing off lunch."

"I need to stress eat."

TWELVE

"According to their website," said Zack, "Clatterbuck Vineyards includes a farm-to-table restaurant. Think you can hold out until we get there?"

"Define *until we get there*."

"Half an hour, max. You going to make it, or should we raid Constantia's kitchen before we leave?"

"I can wait, as long as chocolate is on the menu." Before leaving the dining room, I darted over to the coffee station and grabbed the lone mini muffin Sheriff Granger had left in the basket. "One for the road," I said when Zack raised a questioning eyebrow.

On the drive to the vineyard, I filled Zack in on everything that had transpired after he headed off to Vin de la Terre. "Constantia was rushing off to search the computer Hart kept in the barn when she nearly collided with you. At this point, I need a scorecard to keep track of the countless dangling threads going on around here. And they keep multiplying like rabbits."

"Far worse than rabbits," said Zack.

"Cockroaches?"

"That works, but I was thinking Tribbles. At any rate, very little of what's going on here makes sense. Is it all connected? Is some of it connected? Or is nothing connected?"

"Ever get the feeling you're playing Clue with Monopoly property cards and Dungeons and Dragons dice?"

He shot me a side-eye. "You don't strike me as the D&D type."

I wrinkled my nose. "I'm not. I briefly dated a guy in college who was more than slightly obsessed with the game."

"How briefly?"

"We never made it past the first date. I don't even remember his name." I changed the subject. "Did you learn anything at Vin de la Terre?"

"The operation is even smaller than their brochure suggests. Calling themselves a boutique winery really stretches truth in advertising."

"How so?"

"They're more of a kitchen table operation. I'm no expert, but I suspect they're struggling to compete with the likes of Winely Made, Three Sisters, and the other area wineries."

"That's too bad."

"They're hoping for some national recognition by taking part in the advertorial."

"Is their wine any good?"

"Surprisingly, more than good. Excellent. But are you ready for the plot twist?"

I turned to look at him. "I'm afraid to ask. Does it have anything to do with the murders?"

"I'll let you be the judge of that. Vin de la Terre is owned by Grammy Mead's great-grandson."

"The son of the grandson she cut out of her will? The one who sued the estate? Interesting. How did you discover that?"

"I learned from the best of the best when it comes to sleuthing."

"Meaning?"

"I took a page from your book and eavesdropped on a call he received while showing me around the vineyard."

"You're saying I'm the best of the best?"

"Don't let it go to your head. You ready for this?"

"I'm all ears."

"Apparently, he knew about Hart's venture but refused to invest."

"Okay, that was a drop the mic moment."

"Not quite. It gets even better."

"There's more?"

"Oh, yeah. Remember the personality change we noticed in Shasta after the phone call she received yesterday?"

"When she transformed from Miss Perky to Miss Distracted?"

"I'm guessing, the call was from her husband because as it turns out, he invested with Hart."

"You learned all this from eavesdropping?"

"The guy wasn't exactly whispering into his phone. He had it on speaker."

"He didn't care that you heard both ends of the conversation?"

"He was so incensed that I think he forgot I was there. After he hung up, he seemed surprised to see me standing a few feet away."

"And the caca hit the fan yesterday?"

"From what I gather, all of Hart's investors found out they'd lost everything yesterday."

LOIS WINSTON

"And less than twenty-four hours later, someone murdered Hart. That certainly gives Sheriff Granger a wide pool of suspects."

"Did you see the names on the list Constantia found?"

"I caught a glimpse of the list but wasn't close enough to read the names. Constantia recognized some of the people but not all of them. I wonder how many of Hart's investors also wanted Waylon Oakley dead."

As I gazed out the window while mulling over this additional information, I realized the area looked familiar. "Isn't this the road we took to Winely Made?"

"It is. Why?"

"How would you feel about making a quick stop?"

Zack took his eyes off the road for a moment and shot me a knowing look while shaking his head. "Any chance I can hope that muffin didn't do the trick, and you need the nearest food truck? Or you're craving a dose of country music?"

"Probably not. But I wouldn't mind hitting the taco truck before we leave."

"I was afraid of that." But instead of trying to talk me out of the detour, Zack let up on the gas as we approached the turnoff for Winely Made.

We arrived to find the parking area crammed to near capacity. After driving up and down the rows of parked cars, we finally found a spot at the farthest edge of the field. Once we hiked nearly half a mile to the entrance and flashed the passes Shasta had given us, we made our way to the barn that housed her office.

We found the office door halfway open and Shasta frowning at her computer screen. Zack rapped on the doorframe to get her attention. When she glanced up, she quickly masked her expression, forced an overly bright smile, and said, "I'm so glad you found time to return."

Zack and I stepped into the office and approached her desk. "We're on our way to another photo shoot," he said, "but we were wondering if we could have a minute or two of your time."

Her brows knit together. "About the festival?"

"About the phone call you received while you were showing us around the winery," I said.

Shasta's face hardened. "I don't see why that's any of your business."

I backtracked. "It's not, and we don't mean to pry, but we've been worried about you."

"Why?"

"We couldn't help noticing the change that came over you after the call," said Zack, "and we've since learned of some disturbing news concerning Hart Kingston."

Shasta's eyes welled up with tears, and her lower lip trembled. "You mean like how I might lose the winery thanks to him?"

She then leveled a glare in our direction but not at us, more like at something or someone behind us. I twisted my neck to glance over my shoulder and discovered a tall, lanky man standing in the doorway. He hung his head as he entered the office and closed the door behind him. Speaking to the floor, he mumbled, "I know I messed up, Babe. I just wanted to surprise you."

"Congratulations, Nash. You succeeded. Big time."

"I'll make it up to you. I promise. Whatever it takes."

Shasta scowled, then turned to Zack and me. "Meet my formerly business-savvy husband, Nash Summers. Right now, I don't know who I want to kill more, him for investing our savings without consulting me or Hart for scamming him out of thousands of dollars."

"Someone already beat you to it," I said.

Shasta reached for a tissue from the box on her desk. As she patted the moisture from her eyes, she asked, "What does that mean?"

"Hart Kingston is dead."

Her eyes grew wide, and her mouth gaped open as she struggled to speak. "You don't think I...? I didn't mean literally. I'd never...I wouldn't...."

"No one is accusing you," said Zack. "But we would like to ask you both some questions about the investment."

Nash looked from Zack to me, his expression wary. "Why you?"

"We're here on behalf of Sheriff Granger," I said.

"Are you cops?"

I answered by employing the royal *we*. "We have experience investigating murders." After all, Mama did claim we descended from Russian nobility. However, I figured Nash might be more receptive to speaking with us if he assumed Zack was a member of law enforcement (and for all I knew, he could be.) My credentials as a reluctant amateur sleuth are tenuous at best, no matter what Constantia, her sisters, and the Sleuth Sayer think.

Nash waved us to the two chairs in front of the desk. "Have a seat." He then positioned himself on the corner of Shasta's desk. "What do you want to know?"

"For starters," I said, "what were you investing in?"

"Land. Waylon figured if we all pooled our money, we could buy up available farmland."

"And do what with it?" asked Zack.

"Expand our wineries and at the same time minimize the

suburban sprawl threatening the area."

"A worthy objective but wouldn't Hewitt and other developers outbid you on the properties?" I asked.

"Not if they didn't know about the sales until after the fact."

"Except any farmer looking to sell would want top dollar for his land," said Zack. "Why would they accept your offer without contacting the developers to create a bidding war."

"We planned to offer market price."

"How could you afford to compete with the deep pockets of these developers?" I asked.

"That was the beauty of Hart's plan."

"And its downfall," said Shasta, scowling at her husband. "They invested in cryptocurrency."

"Wait," I said. "Are you saying Hart didn't embezzle the money from his investors?"

"Who told you that?" asked Nash.

"The sheriff. He said the district attorney was investigating Hart for financial fraud."

Nash shook his head. "Not unless stupidity is fraudulent. It never occurred to any of us to ask him which crypto fund he was investing in. All we knew was our return on investment was outpacing the S&P 500 by quite a bit. We expected to have enough money by the end of the year to start acquiring land."

"Until yesterday when they learned the fund went belly up," said Shasta.

"We all knew investing in crypto was risky," said Nash. "We just never expected that the guy who ran the fund was operating a Ponzi scheme. Hart didn't drain our accounts. The fund manager did. Along with the accounts of everyone else who'd invested in his fund."

"Someone accused Hart of fraud," said Zack. "Any idea who?"

"Or why?" I added.

Nash and Shasta stared at each other for a split second before they both shook their heads.

"What about Waylon?" I asked. "Did he know about this venture or have anything to do with it?"

Shasta shook her head. "I wouldn't think so."

Nash stood and slumped against the wall behind Shasta's chair. He shoved his hands in his pockets and stared at his feet as he mumbled, "Actually, Dalton insisted we consult Waylon."

"Dalton Radley?" asked Zack.

Nash eyed him suspiciously. "You know Dalton?"

"We met this morning."

Nash looked like he wanted to grill Zack about how he knew Dalton Radley, but Shasta spun her chair around to face her husband and jumped in before he had the chance. "What did Waylon say?"

Nash glanced up, his voice sounding whiny and defensive as he answered her. "Waylon thought it was a great idea, even offered to invest."

Shasta narrowed her gaze. "And did he?"

Nash grimaced. "No."

"Why not?"

"He said crypto was too risky. He'd only go in with us if we invested in something safe."

Shasta scoffed. "And of course, you didn't."

Nash continued to whine. "Hart argued that crypto was our only chance of making enough money fast enough. He said crypto had been around long enough, and Waylon was plain foolish for not jumping on the one chance we all had to prevent more development in the area."

Shasta's voice rose several octaves. "Waylon was foolish? When had he ever steered us wrong? He's the reason for our success."

Nash grew red in the face. He avoided making eye contact with his wife. "We took a vote. Dalton agreed with Waylon. The rest of us decided to go for it."

"This just gets better and better," said Shasta, unable to keep the bitterness from her voice. Or maybe she didn't care. "You not only ignored Waylon's advice, but none of you bothered to consult with your wives before making the most boneheaded decision of your lives. And now we're all broke, thanks to your greedy frat boy mentality. All of you together don't have the common sense of a gnat. Except Dalton, apparently."

Shasta glanced up at the ceiling and sighed. "Who would've thought the one person among you with any brains would be Lonnie Knox's kid."

"Lonnie Knox?"

Shasta explained. "A local black sheep."

I knew Lonnie was a common Southern name, but what were the chances Lonnie Knox was Grammy Mead's disinherited grandson? I had to ask.

"Would this be the three sisters' cousin?"

Both Shasta and Nash registered surprise. "How do you know about Lonnie?" asked Nash. "He took off years ago."

"All I know is that Grammy Mead cut him out of her will."

"For good reason," said Shasta.

I waited for more. Instead, she turned to her husband. "He's your friend. Maybe you should tell them."

"I don't see why it's any of their business," said Nash.

"You never know what might help lead to finding a killer," said

Zack.

Nash eyed us as he seemed to debate with himself. Finally, he said, "I suppose since you're working with Sheriff Granger, it's okay to tell you about Lonnie and Dalton. It's no big secret around here."

He took a deep breath. "Long story short, Lonnie knocked up his girlfriend in high school. Instead of doing right by her, he took off."

"And Dalton Radley was that baby?" asked Zack.

Nash nodded. "Radley was his mama's name. Bethany Radley. She passed on a few years later. Cancer."

Shasta took over the tale. "Miss Roussanne and Waylon never had any children of their own. They took Dalton in and raised him. When Lonnie disappeared, Grammy Mead changed her will. The money that should have gone to Lonnie went into a trust fund for Dalton. She also left him the property that's now Vin de la Terre."

"Dalton's a good guy," added Nash.

Shasta agreed. "Nothing like his father." She directed her next comment to her husband. "Too bad he couldn't convince the rest of you not to fall for Hart's harebrained scheme."

This set off another round of acrimony between the two of them. Although I felt sorry for Shasta and Nash, the last thing I wanted to do was referee a marital donnybrook. All of this hit too close to home for me, except that I'd never had the opportunity to direct my hurt and anger at the man responsible for it.

Shasta and Nash would have to figure out how to move beyond this major bump in their relationship without any advice from me. Not that they'd asked for any.

Having gotten the answers to our questions—and then some,

Zack and I made a hasty escape. As he closed the office door behind us, we continued to hear Shasta sniping at Nash and Nash repeatedly apologizing. I doubt they even realized we'd exited the office.

By the time we made it back to the taco truck, it was well past lunchtime, and we had our choice of empty picnic tables. We chose one far from any other festivalgoers to avoid curious eavesdroppers.

After silently devouring half of the first of my two shrimp tacos, I'd sated my appetite enough to speak. "Something doesn't add up."

"Something?" Zack paused before taking another bite of his taco. "I'd say more like *nothing* adds up. But I'm all ears. What's niggling on your brain?"

"Hart's business model. As we pointed out, any farmer who wanted to or needed to sell would want top dollar for his land and encourage a bidding war. They'd be foolish not to, given the expansion going on in the county."

Zack nodded. "We're on the same wavelength. No matter how great the return on their initial crypto investment, they'd be competing against developers with both deeper pockets and established banking relationships."

That brought up another problem. "With Hart's track record of business failures, what bank would float them loans, let alone at a decent interest rate?"

Zack spoke around another mouthful. "Good question. Maybe they foolishly thought they'd make enough profit on crypto to pay cash for the land."

Foolishly being the operative word. "Besides," I continued, "even if they secured backing from a bank, how would they pay off the loans? Doesn't it take several years for newly planted acreage to start producing viable grapes?"

"Three, according to what Shasta mentioned in the production facility."

I washed down my last bite with a gulp of water before continuing. "I feel like the kid who pointed out the emperor was buck naked. This business was doomed to fail from the start. If the flaws stood out to us, why were the others blind to them? Given what we've learned about Waylon, I find it hard to believe he only warned them against investing in crypto and not the entire venture."

"Maybe he did. We only have Nash's word that Waylon thought it was a great idea. Greed often blinds people to the truth, and Waylon is no longer around to get his side of the story."

"They were either incredibly stupid, extremely naïve, or both. Hart's heart may have been in the right place, no pun intended, but even if they had bought up some of the local farms, I suspect they'd all eventually wind up having to sell to the very developers they tried to keep out."

We were walking back to the car when another thought walloped my brain. I stopped short.

"What's wrong?" asked Zack.

"What if Hart's heart *wasn't* in the right place?"

"Meaning?"

"Meaning he sold the other guys on this grand idea, playing on either their greed or their altruism, but all along he was planning to abscond with the money."

"Except someone beat him to it."

"Or not. Sheriff Granger said the district attorney was investigating Hart for financial fraud. We only know the fund manager absconded with the money because that's what Hart told his investors. What if he lied to them?"

"I think those countless dangling threads just multiplied again," said Zack.

"More Tribbles?"

"Way more Tribbles."

"Is one of them named Lonnie Knox?"

"Could be."

I pondered over Lonnie Knox. "Shasta and Nash said he flew the coop decades ago, but that doesn't mean he hasn't been in touch with old friends over the years. What if he's returned because he learned Dalton came into his trust fund? If there was history between him and Waylon or Hart, he may have also decided to settle some old scores."

"If so, wouldn't he target his cousins, not their husbands? We know he tried to sue them for his share of Grammy Mead's estate."

"If that's the case, he's already targeted two of the three sisters by killing their husbands."

"Which means Marsala's husband may be his next victim."

THIRTEEN

Once we settled into the car, I pulled out my phone and placed a call to Sheriff Granger. As Zack drove us to Clatterbuck Vineyards, I presented the sheriff with everything we'd learned this morning and asked him about Lonnie Knox.

"I've scheduled a meeting with the district attorney later this afternoon to find out more about that fraud investigation," he said. "I'll ask if he has any new intel on Lonnie. Last I heard, he was doing a long stretch for armed robbery over in Mississippi. As far as I know, he's still locked up."

"Can you find out if he was released?" I asked.

"Easy enough. If so, he may have returned to strongarm Dalton. I'll swing by and have a talk with him after I meet with the D.A."

"What about Waylon and Hart?" asked Zack, his eyes remaining on the road as he joined the conversation. "Did Lonnie have any history with either of them? They would've been about the same age, right?"

Sheriff Granger voice filled with scorn. "Some people walk through life with a chip on their shoulder. Lonnie Knox carried around a two-by-four on his. That kid was born a bully and only got worse with each passing year. He had history with everyone in town. And not in a good way."

"And yet, he had a girlfriend," I said.

"The jury's still out on that one, Miss Anastasia."

"What do you mean?"

"Some of us suspected that relationship was far from consensual, but times being what they were back then, Miss Bethany refused to press charges."

"Do you think he's capable of murder?" asked Zack.

The sheriff answered with a sobering question of his own. "Isn't everyone?"

Half an hour later, we arrived at Clatterbuck Vineyards, a sprawling estate with not only acre upon acre of grapevines but also fields of various other crops and several fruit orchards. Driving along the road that wound through the compound, we passed a barn, stable, paddock filled with half a dozen horses, and various other outbuildings. Nearer the plantation-style main house were a dozen guest cottages, a massive kitchen garden, and a recreational area featuring an Olympic-size swimming pool, kiddie pool, tennis courts, miniature golf, and a well-equipped playground.

"This is more resort than vineyard," I said. "It makes Three Sisters and Winely Made look like also-rans."

"Except if you book a stay here, you have to work for your room and board," said Zack.

"I'll pass."

He chuckled.

A short time later, we arrived at a sign that directed us toward our choice of either valet or self-parking. Zack opted for the latter and followed the arrow to a parking lot filled with vehicles that cost more than what Karl and I had paid for Casa Pollack years ago. I suspected a week's stay at Clatterbuck Vineyards didn't come cheap.

Zack grabbed his camera bag from the trunk, and we trekked the short distance to a white-columned mansion. "I wonder if this Tara clone is an actual Antebellum plantation or a replica."

"Original but renovated, according to the information *Vine* sent me."

"No outhouses?"

"They left one standing as a tourist attraction."

"I'll pass on that, too."

"Where's your sense of adventure?"

"Firmly parked in the land of creature comforts."

We climbed the steps to a wraparound porch and entered through the double doors. A concierge greeted us. "Welcome to Clatterbuck Vineyards. Checking in?"

Zack explained why we were there, adding, "Mariah Clatterbuck is expecting us."

The concierge picked up a phone on his podium. A moment later, he said, "The photographer has arrived." He then listened for a moment. "Yes, ma'am."

After he hung up, he addressed Zack. "Unfortunately, Miss Mariah is tied up in a meeting that's running late, sir. She said she'd be with you as soon as possible. In the meantime, she suggested you wait for her in the restaurant." He waved toward the room on his left. "We're currently serving afternoon tea. Feel free to help yourselves to anything at the buffet. Compliments of

Clatterbuck Vineyards."

Music to my ears, not to mention a belly still not completely satisfied by our visit to the food truck.

A well-laden buffet filled the center of the vast dining room. With its high coffered ceiling, enormous crystal chandeliers, polished wood parquet floor, and rows of floor-to-ceiling windows, the room had most likely originally served as the plantation's ballroom. Individual tables for two, four, or six guests wrapped around the perimeter of the room, many filled with either couples or families. Other guests grazed the buffet, helping themselves to a vast selection of appetizers, salads, sandwiches, and desserts.

After joining the queue, Zack and I each filled a plate with a selection of tea sandwiches, fruit, and crudites. I stared longingly at the pastries and tea cakes but took a deep breath and harnessed my willpower. After all, I'd already eaten two shrimp tacos less than half an hour ago. As soon as we'd settled into our seats, a server arrived to offer us our choice of beverages.

We were finishing up our mini meal when a middle-aged woman approached the table. She wore her silver blonde hair in loose curls that framed her round face. With her rosy cheeks, she reminded me of an adult version of one of Michelangelo's Sistine Chapel cherubs, except she'd traded in her wings and halo for a khaki pantsuit and cowboy boots.

"Mr. Barnes?" She held out her hand to Zack. "I'm Mariah Clatterbuck. Welcome."

Zack stood and shook her hand. "Zack, please." He nodded toward me. "And this is my wife, Anastasia."

"Ah, yes." She smiled broadly and offered me her hand as she joined us at the table. "Constantia Kingston's sleuth. I understand you're helping Sheriff Granger."

I no longer bothered denying it. Thanks to Constantia, I'm sure Mariah Clatterbuck and everyone else in Tennessee had already learned of me through Constantia's social media postings and listened to the Sleuth Sayer podcasts.

Mariah continued. "Such a shame about Waylon. He was one in a million. I can't imagine why anyone would want to harm that man. He was our champion."

Chalk up one more local resident in the Waylon Oakley fan club column. "We've heard he advised many of the local wineries. Did he also help expand your business?"

She nodded. "The farm has been in my family since the early eighteen hundreds. They expanded the vineyard and concentrated on wine production after Prohibition ended. A few years ago, when we were thinking about ways to expand, Waylon suggested branching out into agritourism."

She waved her arm toward the nearest window with its view of the recreational area. "Much of the amenities you see here are a result of taking his advice. We're completely booked for the next two years and are scheduled to add another dozen guest cottages next winter. We now plan to name one of them the Waylon Oakley Memorial Cottage."

"I'm sure his wife will take comfort in that."

"I hope so. I can't imagine Roussanne's grief." No one spoke for an awkward moment before Mariah broke off the silence with a clap of her hands. "Enough depressing talk." She then pushed back her chair, stood, and turned to Zack. "If you're finished with your tea, I'll give you the grand tour. I'm excited to see what magic you create with your camera."

Since Mariah hadn't mentioned the latest murder, I wondered

if she'd heard about Hart. No matter how I wracked my brain, I couldn't come up with a way to insert the news of his death into our conversation, short of blurting it out. Under the circumstances, I remained mum, but I turned to Zack for a second opinion.

As we exited the dining room behind Mariah, I mouthed Hart's name and motioned questioningly toward her back. His brows knit together, and his mouth quirked. I waited as he considered, but after a moment, he whispered, "Let's play it by ear."

Our ears didn't have long to wait. Once Mariah had led us outside and away from her other guests and staff, she stopped beyond the kitchen garden and spun to face us. "Now that we're alone, why don't you tell me about Hart's murder. Do you know who killed him?"

My mouth dropped open. "Word travels fast."

She shrugged. "It's a small community."

Since Sheriff Granger hadn't directed me not to speak about Hart's murder, I filled her in, ending by asking her if she had invested with him.

"He never approached me."

From everything I'd heard, Hart seemed eager to sign on as many investors as possible. "I wonder why."

"I don't."

"Oh?"

"He knew I didn't trust him."

Zack and I both stared at her, waiting for more of an explanation.

After a long pause, she waved her hand as if dismissing the reason like a bad memory. "Ancient history. We dated in college, even talked of marriage—until I caught him cheating on me." She emitted a chuckle of irony. "In hindsight, I'm grateful I didn't wind up with him, given how he turned out."

"Meaning?"

"Meaning you can't go through life trying to recapture the glory days of your youth. You wind up a bitter loser with a reverse Midas touch."

Zack spoke for the first time. "Any idea who'd want him dead?"

"Other than all his investors? How about his wife?"

Maybe I wasn't so off-base thinking Constantia killed Hart. "Why?"

"Rumor has it, he was cheating on her. And not for the first time. Once a cheater, always a cheater."

Funny how Constantia had used those same words to describe Waylon. The circumstantial evidence continued to pile up against her.

But Mariah hadn't finished. "And then there's his business partner."

Zack and I both spoke at once. "What business partner?"

"Beats me, but one thing I can tell you about Hart Kingston, no way was that middle-aged has-been smart enough to cook up an investment scheme on his own, let alone pitch the idea to potential investors."

With that she switched back to tour guide mode and continued leading us across the road toward the vineyards. As we rambled along a path lined on either side with lavender-blue catmint, she effused about her agritourism business.

We spent the next hour and a half hiking through fields, vineyards, and orchards, with Zack clicking away at the panoramic beauty of the Clatterbuck property. The day was nowhere near as hot as yesterday, and a light breeze followed us around. The perfumy scents of herbs, fruits, and florals fought against the omnipresent odors of a working farm. I could do without the latter.

As I followed along, I tuned out Mariah's detailed multi-generational history of both her family and Clatterbuck Vineyards, as well as their prize-winning wines. Instead, I gave my mind free rein to wander over the details I had learned about Waylon Oakley and Hart Kingston.

There was still the frustration of too many missing puzzle pieces and far too much speculation. Such a mixed bag of information also raised the question of ulterior motives among friends and family of the victims. Were one or more of them leading me down a rabbit hole?

And what of Dalton Radley? If Roussanne and Waylon raised him as their own son, why hadn't Waylon offered him any advice regarding his winery? Zack had said Dalton appeared to be struggling. Since he'd taken Waylon's advice concerning the crypto investment, I had to believe the two were on good terms. Why wouldn't Waylon help his son the way he'd helped Shasta and Mariah?

In addition, nothing of what I'd learned aided in tying both murders together. More and more, I began to suspect the two murders weren't connected, and we were dealing with two killers. However, that scenario stretched credulity in a county with such a low homicide rate, especially with both murders occurring on the same property in successive days.

I kept coming back to Mariah's assertion that Hart must have had a partner. If she was correct, did the other investors know about him, or was he a silent partner known only to Hart? Had Hart duped this phantom partner, or had he duped Hart?

I itched to hear from Sheriff Granger to find out what he'd learned from the district attorney regarding the financial fraud investigation. Not only to learn exactly who was being investigated, but who had tipped off the D.A.

By the time Mariah's tour of her sprawling estate ended, the sun had begun to dip behind the Cumberland Mountains, producing the onset of another multi-hued sunset to rival the Impressionists. I inhaled a deep calming breath and soaked in the pastel drenched sky.

Behind me, I heard the distinctive click of a camera shutter and knew Zack was capturing the moment. I sighed. "They do have the most magnificent sunsets around here."

Mariah came up beside me. "We certainly do. Cocktail hour is about to begin. Will you join us?"

I frowned at my pink T-shirt and white capri pants, then glanced over at Zack in his black T-shirt and jeans. "We're really not dressed for a cocktail hour."

"Nonsense. We're not formal here. No one is expected to dress for dinner."

I failed at masking my shock. "Weren't all those field workers we saw your guests?"

She laughed. "Many were. We do request they shower and change into fresh clothes before entering the dining room."

As Zack joined us, she continued. "I'd be honored if you'd be my guests for dinner."

I threw Zack an out in case he preferred not to accept the offer. "Didn't you already make dinner reservations for this evening?"

"I can cancel them."

Mariah smiled at him. "You won't be disappointed. Our chef is famous for his secret rib recipe, and people come for miles around for our pastry chef's crème brûlée, made from the cream of our own cows."

Zack eyed me and grinned. "I think you had her at crème brûlée."

A blush burned my cheeks. The man knows me so well. I don't have a sweet tooth. I have thirty-two of them. And what little willpower I possessed had been drained during afternoon tea.

Mariah led us back to the mansion. At the entrance to the dining room, she spoke to the maître d'. "See that Mr. and Mrs. Barnes are seated at my table for dinner." Then she turned to us. "Cocktail hour is on the side porch. I'll join you for dinner."

Zack and I walked across the foyer toward the double glass doors that opened onto the porch. A long, skirted table held various hot and cold hors d'oeuvres.

Cocktail hour was a misnomer. Instead of the usual mix of cocktails, wines, and hard liquor, the waitstaff wandered around offering only glasses of various Clatterbuck wines. I accepted a rosé, and Zack decided on a Syrah. As I sipped, I glanced around. Guests filled the porch and spilled down onto the flagstone patio below, standing in clusters and seated at the small wrought iron tables scattered around the patio. "Except for everyone in casual dress, you'd think we were at a fancy wedding."

Zack drained his glass and frowned.

"Something wrong?"

"On the contrary. This is the best Syrah I've ever had."

"Then why the face?"

"I was just thinking, whoever had it in for Waylon Oakley did a huge disservice to this community, considering all he did for the area vintners. I would have liked to meet him."

I was about to agree when my phone rang. After pulling it from my pocket and glancing at it, I turned the screen toward Zack. "Let's find somewhere more private." I handed him my glass, and as he led me away from the patio, I answered the call. "Hello."

"You free to talk, Miss Anastasia?"

"In a minute. We're heading toward somewhere more private."

Sheriff Granger waited while Zack and I wandered into the kitchen garden and made our way to the center where we found a bench. We both scanned the area, making certain we were alone except for the company of a few butterflies. Cucumbers, string beans, and tomato plants climbed a long chicken wire support fence between the bench and the house. After settling onto the bench, the lush produce blocked us from view.

Rather than putting the phone on speaker, I rifled in my purse for my earbuds and handed one to Zack before returning to the sheriff. "What did you learn, Sheriff?"

"Plenty. For starters, the district attorney wasn't exactly investigating Hart."

Strange choice of words. "How do you not exactly investigate someone?"

"Let me back up. Turns out it was Hart who went to the D.A."

"Why?" asked Zack.

"He'd grown suspicious of his business partner."

Mariah Clatterbuck had been right. "Who was his partner?"

"Beau Paxton, our state representative."

Something about that name darted around the corners of my brain, but before I could find a connection, Sheriff Granger supplied one. "He's the uncle of that worthless deputy I fired."

FOURTEEN

Talk about an interesting plot twist. "Are you saying the state representative fleeced all the investors? Not Hart and not the guy running the cryptocurrency investment firm?"

"According to what Hart told the D.A."

"What has the D.A. found?" asked Zack.

"Enough to turn the investigation over to the TBI."

"What's that?" I asked.

"Tennessee Bureau of Investigation," said Granger. "Paxton is up to his combover in hot water. Of course, he's denying everything. Claims Hart drained the fund and framed him."

"Did they both have the crypto key to access the funds?" asked Zack.

"Hart told the D.A. Paxton held the code. Said it would be safer with him, given security measures he had in place as a member of the Legislature. Paxton claims they both had a copy."

"How convenient," I said. "Blame the dead man who can no longer defend himself."

I was aware that financial fraud by elected officials, both local and national, happened all too frequently. Many looked on their positions, not as servants of the people, but as a way to line their own pockets. Some are arrested and serve time. Others get away with their crimes. Even though Hart was no choir boy, my gut told me Paxton had scammed him and not the other way around. From everything I'd learned about Hart Kingston, I doubted he had the smarts to pull off a crypto scheme. Time would tell whether or not the law agreed with me.

I didn't voice any of these thoughts, though. Instead, I said, "Sounds like Paxton has a motive for murder. Does he have an alibi for early this morning?"

"Claims he was asleep."

"Can anyone corroborate that?" asked Zack.

"Lyle." The sheriff uttered a sound of derision. "He's crashing with his uncle ever since his wife kicked his no-good, sorry butt out of the house. Claims Paxton didn't wake up until after nine. But I wouldn't believe anything he says."

I thought for a moment. "What about Lyle? Does he have an alibi?"

"You think Lyle killed Hart?"

"From the little I've seen of your ex-deputy, Sheriff, I suspect he's the kind of guy who might do anything for the right amount of money. Did he know that Constantia left the doors of the main house unlocked?"

"'fraid so, ma'am. He was with me on several occasions when I stopped in for a midnight snack."

"Do you think he's capable of murder?"

A long pause followed before the sheriff responded. "I always thought Bates was more coward than anything, but you may be onto something, little lady."

I stifled a groan while resisting the urge to read the sheriff the riot act and drag him into the twenty-first century. Instead, I glanced toward Zack and executed an eyeroll. He placed his hand on my forearm, squeezed, and mouthed, "Courage." I beamed at my husband. At least not all men are chauvinists.

I dug deep for some inner Zen and switched the topic. "What about Lonnie Knox?"

The sheriff cleared his throat. "Paroled three months ago."

"Has he been checking in regularly with his parole officer?" asked Zack.

"As far as I know. We haven't gotten any notification that says otherwise."

Which only means he makes sure he keeps his appointments. "How often does he need to check in with his parole officer?"

"Depends on the officer. Could be weekly, monthly, or every few months."

"Where was he incarcerated?" asked Zack.

"FCI Yazoo City."

Zack whipped out his phone and tapped his map app. "That's only six hours from here. He could easily come and go."

"Has Dalton heard from him?" I asked.

"Claims he hasn't."

"You believe him?" asked Zack.

"Can't see why he'd lie. Knox sure isn't his favorite person on the planet. Anything but."

"Any connection between Knox and Paxton?" I asked.

"They went to school together, hung out in the same crowd, along with Hart."

I suppose in tight-knit rural communities everyone knows

everyone else, but maybe the connections between all these men ran deeper. "Do you think Knox is capable of murder?"

The sheriff huffed a deep sigh. "From what I remember of Lonnie, I think he's capable of anything if it serves his purpose. Even murder."

"Which means Paxton may have paid Knox to murder Hart. With Hart out of the picture, the D.A. has no case against Paxton. They can't prove that Hart didn't drain the account and deposit the funds into some offshore account. Paxton sits back and waits until the investigation blows over and the case against him is dropped."

"What about the crypto?" asked the sheriff.

"My guess is it's hidden in a shell company."

He took a deep breath, and I thought I heard the whisper of an expletive coming from the other end of the phone before he said, "You folks keep your ears open. I'll update you if I learn anything else." He then disconnected the call.

I placed my phone back in my pocket. "If nothing else, at least Constantia has the comfort of knowing her husband wasn't a thief."

Zack raised both eyebrows. "We don't know that. We only have Hart's word that Paxton held the crypto key."

"Do you think, with everything we've learned about Hart, that Paxton would trust him with the keycode?"

"Stranger things have happened."

I pondered the thought for a moment. The deeper we dug, the more possibilities we unearthed.

But how did any of these theories connect to Waylon Oakley's murder?

Zack and I tabled our discussion until later in the evening

when we could speak in the privacy of our rental car. For now, we made our way from the kitchen garden toward the mansion to join Mariah Clatterbuck for dinner. But thoughts of murder and motive continued to ricochet in my brain.

One thing I'll say for the winery owners we'd met so far, they personified Southern hospitality. We were wined and dined as befitted honeymooning newlyweds, even though we hadn't divulged that information to anyone.

Unless the Sleuth Sayer had. I froze. A cannonball landed with a thud in my stomach.

"Is something wrong, Mrs. Barnes?"

Had I groaned out loud? Both Zack and Mariah stared at me. I shook away thoughts of the Sleuth Sayer and tried to will the cannonball out of both my stomach and existence. I forced a smile. "No, sorry."

"If you're unhappy with your meal, I'll have the chef make something else for you."

I glanced down and realized a forkful of asparagus hung in the air, midway to my mouth. For how long? "I'm fine. The food is delicious."

"You're sure?"

"Absolutely. I just suddenly thought of something, and... well, you know how sometimes something comes to you out of the blue and startles you?"

She frowned, obviously not convinced by my babbling. "You're not just saying that? You won't hurt my feelings. I'm happy to send your plate back."

"No, really." Was she kidding? I'd already devoured half the food on my plate. I brought the asparagus to my mouth and savored the perfectly cooked vegetable, then reached for my wine glass. "The rib meat is so tender, it's melting in my mouth, and your wine is the best I've tasted since arriving in Tennessee."

The tension lines around her eyes and mouth relaxed, but her face still held a look of concern. Short of blurting out what had crossed my mind, which I absolutely refused to do, I don't know how else I could assure her.

Besides, I wasn't a Michelin critic in disguise. Or maybe she thought I was?

I turned toward Zack. He, also, showed signs of concern. "Sweetheart?"

What could I say to assure him? As I wracked my brain, both he and Mariah continued to stare at me. *Think, Anastasia!* Finally, I said, "I completely forgot to ask Cloris to water the plants in my office while I'm gone. Remind me to call her when we get back to the B&B."

Zack tilted his head, raised one eyebrow ever so slightly, and quirked the corner of his mouth. "Right. We certainly wouldn't want all those plants to wither up and die while you're gone."

Good thing Mariah Clatterbuck didn't know about my two black thumbs. I had no idea how closely she socialized with Shasta Summers, given they were of different generations, but if I ever came up in conversation, I hoped Shasta didn't out my lack of gardening prowess.

~*~

Throughout our drive back to Three Sisters, Zack continued to enjoy a good laugh over my inability to come up with a more plausible excuse.

"What can I say? My brain deserted me, and I wasn't going to bring up the Sleuth Sayer."

"With everything else the Sleuth Sayer knows, you're worried she might mention our honeymoon? That's a rather minor and innocuous piece of information compared to some of the intimate details of your life she's divulged."

"Not to me. She's dumped enough of my life into cyberspace."

When Zack grunted what sounded like an agreement, I spun to face him. "You've listened to more of the podcasts, haven't you?"

"All three episodes. On my way to and from Vin de la Terre."

I braced myself. "How bad is it?"

"Let's just say she knows enough that she could write a book and call it *Assault with a Deadly Glue Gun*."

I winced. "Are you telling me all the podcasts so far are about Marlys Vandenberg's murder?"

He nodded.

I did a bit of mental arithmetic, going over all the dead bodies I'd encountered in the last year and a half and groaned. At this rate, the Sleuth Sayer could milk my life for podcast fodder for years to come. And that's just adding up bodies to date. Given my penchant for finding them, she'd never have to bother moving on to another sleuth. My life was a goldmine for the woman.

"Maybe I should have thought to do a podcast of my life."

"Seriously? Look at how upset you are over the Sleuth Sayer."

"Yes, but she must be making money from these podcasts. She's got advertisers. And maybe she already has an agent shopping around a book and movie deal. Based on my life! I should be benefiting from my life experiences, not her. I never gave her permission."

The more I thought about it, the more I leaned toward calling a lawyer once we returned home. As long as he or she would take the case on retainer. No way could I afford the obscene hourly rate lawyers charged. I sat and stewed the remainder of the drive back to Three Sisters.

We arrived to discover the entire house lit up. "I suppose we might as well let Constantia know what we found out."

Chaos greeted us in the foyer. And an eerie silence. Someone had tossed the house. "I know Constantia was frantic to find proof regarding the fraud, but unless she's totally lost it, I can't see her turning into a human tornado of destruction in her own home."

"Constantia didn't do this." Zack nodded toward the gift shop where the glass door hung askew on its hinges. Inside, the floor was littered with broken wine bottles. Everything from cookbooks to decorative items, lay covered in shards of glass and soaked in wine.

Zack withdrew his gun. "Stay behind me."

We crept through the downstairs, from one room to the next but found minimal destruction except in Constantia's office where someone had strewn the contents of her desk and file cabinet around the small room. Upstairs, we found similar upheaval in Hart's office, along with the smashing of his numerous trophies and awards. The remainder of the upstairs rooms had only received a cursory sweep, as if the perpetrator wanted the entire house to look ransacked but gave little effort to all but a few select rooms.

The scene reminded me too much of the day I returned home to find similar destruction, along with my sons, mother, and mother-in-law tied up and dumped one on top of the other in the bathtub. "I'm having serious déjà vu."

We doubled back and checked the bathrooms and every nook and cranny that could possibly hide a body, including under each bed. We found neither the culprit nor Constantia.

"Call Granger," said Zack.

After placing the call, I made another to Marsala. The numbers of all three sisters were posted on the Three Sisters website as emergency contacts if guests couldn't get through to the winery on the main number. "Is Constantia with you?" I asked after she answered.

"No. Is something wrong?"

I explained what Zack and I had discovered at the main house. "The sheriff is on his way."

She choked on a sob. "First Waylon. Then Hart. Now Constantia? What's going on?"

"We don't know."

"But where is she?"

"I was hoping she was with you."

"You don't think she—"

"We haven't seen her since early this afternoon. She was headed to the barn to go through Hart's office."

"I'll pick up Roussanne and get right over there."

After reminding her not to touch anything once they arrived, I disconnected the call.

"We should check the barn," said Zack.

"I was about to suggest that."

Instead of walking the quarter of a mile in the dark, we returned to the parking lot and drove the short distance to the barn. On the way, I called Sheriff Granger again to alert him that Marsala and Roussanne were on their way to the winery, and we were checking the barn for Constantia.

After arriving, Zack and I both turned on the flashlight app on our phones. Even with the double bright lights, it took us several minutes before he found a light switch and flipped it on. A row of low wattage bulbs, suspended from a beam that ran the length of the barn, shed a narrow strip of light from the entrance to the far wall.

Most of the area to either side remained submerged in shadows. Since Hart's business operated during the day, I suppose he saw no reason to upgrade the lighting. The barn housed the remains of other structures, not animals that often required tending after dark or before sunup.

We first made a wide sweep of the structure. We slowly walked down the center aisle of the barn, flashing our phone lights left and right, taking care not to trip or bump into various items piled haphazardly along our path. Eventually, we spied a faint glow that drew us toward a back corner. That's where we found the office.

The room looked like it was probably once a horse stall. Random boards nailed to railing created the two walls attached to the back and side walls of the barn. A wooden door, partially ajar, stood centered between one of the jerry-rigged walls. Opposite the door, a printer sat on a short bookcase, a small blue light illuminating the on/off switch. A battered wooden desk and mismatched wooden swivel chair sat to our right. Another small green light glowed from a surge protector connected to the computer on the desk.

A few file folders sat on the desk, but nothing appeared out of the ordinary. Whoever ransacked the house hadn't bothered with the barn office, either because he didn't know about the barn office, didn't care, or had found what he was searching for in the house. Or perhaps the trashing of the house had nothing to do with Hart's murder.

Although the barn was packed to the gills and looked like a hoarder's lair, we saw no evidence of foul play. Nothing was toppled over or broken. The office may have looked exactly the way Hart had left it when he quit work yesterday.

"Let's take a closer look around the barn," said Zack.

As we serpentined around the remains of other people's homes, a system of inventory began to emerge. The assorted stock was broken up into sections, bathroom fixtures in one area, kitchen cabinets piled high in another. One stall held brass and wrought iron bedframes. Another was filled with fireplace mantles and another with stacks of church pews. Hooked and braided rugs were draped over the side of one of the stalls. Another stall contained piles of assorted window frames, some with glass, others without.

We were passing a stall with a wide variety of doors leaning against both sides of the stall when I thought I heard something. "Did you hear that?"

Zack paused, and we both listened. "There it is again," I said, hearing a soft mewling. "A kitten?"

"It's coming from behind that stack of doors." Zack squatted and shined his phone into the empty space between the bottom of the doors and the side of the stall.

I leaned over him, peered through the triangular gap, and gasped. "That's no kitten."

FIFTEEN

I placed a third call to Sheriff Granger. "We're going to need an ambulance at the barn."

"Constantia?"

"Most likely but no way of knowing yet. Gotta go."

After I ended the call, Zack handed me his phone. He stripped off his shirt and tossed it to the side. With me juggling two phones to provide enough light, he began to remove one door at a time and haul it to the opposite side of the stall.

These weren't modern hollow-core doors. They were mostly antique solid wooden doors made from dense, heavy hardwoods. Some were hand carved, standing at least eight feet tall and too wide for Zack to grasp on either side with both hands. They looked like they came from old churches.

Zack maneuvered those by bracing each one with his body, tipping up one end a few inches, and pivoting it before lowering. In this manner, he painstakingly moved each side a few inches at a time until he'd hip-hopped the door across the width of the stall and stacked it against the opposite side.

Unlike me, Zack didn't have an ounce of fat on him. The guy was all lean, sinewy muscle with six-pack abs. As I watched him struggle with the doors, I knew the assailant had to be equally buff. Either that, or he had help.

Three columns of doors, each at least six or eight doors deep, spanned the length of the stall. I felt helpless watching Zack struggle with one huge door after another, but someone needed to provide the light as he worked. Otherwise, he'd run the risk of either injuring himself or the person hidden behind the doors.

Was it Constantia? If not, then who? One of the winery guests? And if so, where was Constantia?

Zack had tackled the group of doors closest to the stall entrance first. Once he'd removed those eight doors and exposed the woman's legs, I asked, "Do you think it's safe to drag her out by her legs?"

He shook his head. "Better not. We have no idea as to the extent of her injuries. The soft moaning tells me she may have sustained a concussion. She might also have broken bones. We'd run the risk of causing more harm by dragging her, maybe even puncturing a lung if she has any broken ribs."

He continued to work. By the time he'd removed the last door in the last column, a sheen of sweat covered his exposed flesh and dripped from his face.

We stared down at the body. A feed sack covered the woman's head and torso. A series of thick knotted ropes ran from her shoulders to her thighs, securing the sack and pinning her arms to her body.

"She needs air." I handed Zack his phone. "I think I saw scissors in a pencil cup on the desk."

I ran toward the office, found the scissors, and returned. I squatted on the floor and began carefully snipping at the woven burlap strands at the top of the sack. The scissors were quite dull, and it took me several minutes to cut a long enough slit to expose the victim's face and verify it was Constantia. She squeezed her eyes shut against the light from the phones as she coughed and fought to fill her lungs with air.

Constantia was bathed in sweat, her hair plastered to her head. I grabbed Zack's discarded shirt and wiped her face. "Don't try to move. An ambulance is on its way."

Zack gingerly picked away at the knots to loosen the bindings around her chest, taking care not to jar her body. The more he worked, the more her chest expanded with each breath as her lungs fought to inhale air.

I didn't notice any visible injuries except a goose egg protruding from the side of her head. She didn't wince as she began to flex her muscles. Although someone had taken his time to make sure she had no way of escaping, he hadn't beaten her up. Still, if we hadn't discovered her when we did, she would have eventually suffocated to death.

Her cracked lips moved. She tried to speak, but the effort proved too much of a struggle, producing nothing more than a whispered moan. Finally, she mouthed what I interpreted as *water*. While Zack continued to work on the knots. I sprang to my feet and raced to the car to retrieve a nearly empty water bottle sitting in the console. Returning, I held the bottle to her lips and dribbled in a few drops at a time.

In the distance, we heard sirens approaching.

~*~

After the EMTs had stabilized Constantia and tranfered her into the ambulance, Zack and I returned to our guest cottage. He quickly toweled off and threw on a fresh shirt before we drove to the hospital.

Once we arrived in the waiting room, we sat with Roussanne and Marsala, offering moral support as they awaited word on their sister's condition. They spent the time alternating between shedding tears and offering Zack and me profuse thanks for finding Constantia in time to save her life. I didn't know if that was true, but I didn't contradict them. They needed to believe their sister would pull through the assault.

Half an hour later, both the doctor and the sheriff entered the waiting room. The sheriff held back near the entrance as the doctor walked over to the two sisters. They jumped to their feet and reached for each other's hands. He offered them a smile of assurance as he clasped their joined hands. "She'll be fine. She sustained a slight concussion, and she's severely dehydrated, but she has no other injuries."

The sisters hugged each other, then the doctor. "You're sure?" asked Marsala.

"Now, Miss Marsala, have I ever steered you ladies wrong? You know your sister is one tough steel magnolia. It would take a lot more than a conk on the head to slow her down."

"May we see her?" asked Roussanne.

"Absolutely. We're going to keep her overnight as a precaution, but you can go in now."

They started to dash from the room, but Marsala stopped and turned back to us. "Again, thank you both."

Once the sisters and the doctor departed, the sheriff strode across the waiting room and settled into a chair cattycorner to us. "You folks must think you landed in the crime capital of

Tennessee."

I had begun to wonder if that were the case, but I kept my thoughts to myself. I saw no point in putting the sheriff on the defensive. Murder and mayhem happen. Even in places no one expects. However, we'd certainly come across an inordinate amount of violent crime in the past three days, especially given the outwardly bucolic tranquility of the area.

When neither Zack nor I commented, the sheriff turned to Zack. "If you don't mind, I'd like to fingerprint you. I'm hoping our assailant got sloppy and left his prints all over those doors. We'll need to exclude yours."

Zack nodded. "No problem. I was going to suggest that if you didn't bring it up. When would you like to do it?"

"Tomorrow morning at headquarters is soon enough."

Sheriff Granger next turned to me. "Miss Anastasia, no need to get your prints. I'm assuming a little thing like you wouldn't have the strength to haul any of those massive doors away from Miss Constantia."

Little thing? For a split second, I thought about telling him that I routinely bench-press double my weight, but no one looking at my slightly overweight pear-shaped self would ever believe such a whopper. Instead, I decided to overlook the chauvinism and accept the comment as a compliment. I offered him a smile. "Alas, Sheriff, the spirit was willing, but the flesh is far too weak."

Zack shot me a side-eye, before addressing the sheriff. "I don't suppose Constantia identified her assailant."

The sheriff huffed. "That would make my job too easy. All she remembers is hearing a noise shortly after she arrived in the barn this afternoon. The next thing she remembers is coming to, trussed up like a turkey, unable to move, and barely able to breathe."

I gasped and reached for Zack's hand. "Constantia headed to the barn around lunchtime. That means she was tied up for nearly nine hours."

The sheriff's brows drew together, and his voice grew serious. "You folks really did save her life. Doc doesn't think she would have made it to morning. We need to find this creep before he strikes again."

Was that the royal *we*, or was Sheriff Granger suggesting he wanted to deputize Zack and me? One look at the hard set of Zack's mouth and I knew we were on the same wavelength. Neither one of us cared to get more involved in this recent Middle Tennessee wine country crime spree. Brainstorming with a sheriff inexperienced in murder investigations was one thing. Deliberately poking a hornet's nest was quite another. I was convinced that if Zack didn't still have a few wineries to photograph, he would have already booked us on the first flight back to New Jersey.

Before either of us could object to the direction I feared the conversation was veering, Sheriff Granger started peppering me with questions. "What's your gut feeling, Miss Anastasia? Do you think both murders, the assault on Miss Constantia, and the vandalism of her home are connected?"

I had wracked my brain in search of a common thread that wove together all the crimes. "If there is, I'm not seeing it."

"What about the fraud?"

"What about it? The only way Waylon Oakley is connected to the crypto investment is that he dissuaded one of the potential investors from going in on it. I don't see that as a motive for murder, do you?"

He shook his head. "Unless we're missing something. Which means we've got two killers out there."

"Possibly," said Zack.

Confusion spread across the sheriff's face. "Possibly?"

"Until you figure out the motive or motives behind each of the crimes, you have no way of knowing whether they're connected."

"Also," I added, "what about Constantia? If the perpetrator had tossed the house because he was searching for something related to the investment, why didn't he ransack Hart's office in the barn after he knocked Constantia out and tied her up?"

Sheriff Granger pondered my question. "Maybe he found what he was looking for in the house."

"Then why go to the barn?" asked Zack.

The sheriff nodded. "Valid point. He'd have no reason to."

"Constantia's assault was personal," said Zack. "Her attacker left her where she would die before anyone found her."

I nodded in agreement. "And because her attacker didn't bother to go through Hart's papers or grab either of his computers, I don't think the attack is connected to the crypto fraud."

"But you're forgetting he ransacked the house, Miss Anastasia."

I'd had the glimmer of an idea playing peekaboo in the far recesses of my brain. Now, the more I thought about it, the more it began to formulate. "Unless he wasn't looking for something."

"I'm not following you."

"He only ransacked select areas of the house. What if he was looking to get even?"

A puzzled expression settled across Sheriff Granger's face. "For what?"

"You tell me."

It's amazing how sometimes you can watch the invisible wheels spinning in someone's brain and witness the exact moment the eureka lightbulb flips on. With Sheriff Granger, he scrubbed his jaw and chewed on the inside of his cheek. Then his eyes grew wide as the wattage finally burst forth. He slapped his thigh. "Of course. Lyle. He blames Miss Constantia for getting him fired."

"Even though he has no one to blame but himself," said Zack.

"He's not the sort of person who takes responsibility for his own actions. Never has." Granger stood. "Looks like my night just got longer."

As the three of us exited the hospital, we heard thunder rumbling in the distance. Granger scanned the heavens. "We've got some bad storms headed our way shortly."

I followed his gaze, not sure what he saw. Maybe the sheriff could read cloud cover like fortune tellers could read tea leaves. I viewed both with a huge dollop of skepticism. Still, we were in the South, and that could mean only one thing. "Tornadoes?"

"Possibly. Low chance according to the latest weather report, but you never know. You folks take care getting back to Three Sisters."

The moment we went our separate ways in the parking lot, a huge bolt of lightning lit up the sky. I yelped at the clap of thunder that followed. Zack grabbed my hand, and we raced to the car, beating the downpour by seconds. As we pulled away from the hospital, the rain quickly turned to marble-sized hail, pelting the car from all sides as the wind picked up force.

We managed to arrive back at Three Sisters without a detour to Munchkinland. However, we still had to traverse the distance from the paved parking lot to the guest cottage. Neither the wind nor the hail had abated, and some of the pellets hitting the windshield looked concussion-inducing. "I suppose it's not a good idea to camp in the car tonight."

"I wouldn't advise it."

"I was afraid you'd say that."

Zack unlocked the door, and we made a mad dash through the blinding rain, hail, and ankle-deep puddles.

The next morning, Zack and I awakened to the sun streaming in through the windows. As we walked over to the main house for breakfast, evidence of last night's storm, mostly in the form of toppled patio furniture and fallen branches, dotted our path. Once on the porch, we found the house locked and a note tacked to the front door.

> *Dear Guests,*
>
> *Due to a family emergency, we're unable to serve breakfast today. The main house will reopen tomorrow morning. In the meantime, we apologize for this inconvenience. Please patronize any of the many fine restaurants in town this morning. If you present us with a receipt, we're happy to reimburse you for your meal.*

The note was signed by all three sisters and included a number, which I recognized as Marsala's, to call in case of emergencies. The house, however, was not empty. Although the blinds were drawn on the front-facing downstairs windows, I heard activity coming from the gift shop. Given the amount of destruction we'd noticed last night, Marsala and Roussanne had their work cut out for them today. Hopefully, they had enough inventory set aside to restock the gift shop in time for tomorrow morning.

As we descended the porch steps, I noticed the group of crime junkie women round the corner of the garden on their way toward the main building. Coward that I am, I grabbed Zack's arm and hustled him toward the parking lot.

He glanced in the direction of the chatter. "Not up for an interrogation this morning?"

"From my previous encounter with the one I suspect is their ringleader, I'd rather have a sit-down with Torquemada."

"Lucky for you, the guy died more than five hundred years ago."

"Nice to know I have some luck."

He chuckled as he unlocked the rental car and held the door open for me. Once he settled behind the steering wheel, his features tightened. "What previous encounter?"

"Not worth mentioning."

"I'll be the judge of that. Where was I during this encounter?"

"Either off saving the world or at Vin de la Terre."

He started the car but made no effort to pull out of the parking space. I sighed. "I take it I'm not getting breakfast until I say more?"

He grinned. "You're a quick study."

"Fine. You win." I proceeded to explain my one and only brief encounter with the woman. "As you can see, it was a nothing burger. Now, can we please find a place for breakfast?"

"Of course." He threw the car in reverse and pulled out of the parking lot.

On the short ride into town, we passed the aftermath of last night's storm. Road crews were out in force, dealing with the multitude of downed limbs and branches, as well as the occasional felled tree, that dotted either side of the road, often closing a lane of traffic. The sound of chainsaws buzzed around us, but the damage seemed confined to the landscape. The storm had spared both utility poles and structures, at least along our route.

Sunday brunch was a big deal in the New York metro area, but Middle Tennessee took brunch to a completely new level. I'd never seen so many restaurants specifically catering to the breakfast and lunch crowd. Many included live music, and most only remained open until mid-afternoon. Zack and I had our choice of half a dozen within a few square blocks of the downtown area. After peering in windows and checking out menus, we settled on one with next to no ambiance but the most tantalizing aromas wafting from the building and no wait for a table.

Once inside, we were greeted by a server winding her way through a labyrinth of tables to deliver an order to one of the booths that lined the back wall. "Morning, folks. Sit anywhere you like."

A counter with barstools filled the area to the right. Booths ran around the remaining three walls with tables filling the floorspace in-between. We chose a booth along the front wall with a view of the street. The moment we slid into the red vinyl booth with its retro boomerang-design Formica tabletop, another waitress appeared with menus, two water glasses, and utensils. "Coffee?"

"Two," said Zack. "Cream, no sugar."

She returned shortly with the coffee, a complimentary basket of biscuits and small ramakins of butter, honey, and jam, then took our order. After everything I had eaten yesterday, I harnessed what little willpower I possessed and chose a spinach and mushroom omelet with a side of fresh fruit. Zack opted for a cheese omelet with fried green tomatoes and grits with gravy.

I'd never tasted either fried green tomatoes or grits. After the waitress left to place our order, I asked, "When in Rome?"

"Absolutely."

"You will let me taste both, won't you?"

"Of course."

"Good. I've heard that calories don't count if you sample from someone else's plate."

He raised an eyebrow. "Is that so?"

Less than ten minutes later, our food arrived. Zack placed one of his three slices of tomato on my plate along with a large spoonful of grits. I stared at the grits. "This looks like cream of wheat."

"Similar. Grits are made from ground corn, not wheat."

Cream of wheat had been a Periwinkle breakfast staple on cold wintry mornings when I was a kid, mostly because the instant variety was one food Mama rarely ruined—as long as she didn't accidentally hit the wrong button on the microwave. Many a morning, I left for school while Mama dealt with the fallout of a nuclear disaster. I sampled a spoonful of grits. "Tastes like cream of wheat, except coarser."

I moved on to the fried green tomato. Although skeptical about eating an unripe tomato, I cut a quadrant, popped it into my mouth, and became an immediate convert. "I hope you know how to make these because I'm not waiting until we find ourselves in the South again to have more."

Zack chuckled as he waved over the waitress. "We'll have another side of fried green tomatoes, please."

At least this wasn't a restaurant that listed calorie counts on the menu. I could enjoy my fried green tomatoes in ignorant bliss.

I was doing just that when a boisterous group waving flags and signs, carrying balloons, and wearing assorted campaign paraphernalia entered the cafe. There was no mistaking the man's identity.

SIXTEEN

Zack and I watched as State Representative Beau Paxton, a portly man in his late forties or early fifties and sporting a thinning silver pompadour, made his way from table to table and booth to booth, gladhanding constituents in the time-honored tradition of voter-courting. Like any good politician, he kept a wide smile pasted across his face, addressed each constituent by first name, and had brought along a gaggle of campaign staffers and a local news crew to record everything. His nephew, the former sheriff's deputy, and another man brought up the rear but hung back from the crowd.

Bates looked in need of a razor and a bar of soap, followed by a date with his pillow. His burly companion was equally unkempt, with scraggly dishwater-colored hair and an equally scraggly beard. The beard, a pair of dark shades, and a ratty ball cap pulled low over his brow, masked most of his facial features. Neither man gave off the image of a typical campaign staffer, and both looked like they'd rather be anywhere else on the planet than playing devoted puppy dog to a campaigning politician.

I wondered if they were enlisted for security purposes in case Paxton happened upon one of the fleeced investors. How many of the duped men would buy into Paxton's version of events, that Hart had masterminded the financial fraud, and he, too, was a victim?

"Looks like the damage control phase of the campaign has begun," I said as I strained to listen to the brief conversations between the representative and his constituents. Would any of them bring up the fraud allegations or Hart's murder? However, from my vantage point, it appeared everyone in the café was firmly planted in Paxton's camp. I witnessed plenty of backslapping and some selfies. Not a single diner frowned at Paxton, refused to accept his extended hand, or spewed venom.

I leaned across the booth and whispered, "They're all acting as though nothing out of the ordinary has occurred. Is it possible they don't know their representative is under threat of indictment?"

Zack shook his head. "Hard to believe. Word travels fast in small towns, and too many people around here are out huge sums of money."

"Obviously, none of these people." I watched as the crowd cheerfully engaged with Paxton, then accepted the campaign flyers, bumper stickers, and window signs his staffers passed out as he moved on to the next group of people.

"Maybe they already believe he's innocent. I'm sure part of the damage control campaign is planting the idea that Hart scammed Paxton and not the other way around."

I scoffed at the idea. "Whether or not it's the truth?"

Given what I'd learned about Hart Kingston in the short time since we'd arrived in Tennessee, I found it inconceivable that anyone in the community would think him capable of orchestrating a cryptocurrency scheme to defraud investors. If the guy had been such a financial mastermind, he wouldn't have failed at one business after another for most of his life.

"When has a politician let truth get in the way of campaigning?"

"Touché."

When Paxton arrived at our booth, he held his hand out to Zack, nearly colliding with the forkful of omelet that was midway to Zack's mouth at the time. "I don't believe we've met. You folks must be new. Beau Paxton, State Representative."

He quickly flashed me his pearly whites before returning his attention to Zack. "Hope I can count on your votes in November."

With his other hand, he pulled a couple of campaign buttons from his suit pocket and slapped them onto the table. I glanced at the red, white, and blue disks emblazoned with the less-than-creative slogan of *Vote Paxton*.

Zack ignored Paxton's outstretched hand, but he did manage a slight upward quirk of his lips. "Afraid not. We're only passing through."

Out of the corner of my eye I noticed Ex-Deputy Bates muscling his way past the camera crew and staffers. When he arrived at the booth, he leaned in and whispered something in his uncle's ear. The smile faded from Paxton's face. He quickly withdrew his hand, scooped up the buttons, and moved on without another glance or word to either of us.

As I stared at Paxton's departing back, Bates speared us with a glare before following his uncle. The burly scraggly guy dogged his heels. "What was that all about?"

Zack eyed the entourage as they quickly exited the café, bypassing the three remaining booths. "Beats me, but he's suddenly in a hurry to leave."

~*~

Zack had two more wineries to shoot before we flew home the next morning. So far, he'd only taken a few quick shots at Three Sisters, and he still had to photograph Grape Expectations. Given yesterday's events, he decided to leave the Three Sisters shoot for last.

We had two stops to make before heading out to Grape Expectations. "Ever been fingerprinted?" I asked as we drove to the county offices.

"I'm in the system. And before you ask, it's not because I'm a member of any alphabet agencies."

"Do all photojournalists get fingerprinted?"

"Only those who travel to foreign lands and are licensed to bring along protection."

"I see."

"Good."

Not that it meant I believed him. Someday I wouldn't be surprised when my suspicions were confirmed. I just prayed that it wasn't when some men in uniform showed up unexpectedly at my door to offer their condolences.

When we arrived at the county building, we were ushered directly into the sheriff's office. While Deputy Norwood fingerprinted Zack, we told the sheriff about our breakfast interaction with Paxton and Bates, also mentioning the man who appeared shoulder-to-shoulder with Bates.

Sheriff Granger muttered a few choice words under his breath as he rifled through a set of papers on his desk. "Typical Paxton

M.O. He'd ignore a drowning man if the guy had voted for his opponent in the last election."

Finding what he wanted, he pulled out the sheet and handed it to us. "Did the guy with Bates look anything like this fellow?"

We stared at the mug shot. Lonnie Knox. A phrase I once heard in a song crossed my mind. *Meaner than a junk yard dog.* I wouldn't want to cross paths with Lonnie Knox on a crowded street in the middle of the day, let alone in a dark alley.

"Hard to say," said Zack.

I agreed. The mug shot showed a clean-shaven man with a shaved head and beady pale blue eyes.

"How so?" asked Granger.

Zack explained. "The guy with Bates had a beard and shoulder-length hair. Light brown with streaks of gray."

"An extremely scraggly beard," I added. "And the remainder of his face was hidden behind dark sunglasses and a ball cap pulled low over his brow."

The sheriff returned the mug shot to the top of the pile. "I dropped by Paxton's home last night to have a chat with Lyle."

"Did you learn anything?" I asked.

"Not much. Claims he never left the house all day. Paxton backed up his story."

"Can anyone corroborate their alibi?"

"They didn't offer up any names."

"Did you believe them?" I asked.

"Heck, no. I also saw evidence of a third person in the house."

"What sort of evidence?" asked Zack.

"A third plate and beer can on the coffee table." His features tightened. "I suspect Knox was hiding out in one of the other rooms but not much I could do about it. I couldn't search the house without a warrant, and I have no justification for getting one, at least not yet. So far, we have no evidence tying Bates to Miss Constantia's attack."

"Is Knox allowed to travel out of state?" I asked.

"He showed up for his last meeting with his parole officer. He's not currently in violation of his parole, and the terms of his release don't confine him to Mississippi. According to the law, the guy's got every right to visit old friends."

He waved the fingerprint card that Deputy Norwood had handed him. "However, I won't be surprised when we get a hit on both his and Bates's fingerprints from those doors in the barn."

~*~

After leaving the sheriff's office, we swung by the hospital to check on Constantia. We found her sitting up in bed. Her face beamed when we entered the room. "I hear I owe my life to both of you."

"Luckily, we were in the right place at the right time," said Zack.

Her body gave off an involuntary shudder. "Amen to that." Then her features tightened. "Who would do such a thing? I can understand someone attacking Hart, given the fraud, but why me?"

"Your attacker might have believed the two of you were in cahoots," I said.

Her brows drew together. "Is that what you believe, Anastasia?"

"No, of course not. Besides, I don't believe Hart defrauded all those investors."

"Why not?"

"Didn't Sheriff Granger tell you?"

"Tell me what?"

200

"The D.A. wasn't investigating Hart, Constantia. Whoever told that to the sheriff, was either misinformed or deliberately lied."

"Are you saying there was no fraud?"

"Not exactly. The money is missing, but Hart suspected his partner of embezzling the funds. It was Hart who went to the D.A."

"His partner? What partner?"

"State Representative Beau Paxton."

Constantia leaned forward, her eyes widening. "Hart was innocent?"

"Most likely," said Zack. "You'll have to wait until the investigation wraps up. As of now, Paxton's claiming he's also a victim, that Hart stole the cryptocurrency. We don't know what evidence Hart supplied the D.A."

"It had to be very convincing, though," I said, "because the D.A. has turned the investigation over to the TBI."

Constantia slumped back into her pillows and closed her eyes. "Paxton has powerful friends in high places. He'll walk."

"Don't be so sure," I said.

"Does it matter?" She expelled a ragged sigh. "All those people still lost their money. Learning who stole it won't get it back."

I squeezed her hand. "You don't know that the TBI won't be able to recover at least some of the money. I'm sure they have forensic accountants scouring Paxton's records. And I suppose they could also call in the Feds if they need help."

She shook her head. "Maybe if Paxton had robbed a bank. From what I've read about cryptocurrency, it's the ideal investment for anyone looking to launder money or commit fraud."

"At least the victims will have some satisfaction in seeing the perpetrator convicted and sent to prison," said Zack.

Constantia harrumphed. "I've known Beau Paxton too long, and I'm not sure I have enough faith in the system, not when it comes to someone like him. The guy's spent his entire life flashing his phony smile to wheedle people into doing his bidding. Guys like that know how to keep their hands clean and let others do their dirty work. The only thing that amazes me is how people around here continue to vote for him."

She squeezed her eyes shut again but not in time to prevent a lone tear from escaping and traveling down her cheek. "Besides, it doesn't negate the fact that Hart cheated on me. And right under my own nose. I'm a blind fool."

For years, apparently, according to Mariah Clatterbuck, but people see what they want to see. I'm a prime example of that. I patted Constantia's hand. "People make mistakes, and we never want to think the worst of those we love. Try to hold onto the good memories and not dwell on the bad."

Too bad I seemed incapable of taking my own advice. I'm sure Karl and I had many happy moments together over the course of our marriage, but his ultimate betrayal had wiped my memory banks clean of all but his deceit. I wondered if I'd ever truly get over the anger and bitterness, not just toward Karl, but at myself for not realizing what was going on under my own nose.

We stayed with Constantia a few minutes longer, only leaving after a nurse arrived to take her vitals. As we walked down the hall to the elevator, Zack reached for my hand and gave it a squeeze. Maybe Constantia would also find a second chance at love.

~*~

Once in the car, as Zack brought up the navigation system and programmed in the address for Grape Expectations, I asked, "Anything special I should expect at Grape Expectations?"

"This one is right up your alley."

"Oh? I hope you're referring to my crafts and editorial expertise and not my penchant for finding dead bodies."

He shot me a serious side-eye. "You'd better not find another dead body."

"Hey, it's not like I go looking for them."

"I know. That's what worries me."

"So back to my alley..."

"The winery is part of a crafting co-op. They rent out studio space to crafters and sell their wares in the gift shop."

"No dead bodies, then. Good to know."

With fields of crops or sub-divisions on either side of the highway, we came upon very little in the way of storm debris, but I noticed Zack continually glancing into the rearview mirror. "Something wrong?"

"I'm not sure."

"But?"

"Someone is following us."

I glanced in the sideview mirror. "The gray pickup? He's not that close."

"He's been following us since we left the hospital."

"What should we do?"

"I'm going to pull into the next gas station. Let's see what he does."

We drove for another five miles before the fields gave way to a commercial area. Zack stopped at the first gas station. The pickup continued down the street and made a right at the next intersection. I exhaled my relief. "Probably just coincidence.

Maybe he was visiting someone at the hospital or picking up a discharged patient."

"Maybe," muttered Zack, as he exited the car to fill the gas tank, but he didn't sound all that convinced.

Once we were again on our way, Zack slowed as we approached the next intersection. A two-story motel ran the length of the perpendicular block on the near side of the intersecting street, a strip mall filled the far side. As we coasted through the intersection, I quickly scanned the parked vehicles in both parking lots. "There's a gray pickup in front of the tattoo parlor and another parked at the motel."

Zack relaxed his grip on the steering wheel, pressed down on the accelerator, and we picked up speed.

We drove along the highway for another fifteen minutes, vehicles continually whipping past us on either side. I glanced over at the speedometer. "You're doing ten miles above the posted speed limit, yet everyone is passing us."

"I noticed." He let loose with a few choice words as a black pickup zoomed past on our left and a Mustang cut in front of us after passing on our right.

"You sure you didn't make a wrong turn and land us in the middle of the speedway at Talladega?"

"I'm beginning to wonder that myself."

We eventually exited the highway onto a two-lane county road. A few lefts and rights took us onto more rural roads that still showed signs of last night's storm. Zack was forced to zigzag around scattered brush and a few downed limbs until a large branch in the middle of the road forced us to come to a complete stop.

I knew immediately that something wasn't right.

I followed Zack's gaze as he scanned the area and saw what he saw. Not only had no tree on either side of the road, recently lost a limb, but the large branch in the middle of the road showed signs of a clean fresh cut from a power saw. My heart pounded in my chest. "Someone deliberately blocked the road."

Zack grunted in agreement. Given the topography and our lack of an off-road vehicle, driving into the surrounding wooded area to maneuver around the tree wasn't an option. After last night's storm, the area between the road and the woods had transformed into a swamp, making it impossible to execute a K-turn without the likelihood of getting stuck in the mud. All Zack could do was back down the road in the direction we'd come.

He threw the car into reverse. As he slowly backed up toward the last intersection, a black pickup sped onto the road, squealing to a stop inches from our back bumper. Two men wearing ski masks jumped from the pickup and rushed the passenger side of the car. They began rocking the car from side to side, attempting to flip it.

"Get down," yelled Zack. With one swift motion, he released my seatbelt and pushed me to the floor.

A moment later a shot rang out.

SEVENTEEN

The car thumped back onto the ground. Zack jumped from the car, shielding himself behind the open door, and fired off another round behind the car.

I remained on the floor, sandwiched between the front seat and the dashboard, angling my neck to gain a partial view. No one returned fire, but within seconds of Zack's second shot, I heard a door slam. A moment later, the pickup's engine roared to life.

"Stay down!" Zack darted from behind the car door and out of my field of vision.

I watched in horror as the pickup swerved past where I'd last seen Zack. The crack of another shot roared in my ears, then the squeal of brakes, followed by a loud crash. Only the wail of a car alarm pierced the ensuing silence.

A moment later, the front passenger door swung open. I crawled onto the seat, took one look at Zack, standing tall and unharmed, and burst into tears. Concern immediately clouded his face. "Are you hurt?"

I shook my head, unable to voice anything other than tearful blubbering. He helped me from the car and enveloped me in his arms, holding me against his chest until my sobs dwindled down to ragged, breathy sniffles.

Eventually, I opened my eyes and peered around Zack's shoulder to the body on the ground. "Are they both dead?"

"I don't think so." He released his grip on me and checked the first assailant. He lay sprawled supine in a muddy patch of storm debris on the side of the road. Blood soaked the left side of his upper body from his shoulder to his collarbone, but on closer inspection, I noticed his chest moving up and down ever so slightly. Zack kicked at the man's leg. He didn't move, didn't make a sound. "This one's unconscious. Looks like he hit his head when he fell backwards."

As he stepped onto a pile of twigs and branches, mud oozed through the woody debris and around his sneakers. Ignoring the gooey mess, Zack leaned over the body and lifted the ski mask to expose the face of Lyle Paxton Bates.

No big surprise, considering what I'd personally observed of the man and learned from Sheriff Granger. The guy in the pickup was probably the one from the café this morning. "You think this has something to do with finding Constantia last night?"

"If he left her to die? Definitely. Especially if he learned we saved her."

I shuddered. "I don't suppose we can leave him here for a taste of his own medicine?" I'd spoken in jest, which I chalked up to a combination of fear, anger, and shock. After all, the dirtbag had just tried to kill Zack and me. Even so, once the words passed my lips, the coldblooded suggestion rocked me.

Zack glowered at the man. "Not with a bullet from my gun

lodged in his shoulder."

"There is that."

He ignored my quip. "We need to check on the other guy, then call Sheriff Granger."

The second assailant had crashed the pickup into a tree and slammed his head into the windshield. Zack reached into the truck and felt his neck for a pulse. "He's alive."

He pushed the man back against the seat. When he lifted the driver's ski mask, it came as no surprise to see the burly guy with the scraggly hair and beard. Aside from the injuries to his face, I saw no evidence of a bullet wound. "I heard three gunshots."

Zack pointed to the man's sleeve. "The first shot hit Bates in the shoulder, the second grazed this guy's arm."

"And the third?"

"I shot out his tire."

"So you weren't trying to kill either of them?"

"Not if I didn't have to. Better to get answers. Let the courts deal with them."

"Unless they somehow get off. Constantia suspects Paxton will weasel out of the fraud charges. Let's assume our mystery man is Knox. Bates and Knox are connected to Paxton. Won't he pay them off to keep them quiet?"

"If the D.A. knows what he's doing, he'll play these two against each other and Paxton. Bates and Knox—or whoever he is—will trip over each other to cut a deal. Paxton will look out for himself and no one else. If that means throwing these two under the bus, he'll do it and hope the jury buys his story."

"You think they're involved in more than the attack on Constantia? That they have something to do with the fraud and the murders?"

Zack shrugged. "I think we don't know what we don't know. And that includes the attack on Constantia. Bates and Knox may be completely innocent. Same for Paxton when it comes to the fraud. We need to wait on the evidence."

"What do you believe? In your gut."

"In my gut?" Zack's mouth tightened. "We're not dealing with any Mensa masterminds here. One look at those two and you know they aren't financial geniuses, but they're both connected to Paxton, and we know Paxton was Hart's partner, Hart accused Paxton of fraud, and now Hart is dead. One or both may be connected to his murder."

"And Waylon's murder?"

"Could be."

"My gut tells me both murders are connected, and those three are the likeliest candidates. I just can't figure out how."

"That's why we need to wait for the evidence before jumping to any conclusions."

"You're sounding like a lawyer."

His eyes twinkled as his mouth cocked a grin. "I don't even play one on TV."

He pulled out his phone and placed a call to Sheriff Granger. As soon as the sheriff answered, Zack hit the speaker button, then filled him in, giving a brief account of the situation and our location. "You're going to need a couple of ambulances."

"Are either of you injured?" asked Granger, his voice filled with concern.

"We're fine," I said, "but Bates and his buddy are going to regret tangling with my husband."

The sheriff guffawed. "I'll bet."

The comment caught me by surprise. What did Sheriff

Granger know about Zack that I didn't? Did it have something to do with running his fingerprints? I shot Zack a quick look, but his expression remained passive and unreadable. I bit down on my tongue.

After ending the call, Zack returned to the black pickup and began searching through the truck bed's contents while I pondered a theory. "Do you suppose those two were in the gray pickup and switched vehicles at the motel?"

"It's possible."

"That would mean they knew where we were headed after leaving the hospital." Which in turn would suggest someone had shared our itinerary with them. "Who knew we were going to Grape Expectations this morning?"

"Probably anyone who follows the local wineries on social media. Grape Expectations has tweeted all morning in anticipation of today's photo shoot."

"Well, that certainly narrows down the list to a few thousand people."

"More like a few million when you add up all the wine connoisseurs, travel bloggers, influencers, and handcrafts enthusiasts. And that's before the retweets and the posts on other social media sites." He jumped out of the pickup bed and held up a fistful of white plastic.

I raised both eyebrows. "Zip ties?"

"Interesting, huh?"

"You think they were meant for us?"

"Quite possibly. I also found two additional feed sacks like the one used on Constantia, several lengths of rope, a chainsaw, and a tacklebox filled with assorted hunting and fishing knives."

A shiver coursed through my body. "What exactly had they

planned to do to us?"

"Nothing good. These guys came prepared." Zack rounded the truck and secured the wrist of the man who may or may not be Lonnie Knox to the steering wheel. Then he walked back to Bates and secured both his wrists and ankles. When he'd finished, he said, "At least it's a partial taste of their own medicine."

Both men began to regain consciousness while we waited for the sheriff and the assorted cadre of first responders to arrive. Bates opened his eyes first, took one look at Zack and me, and began hurling death threats at us.

Once Bates begun to stir, Zack had had the forethought to press the Record button on his phone. When Bates paused in his tirade to take a breath, Zack pointed to the phone, still recording. "Anything else you'd like to say?"

Bates then let loose with a string of four-letter words before clamming up.

A few minutes later, we heard shouting coming from the pickup. Zack once again set his phone to record. However, as the two of us walked the short distance to the passenger side door, Bates yelled out, "Lonnie, keep your f'ing trap shut!"

"You might want to ignore him," suggested Zack. "He's only out to protect himself. Now's your chance to tell your side of the story."

Instead of unburdening himself, Lonnie suggested Zack perform an anatomically impossible maneuver.

When Sheriff Granger arrived, he took one look at the situation, shook his head, and muttered under his breath before asking, "You sure you're both okay?"

My repertoire of rotating nightmares had increased significantly since arriving in his jurisdiction, but I put on a brave face. "As long as you take those two into custody and they remain locked up, I'm good."

"Attempted kidnapping and murder should do the trick," said Zack. He pointed out the clean cut of the tree branch that blocked the road before adding, "If you check out the contents of the pickup, you'll find a chainsaw with freshly cut wood clinging to the teeth."

While the EMTs strapped Bates and Knox onto stretchers and loaded them into the ambulances, I asked Sheriff Granger if the crime team had found either of their fingerprints on the doors that had trapped Constantia in the barn.

Granger scowled. "Given the age of those doors, where they were stored, and the number of people who had access to them, we're dealing with dozens of different prints on each one." He pitched his chin toward the departing ambulances. "But none from either of those two. I guess Bates learned something in the police academy after all."

"What's that?"

"To avoid contaminating a crime scene. My guess is, they both wore gloves."

"Which would mean you can't place them in the barn last night," said Zack.

"At least not yet. But we've got them dead to rights here." He pointed to what remained of the car's bullet shattered passenger window. "Looks like you'll need the incident report to explain that damage to the rental company. I'll see you get a copy as quickly as possible."

After taking our preliminary statements, Granger cleared us to leave the crime scene, but a fleet of police vehicles blocked the road. Once they'd performed a chessboard-like jockeying of vehicles, the county tow truck arrived to remove the pickup.

Eventually, the tow truck departed, and we were able to leave. Too bad the car refused to cooperate.

Granger stated the obvious. "Looks like you have more damage than just a shattered window."

He called in a second tow truck. Then he placed a call to the nearest location of the rental company to explain the situation and arrange for another car for us. He then ordered one of the officers to give us a lift to the rental office.

"Least I can do," said Granger after Zack and I thanked him. "You folks don't need the hassle of bureaucratic red tape after what you've just gone through. You have any problems once you get there, call me."

After arranging to meet the sheriff later at headquarters to sign our statements, we followed one of the officers to her cruiser. While she drove us to the car rental location, Zack called Grape Expectations to postpone the shoot until tomorrow. Then he contacted the airline to reschedule our flight.

Once we had confirmation of the flight change, I texted Nick, Alex, Shane, and Mama with the change in plans. "I'm not saying why."

"Maybe you better tell them something innocuous," Zack suggested. "Otherwise, your phone will blow up with incoming texts and calls."

I didn't like lying, but Zack was probably right. Before hitting Send, I mentioned last night's storm and a scheduling conflict today with one of the wineries. Not exactly the truth but not exactly a lie. A severe storm had hit the area last night, and our run-in with Bates and Knox had caused us to reschedule with Grape Expectations. Besides, I could pull off a slight stretching of the truth via text. Not so much with a face-to-face fib where I could never seem to keep a straight face.

~*~

The car rental company required Zack plow through reams of insurance paperwork before they'd hand over the keys to another vehicle. By the time he'd finished, my stomach was channeling Audrey from *Little Shop of Horrors*, loudly demanding, "Feed me."

He stole a quick glance my way but lost the battle to suppress a grin as he signed the last document. At least he didn't laugh out loud. I couldn't say the same for the clerk behind the counter, although she did try to mask her wide-eyed amusement with a faux cough.

Once she accepted the paperwork from Zack, she handed him the keys. "Y'all have a nice day."

Really? I raised both eyebrows. We weren't swapping out vehicles due to AC problems or a faulty seatbelt. Two thugs had tried to kill us. Luckily, they only killed the car. Hence, all the paperwork. I gritted my teeth and muttered under my breath, "The day can't get much worse."

Too late, I realized I may have just tempted fate. Then again, I'm not at my best when I'm fighting a headache from lack of calories and caffeine. Not to mention the stress of nearly getting killed.

Ever the diplomat, though, Zack smiled at the clerk and thanked her. He then reached for my hand, and we exited the building. The lot had few cars in it, and we quickly found the silver Camry she'd assigned us.

Once settled inside, I fastened my seatbelt, closed my eyes, and attempted a few calming breaths. Too bad my inner Zen had flown the coop.

Zack started the engine but didn't back out of the parking space. "Why aren't we moving?"

When he didn't answer immediately, I opened my eyes to find him staring at me, concern written across his face. "Are you all right?"

I sighed. "I will be. Eventually."

"But?"

"There are days when it isn't easy being the Typhoid Mary of murder and mayhem. This is one of them."

He squeezed my hand. "Do me a favor?"

"I hope it involves the two of us spending the rest of the day in bed. After you feed me."

"That can be arranged but promise me you won't listen to the remaining two podcasts."

"Are you worried I can't handle them?"

"No, but they're not worth the added aggravation they'll cause you. There's enough going on here."

"Agreed. I promise."

Of course, forcing me to promise not to listen to the podcasts only increased my curiosity about them. I needed to figure out who had spilled the private details of my life to the Sleuth Sayer. I could wait until we returned home, though.

Zack drove us to an outdoor mall that boasted a wide variety of restaurants. We chose one that also featured a deli and bakery, deciding to place a take-out order and bring our lunch back to Three Sisters for a private picnic.

We were passing the main house, on our way from the guest parking lot to our cottage, when a tearful Jolene bounded down the porch stairs and collided with me. This time I managed to remain upright, but my coffee cup lid popped off, and hot latte sloshed over my hand and splattered onto my T-shirt.

She stared wide-eyed at me for a fraction of a second before darting around the house. A moment later, a battered sedan flew around the side of the house. Zack and I jumped out of the car's way as Jolene sped toward the road. I stared after her. "I'm guessing Constantia is back and fired her."

Zack zeroed in on my coffee-soaked hand and shirt. "I'm more concerned about you right now."

I waved away his concern. "I'm more upset over the loss of my latte than a stained shirt."

"I wasn't talking about the shirt. Or the latte." He pointed to my hand. "Were you burned?"

I'd experienced far worse, having survived my share of glue gun burns. I dried my hand on my T-shirt. The pain barely registered. "Nothing a little ice won't cure."

He handed me the guest cottage key and the bag of food. "Go change. I'll grab some ice for you."

"And a cup of coffee, please."

He offered me his cup. "This should tide you over until I get back."

I blew him a kiss. "My hero."

By the time Zack returned to the cottage, I'd changed my clothes, set out the food on the small table on our porch, and downed his entire cup of coffee, even though he takes his black and I like mine with a generous amount of cream. Beggars can't be choosers.

I had also exerted extreme willpower not to wolf down my entire lunch as the minutes ticked by and he hadn't returned. However, I eventually polished off the bag of chips and pickle that had come with my sandwich. As Zack bounded up the porch steps,

I asked, "What took you so long?"

"You were right. Constantia is home from the hospital, and she fired Jolene."

"I'm not surprised. What woman would continue employing her husband's girlfriend once she found out about their affair? Still, you were gone much longer than it takes to learn that limited amount of information."

He handed me one of the two to-go cups he carried. "When she heard about the collision, she insisted on making you another latte."

"You're forgiven. Now can we eat?"

He glanced at the empty bag of chips. "Looks like you've already started."

"You were gone quite some time."

He glanced at his phone before settling into the chair across the table from me. "Less than ten minutes."

"Time is relative."

"Especially when you're starving?"

"You catch on quickly." I grabbed half my tuna sandwich and took a rather large and unladylike bite. "Did you tell Constantia what happened to us this morning?"

Zack unwrapped his Italian hoagie. "She was horrified. Blamed herself."

I took a sip of my latte. "Nonsense."

"That's what I told her."

Then again, was it nonsense? One act of defiance on Constantia's part, had triggered a cascade of terrible events. I voiced my thoughts. "On the other hand, she has a point. If Constantia hadn't ignored Bates and had gone to the dining room as directed yesterday morning, Bates would still have his job and wouldn't have retaliated against her or tried to kill us."

"Valid points. Fingerprints or no fingerprints, after this morning, it's obvious Bates tried to kill Constantia. Why else would he go after us?"

"No other reason than because he somehow discovered we thwarted his revenge plans."

Zack opened his bag of chips and popped one into his mouth. "Too bad *obvious* doesn't hold much sway in a court of law. To get a conviction, the D.A. needs to provide the jury with facts, and right now the sheriff has no evidence placing Bates in the barn last night."

"Maybe he'll have some by the time we finish lunch and drive over to headquarters to sign our statements."

Not that I was optimistic, but you never know. Stranger things have happened. We could arrive at Granger's office to find he'd gotten full confessions from both Bates and Knox.

I craned my neck and scanned the vast cloudless heavens.

Zack aped my efforts. "I'll bite. What are we searching for?"

"A flock of winged pigs soaring across the sky."

"Do I want to know why?"

"It's an optimism thing."

"Have you ever seen any flying swine?"

"Never. But hope springs eternal."

He reached for my hand. "I have a much better idea."

~*~

Two hours later, we drove back into town to sign our statements. A frustrated Sheriff Granger greeted us. "My gut tells me Bates and Knox are behind everything, but I have no proof to charge them with anything other than the attack on the two of you."

"It's a start," I said.

"Not much of one. Bates was already released from the hospital and made bail."

Zack narrowed his eyes at Granger. "You've got Knox locked up, though, right? The guy violated parole."

The sheriff grimaced. "Yeah, that was the plan."

"But?"

"I assigned a cop to guard him at the hospital. Knox gave him the slip."

I gasped. "How?"

"The cop unlocked Knox's handcuffs so he could use the bathroom. Once in the bathroom, Knox closed the door, then faked a fall and screamed for help. Only he hadn't fallen, knocked the cop out, grabbed his gun, and ran. We've got an APB out on him."

My voice climbed two octaves. "So the two guys who tried to kill us hours ago are both free, who knows where, doing who knows what?"

Granger scowled as he scrubbed his jaw. "We'll get Knox. I've got everyone out looking for him. As for Bates, the judge set bail at a hundred grand, thinking that would be enough to keep him locked up. It wasn't."

"Who posted his bail?" asked Zack.

Granger spit out the name. "Paxton."

Before either Zack or I could respond, Deputy Norwood rushed into the office. "Something may be going on at Three Sisters."

EIGHTEEN

"What kind of something?" asked Granger.

"Not sure, sir. A 9-1-1 call came in but before the caller said anything, dispatch heard a scream. The operator tried calling back, but the phone went directly to voice mail."

"Do we know whose phone?"

"Unknown. It wasn't a local number."

"Did dispatch try calling the winery directly or any of the sisters?"

Deputy Norwood nodded. "She did, sir. No one answered any of the phones."

Sheriff Granger muttered a string of expletives, then began barking orders, ending with one for Zack and me as he raced out of the office. "You two are with me." A split second later, he stopped short, pivoted back toward us. Almost as an afterthought, he added, "If you folks wouldn't mind?"

When we both agreed, he told us to meet him at the entrance. He joined us two minutes later. He'd donned a bulletproof vest and clutched two more in his arms, passing one to me and one to Zack. "I'm hoping we won't need these but better safe than sorry."

After donning the protective gear, Zack and I left the new rental in the visitors' parking lot and piled into Sheriff Granger's Suburban. We sped off to the winery with two other department vehicles following behind us.

No one spoke during the short drive. However, I didn't need mindreading abilities to know all three of us were on the same wavelength in believing Bates and Knox had set out to finish what they'd started last night.

We arrived at Three Sisters to find no cars in the guest parking lot and no fieldhands working in the vineyards visible from our vantage point. Given the extreme heat that had blown in shortly after noon, the winery staff had probably quit for the day. Current guests were either still out sightseeing or off to extremely early bird dinners.

Before parking in front of the main house, the sheriff radioed to his deputies to wait in their vehicles. He then pulled around the side to check the employee parking area behind the house. We found only two vehicles. Granger inclined his head toward them. "That's Hart's pickup and Miss Constantia's car."

A sickening sense of dread coursed through my body. If Constantia's car was here, she should be somewhere on the property. Why hadn't she answered her phone when the 9-1-1 dispatcher had called her? Were we too late?

Granger looped around the nearly empty parking area, returned to the front of the house, and parked the Suburban. Before exiting the vehicle, he turned to us. "Best if you two wait here until we do a sweep." He then stepped from the vehicle and drew his gun. The other law enforcement personnel stepped from their vehicles. With guns also drawn, they joined the sheriff.

Granger ordered two of the deputies to cover the back door. He and the remaining two deputies, including Deputy Norwood, climbed the porch steps and entered the house through the unlocked front door.

I'm very much aware of my own shortcomings. Patience has never been one of my virtues. For me, each second that Zack and I waited in the Suburban was akin to watching paint dry. I itched to jump from the car and do something—anything—to help. If only I had a clue as to what I could do.

After a few minutes, Deputy Norwood emerged from the house and waved us over. We exited the Suburban and joined her on the porch. "The sheriff wants to see you both in the kitchen."

We followed her through the house and found the sheriff bent over a woman's prone body. As we approached, he stood and stepped aside. "Either of you recognize this woman? Deputy Norwood seems to think she may be one of the guests."

I stared down at the woman who'd acted hostile toward me after Hart's murder. "Is she dead?"

He shook his head and pointed to a lump the size of an ostrich egg on the back of her head. "Knocked out."

"She arrived with three friends sometime after Waylon's murder. All crime junkies."

Granger raised an eyebrow. "You've spoken with them?"

"I wouldn't call it a conversation. We exchanged words. After Jolene discovered Hart's body, they raced upstairs, hoping to view the crime scene. Others followed behind her."

"And you barred them from the room?"

"Zack ordered them back downstairs. They weren't exactly pleased."

I glanced back at the woman. From the size of the lump, I doubted the wannabe sleuth would regain consciousness anytime soon. "It looks bad."

Granger agreed. "I've radioed for an ambulance."

"What about Constantia?" asked Zack.

"She's not here. We've searched every nook and cranny of the house. My other deputies are checking the barn and the various outbuildings. I've called in reinforcements. Once they arrive, we'll comb the vineyard, the woods, and the walking trails."

"That's probably a waste of time," I said. "If Bates and Knox are behind this, do you think they're stupid enough to leave her on her own property again?"

He frowned. "Probably not but we still need to rule out the winery grounds before we figure out where else to look. They also wouldn't be dumb enough to bring her to Paxton's house. That leaves about a million places in the county they could dump her body."

My heart skipped a beat, and not in a good way. I glanced around the kitchen but saw no signs of a struggle or any other evidence to indicate a murder had occurred. From what I could tell, the tourist lying comatose on the floor was the only thing out of place in the spotless kitchen. "You think Constantia is already dead?"

Granger sighed. "I hope I'm wrong."

That made three of us. We needed some way to narrow down where to search for her. "Can't you track her phone?"

"I'd first need a warrant. That takes time."

My mind began scrolling through the hours since we'd discovered Constantia in the barn last night. As I began going over what had happened to Zack and me this morning, an idea surfaced. "What type of vehicle does Bates drive?"

"A late model gray Ford pickup. F-150. Why?"

I turned to Zack. "Was that pickup truck this morning a Ford F-150?"

"It was." He then explained to Granger how we suspected someone of following us when we left the hospital. He opened his phone, brought up the GPS app, and turned the phone toward Granger. "This is the road they turned off when we pulled into the gas station."

I took over. "When we drove through the intersection afterwards, I noticed two gray pickups, one parked at the motel down the street and the other in front of the tattoo parlor across the street."

Granger squinted at the screen. "You think they switched trucks and got far enough ahead of you to chop down a tree and block the road before you arrived?" He sounded skeptical. "Seems highly unlikely."

"Actually," I countered, "it's extremely likely. Cars and trucks were whipping past us left and right. Some doing at least ninety miles an hour or more."

Zack agreed. "Especially if Bates and Knox knew our destination."

Again, Granger looked skeptical. "That's one of the many things puzzling me. How did they know where you were headed this morning?"

"It's not rocket science," said Zack. He once again brought up an app on his phone and showed the screen to the sheriff. "They'd only have to check the wineries' social media accounts. As you can see, Grape Expectations posted that I'd be photographing there today so all the crafters knew when to show up if they wanted their wares photographed."

Granger grew silent. He scrubbed at his stubble, his mouth skewed and his brows forming a deep vee. After a moment, he turned to Deputy Norwood. "You wait here for the ambulance. I'm heading over to the Rest-a-Spell. Join me once the ambulance leaves."

"Yes, sir."

As we followed the sheriff back to his Suburban, he reached for his radio and issued updated orders, diverting half the backup to meet us at the motel.

~*~

In less than fifteen minutes, the sheriff arrived at the gas station where Zack had topped the tank off that morning. He hung a right at the intersection and slowly cruised down the street, passing the Rest-a-Spell Motel on our right. The one-story structure consisted of twelve units, probably built back in the middle of the last century. The peeling paint and rusted wrought iron trim suggest that was also the last time the building had seen a fresh coat of paint.

A battered green pickup was parked in front of the motel office, but all the parking spaces in front of the units were empty. No gray Ford pickup was parked across the street at the strip mall. Granger hung a right at the next corner, stopping at the driveway leading to the alley behind the motel. No vehicles hid in the alley, but a Dumpster sat a few feet from the driveway.

I held my breath as Zack hopped out of the Suburban and jogged over to the Dumpster. he raised both lids and peered inside before returning to the vehicle. "Nothing suspicious. Only a day or two worth of pizza boxes, beer cans, and empty whiskey bottles."

I let loose a lungful of relief.

Granger radioed his backup for their ETA, then issued orders for when they arrived. He directed two officers to cover the alley. Norwood and her new partner were to position themselves out of sight but in view of the motel. He then drove a block away, turned down another side street, and parked. "Let's mosey on over to have a friendly chat with the manager."

Bulletproof vests are not exactly standard issue for magazine crafts editors. I had no idea how heavy and bulky they were until I'd strapped myself into one. On a day when the mercury had climbed near three digits, walking the short distance back to the motel was akin to running a marathon. In a sauna. While wearing a snowsuit. I glanced at Zack and Granger. Neither man appeared bother by the heat. Was the Y chromosome devoid of sweat glands?

Visions of the air-conditioned motel office spurred me forward. That and the silver lining of the pounds literally dripping off my body. However, when we arrived at the office, we were met not by a welcome chill but with a blast of warm air from an ancient wall-mounted AC unit. I stifled a groan.

The clerk on duty, a pimple-faced kid barely out of puberty, ignored us. He sat at a computer behind the counter, his feet propped on a desktop, a video game controller balanced on his thighs as he defended the planet from neon green insect-like space aliens. Given the decibel level from a combination of heavy metal music and laser cannon fire, perhaps he hadn't heard us enter the shabby lobby.

The sheriff walked around the counter and grabbed the controller. The kid jumped up, about to deck the sheriff when he stopped short, fists in midair, his eyes bulging. He took a step back and lowered his arms.

Granger reached across the desk and switched off the computer. "Smart move, Rusty. I sure wouldn't want to lock you up for assaulting an officer."

"No, sir. Sorry. I thought someone was robbing me."

"Your daddy here?"

Rusty looked around the small room, as if he'd find his father hiding behind the dead potted plants on the large plate-glass windowsill or sitting on the two rickety wooden folding chairs in the waiting area. "Guess not."

Sheriff Granger pulled out his phone and brought up a photo of Knox he'd snapped at the hospital. "Is this guy staying here?"

Rusty nodded. "He checked in about a week ago. He's our only guest right now."

"Which room?"

"Seven."

"We need to get into that room."

Rusty squinted at the sheriff. "Don't you need a warrant or something?"

"Not for a wellness check."

Rusty hesitated. "I don't know. I'm not supposed to leave the office. Besides, he ain't here. I saw him drive off earlier."

"You have three options, Rusty. Either you unlock the door for me, or you give me the key."

The kid squinted. "That's only two."

"The third option is I toss your hiney into lockup for impeding a police investigation."

Rusty reached under the counter, retrieved a set of keys, and handed them to the sheriff.

"Now, I want you to leave, lock the office behind us, get in your truck, and head home."

"I can't do that. My daddy will skin me alive if I leave before he returns."

"I'll square things with him. I don't know what's about to go down here, and I don't want you anywhere nearby if bullets start flying."

"B...b...bullets?"

"You heard me, Rusty. Now, move."

"Yes, sir." He grabbed his keys from his pocket, then held the door for us. Once we'd all exited the office, he locked the door, jumped into his pickup, and sped out of the parking lot.

The sheriff pointed down the street. "Miss Anastasia, there's a small park half a block from here. I'd appreciate it if you'd head over there and wait until we check things out here."

I crossed my arms and turned to Zack. "I'm not leaving you."

"I need to know you're safe."

"While you play James Bond? I need to know *you're* safe."

"I will be. I have training. You don't."

"Wow! You do realize you just proved my alphabet agency theory?"

"We'll discuss that later."

"And you're not denying it this time."

Zack pointed in the direction of the park. "Please. I'll call you once we know it's safe."

"You'd better." Part of me couldn't tear my gaze from his face, but tears had begun to gather behind my eyes.

Not knowing how long I could stave off the waterworks, I broke eye contact and laced into Granger. "I'm holding you responsible. You'd better make sure nothing happens to my husband."

"Yes, ma'am."

I turned my back on both men. With my head held high and forcing myself not to glance back, I headed across the parking lot toward the sidewalk. I'd only taken a few steps down the street when my phone rang. "Tell me you're alive," I demanded.

"Get back here and see for yourself. We need your help."

Zack hung up before I could ask him anything. I ran the short distance back to the motel, swung open the door to Room Seven, and gasped.

NINETEEN

Constantia, Roussanne, and Marsala sat propped on the floor, their backs against the wall to the left of the room, their mouths gagged, their arms outstretched and crossed with their wrists trussed to their ankles, simulating human pretzels. On his knees, Sheriff Granger bent over Constantia, working with a Swiss Army Knife to remove her gag, while Zack worked on Roussanne's gag.

Zack and I locked eyes for a moment before he said, "See if you can loosen Marsala's gag."

I dropped to the floor beside her. "Did Bates and Knox do this?"

She punctuated a nod with a grunt.

The sheet from one of the two twin beds in the room had been stripped and torn to form the gags. I set to work, but her captors had wet the cotton before tying the gag with multiple knots, making it nearly impossible to untie.

What I wouldn't give for a pair of scissors or my trusty X-acto knife. At least I had both fingernails and experience dealing with knotted yarn and embroidery floss. All I needed was time and good lighting. Unfortunately, I had neither. Bates and Knox might return at any moment, and the lighting in the room consisted of one low-watt overhead bulb. Pulling back the drapes wasn't an option. It would act as a red flag, alerting the two kidnappers when they returned to the motel.

I'd finally picked away at the first of the five knots securing Marsala's gag, when Sheriff Granger finished cutting through Constantia's gag. As she gulped in a deep lungful of air, he tossed me his knife.

Ever the Southern lady, in a shaky voice Constantia first thanked the sheriff before asking, "How did you find us?"

Granger nodded toward me. "You have Miss Anastasia to thank for that."

Constantia's voice grew stronger. "See, Buck? I told you she'd be a help, didn't I?"

"Yes, you did, ma'am. The sheriff briefly locked eyes with me. "And you were right."

Zack had freed Roussanne from her gag. After a few deep breaths, she asked, "Where exactly are we?"

When Granger gave her the location, she gasped. "How in the world did you figure that out?"

"Long story," said Zack.

"We'll fill you in later." I continued to snip away at Marsala's gag. Cutting through multiple layers of soggy cotton with miniature scissors proved harder than I'd expected. No wonder Zack and Granger had struggled.

"They came up behind me," said Roussanne, "and threw a feed sack over my head. Then they grabbed my purse, hogtied me, tossed me in the back of a pickup, nearly smothering me with horse blankets."

She rubbed her arms. "I swear, my bruises have bruises."

Constantia suddenly choked back a sob. "I think Knox killed one of our guests."

Granger had begun to remove her zip ties, first releasing her wrists from her ankles. "She's alive and at the hospital."

Constantia groaned as she flexed her muscles. "Thank goodness. Will she be all right?"

"Hopefully. I haven't heard anything yet."

"Where were her friends?" I asked.

"Gone to dinner. She stayed behind with a migraine. Or so she claimed. I suspect she planned to snoop around looking for clues to the murders. She wandered into the kitchen as I was struggling with Bates. Knox coldcocked her from behind with a gun. The poor woman never saw it coming."

As Zack worked on Roussanne's zip ties, she explained how each of them had wound up at the motel. "They grabbed us one at time. I was grabbed as I left home this morning. Marsala was already here when they dumped me. Then they left and returned with Constantia."

"Any idea where they are now?" asked Granger.

I'd loosened Marsala's gag enough to pull it away from her mouth. She moistened her lips, then spoke for the first time. "Out getting drunk."

Constantia elaborated. "They were arguing about the best way to dispose of our bodies after it got dark tonight and decided they'd think better over tequila shots and nachos."

Zack and Granger had both finished freeing Constantia and Roussanne and set to work on Marsala's zip ties as I finished removing her gag. I stood and stepped into the bathroom in search of a glass. All three women needed water, but when I noticed the disgusting condition of the bathroom and the one cloudy glass sitting on the sink, I decided after the ordeal they'd suffered, the sisters didn't need to risk contracting a parasitic or bacterial infection.

As I turned to leave the bathroom, something shiny caught my eye. I flicked the light switch and took a closer look. Fragments of plastic, glass, and circuitry floated in the rusty toilet water. Returning to the main room, I gave the sisters the bad news. "Looks like they flushed your phones."

"We know," said Roussanne. "They took turns smashing them with a hammer. Gleefully."

"Like back in the day," said Constantia, "when they used to pull the wings off butterflies."

Granger's radio crackled to life. He listened as his backup indicated they were now in position. "I radioed for additional backup. The sisters are here and safe. Norwood, we're in Room Seven. Come get my keys and drive them home. The rest of you sit tight. We're going to set a trap for Bates and Knox."

Constantia still sat on the floor, rubbing the circulation back into her hands and feet, but Roussanne and Marsala had risen and were leaning against the wall.

Granger reached a hand down to Constantia and helped her to her feet. He then addressed all three women. "Are you ladies capable of walking a couple of blocks?"

The three took a few tentative steps across the room. "I'll run if I have to," said Marsala. "I'm not staying here a moment longer than necessary."

The others agreed as Deputy Norwood entered the room. She quickly scoped out the situation without commenting. After

Granger handed her the keys to his Suburban and told her where he'd parked, he turned to Zack and me. "Thank you. We'll handle things from here. You two go with them. I'll catch up with you later."

I didn't argue and was more than happy to comply. We knew Knox had a gun. Although Bates had turned over his service weapon to Granger, he struck me as the kind of man who owned an arsenal. I had no desire to stick around for the gunfight at the Rest-a-Spell Motel. This time Zack agreed with me.

As we headed toward the door, Constantia stopped, turned back to Granger, and wrapped her arms around him. "You be careful, Buck. You hear?"

"Yes, ma'am."

No one spoke during the short walk to the Suburban. We were all too busy scanning our surroundings, on alert for any gray pickup trucks. If Bates and Knox drove past us on their way back to the motel, we were sitting—or rather, walking—ducks. Hopefully, they were still throwing back tequila shots and stuffing their faces with nachos.

Six huge sighs of relief filled the interior of the sheriff's vehicle once we'd piled in and buckled our seatbelts. As soon as Deputy Norwood pulled away from the curbside parking space and drove toward the highway, the sisters began bombarding us with questions.

After we'd caught them up, Roussanne asked, "Do you think they killed Waylon?"

"And Hart?" added Constantia.

I had continually pondered these same questions, but motives eluded me. I hadn't uncovered any connection between Waylon and either man to suggest a reason for his murder. From everything I'd learned, the one person who stood to gain from Waylon's death was Carter Hewitt, the land developer. However, according to Sheriff Granger, the man had a solid alibi.

As for Hart, I'd heard enough about his past to suggest he may have had some sort of altercation with Bates. But over what? Had Bates invested in the cryptocurrency scheme? I'd only caught a glimpse of some of the names on the spreadsheet listing the investors. If he'd invested, I would have thought either Constantia or Sheriff Granger would have mentioned such a pertinent fact.

Had Bates acted at the behest of someone else? Perhaps his uncle? Would former Deputy Lyle Paxton Bates murder for money? Sheriff Granger hadn't ruled out the possibility, and he certainly knew Bates better than I did.

One thing was obvious, though. Since Hart was killed before Granger canned Bates, the ex-deputy hadn't killed Hart to get back at Constantia. If Bates killed Hart, he had another reason.

And where did Lonnie Knox fit into all of this? If he'd wanted revenge on the three sisters, even though they had nothing to do with Grammy Mead cutting him out of her will, why not exact that revenge as soon as he'd learned he was disinherited?

What did he hope to gain by killing the sisters? Did he believe that if he got away with murder, he'd inherit the winery? Or maybe he thought Dalton would inherit, and he'd wheedle his way back into his son's life to get his hands on the sisters' estates. Or perhaps he also planned to cause the demise of his own son. He'd had nothing but time the last twenty years for his anger and bitterness to fester into fantastical revenge plots. Had he chosen to enact one of them?

I needed more information about Knox, and who better to ask than his cousins? "We know Lonnie Knox is your cousin, that your grandmother disowned him, and he tried to sue for a share of her estate. We also know that Dalton Radley is his son and Roussanne and Waylon raised him after his mother's death."

Deputy Norwood glanced into the rearview mirror, and our eyes met. She raised one eyebrow. "You are good. How'd you learn all that in four days?"

I shrugged. "People talk. I listen." And sometimes I prod them along with the right questions, but instead of adding that, I directed my attention back to the sisters. "What more can you tell us about Knox?"

Constantia rode shotgun. She twisted in her seat to face toward the back of the Suburban where Zack and I sat in the third row of seats. Before speaking, she scowled. "He's the family bad seed. Looks like prison failed at rehabilitating him."

"Did any of you know he'd returned to the area?"

Roussanne and Marsala looked over their shoulders at us. "We hadn't seen him in years," said Roussanne. "But Waylon kept track of him. He figured at some point after Dalton came into his inheritance, Knox might show up and try to manipulate Dalton."

"When did Dalton come into his trust fund?" asked Zack.

"He hasn't," said Constantia. "Not until he turns thirty-five in three years, but as trustees we have discretion to tap into the fund for educational purposes."

"Dalton grew up working at Three Sisters," said Roussanne. "He's always shown an interest in becoming a vintner. After he graduated college with a business and marketing degree, we sent him to the same program Constantia attended in France."

"Once he completed the program," added Marsala, "we also gave him money to start Vin de la Terre on the land Grammy Mead left him."

"You have no idea why Knox suddenly showed up here?" I asked.

"None," said Roussanne. "The last time we saw him was at the reading of Grammy Mead's will. No one knew how he'd even found out, but it was the first time he'd returned since running off. He didn't stay long. As soon as he learned she'd disinherited him, he stormed out of the lawyer's office. The next day, the three of us were served with papers. He'd filed suit to contest the will."

"He didn't show up for the court case?" asked Zack.

"He couldn't," said Roussanne. "It took several years for the case to come up on the court docket. By then, Lonnie was doing twenty-five years in a state penitentiary in Mississippi for armed robbery and assault with a deadly weapon. He'd robbed a liquor store at gunpoint and nearly killed the clerk."

"Until today," added Marsala, "we had no idea he'd been released. He still had five years left on his sentence."

Constantia scoffed. "Must have been due to prison overcrowding. Or maybe he bribed someone. I can't imagine they let him out early for good behavior. Lonnie was never good a day in his life."

Constantia's sisters nodded in agreement.

~*~

After Deputy Norwood dropped Zack and me off to pick up the rental, we followed her back to Three Sisters. By now the sun had begun its dip toward the mountains, and the sky had once again transformed into an Impressionistic painting.

I leaned my head against the headrest, closed my eyes, and sighed. "Could've been worse."

Zack reached for my hand and laced his fingers through mine. "Could've been much worse."

"I've had worse."

"We both have. Still, some honeymoon, huh?"

I swiveled my neck toward him and opened one eye. His eyes projected a mischievous twinkle. "On a scale of one to ten? I'd rank it a negative fifty."

"You're being generous."

"I didn't want to hurt your feelings."

He lifted my hand and brought it to his lips. "I owe you."

"We owe each other, but for now, I'll settle for dinner and a bottle of wine. Or two or three."

He quirked an eyebrow. "Two or three?"

"Maybe four. It's been one of those days."

As we drove down the driveway at Three Sisters, we saw several cars parked in the visitor lot and a man pacing back and forth in the shadows of the porch. He froze when Deputy Norwood pulled the Suburban in front of the main house. As soon as Marsala jumped from the Suburban, he ran down the steps and scooped her up in his arms. I recognized him as her dinner companion from the other night.

Constantia and Roussanne joined them, all three sisters verbally tripping over each other as they explained their harrowing ordeal. As Zack and I stepped from the car, we heard the man say, "Buck called and told me what happened and to meet you here."

In the background, I heard the crackle of Deputy Norwood's radio. Once the communication had ended, she joined Zack and me. "Sheriff Granger said Bates and Knox are back behind bars. He'll stop by later."

She paused as she made her way back to the Suburban, turned around and said, "I'm glad everyone is safe."

Not quite, I thought. Waylon Oakley and Hart Kingston were

still both dead. So far, there were no suspects. However, the more I puzzled together the bits and pieces I'd learned and overheard, the more I believed one motive—revenge—tied all the crimes together. The problem was proving it.

Once Deputy Norwood drove off, Marsala's mystery man approached us. He held out his hand to me. "Fisk Rutledge, ma'am. I hear I owe you for saving my wife and her sisters."

"I can't take all the credit." I smiled toward Zack. "It was a group effort."

"With quite a bit of help from the sheriff," added Zack.

"Nonsense." Constantia joined us. "You're too modest, Anastasia."

"True," said Roussanne. "Without you figuring out where they'd taken us, Bates and Knox would have succeeded in their plot to kill us."

"I can't wait for the Sleuth Sayer to interview us for a future podcast," said Constantia. My mouth dropped open, but before I could utter a single word, she added, "but for now, let's all go inside, open a few bottles of wine, and scrounge up some dinner."

Fisk wrapped his arm around Marsala's shoulders and begged off. "If you don't mind, I'd like to take my wife home and spend a quiet evening together."

Constantia nodded. "Suit yourself."

Sadness clouded her eyes. As I glanced toward Roussanne, I noticed an identical expression on her face. Neither woman would ever again spend a quiet evening at home with their husbands. My heart ached for them. I wanted to offer them closure before we returned to New Jersey, but there were still too many loose threads to this story.

Once Marsala and Fisk left, Constantia herded us into the

house. Roussanne tasked herself with opening a few bottles of wine while Constantia raided the fridge. Within minutes, she'd compiled a massive charcuterie board, complete with assorted cheeses, dried fruits and grapes, preserved meats, nuts, pickles and olives, veggies, assorted spreads, jams, honey and mustard, crackers, and a sliced baguette. Roussanne poured four glasses of wine as the four of us settled around the kitchen island.

Before any of us had taken more than a sip or a bite, we heard the front door open and the sheriff call out, "Anyone home?"

Constantia answered. "In the kitchen, Buck."

A moment later, the sheriff stood in the doorway, his arm bandaged and in a sling. Constantia scowled at him. "Didn't I tell you to be careful?"

"Yes, you did, ma'am."

Constantia pulled a face and muttered under her breath loud enough for all to hear. "Typical man. Never listens."

Granger blushed. "Tried my best."

"Who did what to you?"

"Knox winged me." He smiled. "Along with everything else, now we've got him on attempted murder of a law enforcement officer."

She stared wide-eyed at him. "You didn't deliberately get in the way of a bullet, did you?"

"Now, Miss Constantia, I may be a good ol' country boy, but I'm not stupid."

She nodded. "Just making sure. With you boys, I never know." She shook her head and corrected herself. "Knew. Pull up a stool and join us for some dinner. You off duty?"

"Yes, ma'am."

She sidled off her stool and grabbed another wine glass. Not bothering to ask his preference, she poured a glass of Merlot and handed it to him.

Meanwhile, Constantia's slip of the tongue had given me the opening I needed to tie together a few of the dangling threads of this crime wave. I turned to Sheriff Granger. "Connect the dots for me. Exactly how far back do all of you go?"

"All of whom?" asked Roussanne. "Us?"

I threw out the names of every man somehow connected to the various crimes—both past and current—that had occurred in this seemingly quiet and picturesque region. "The sheriff, Waylon Oakley, Hart Kingston, Lonnie Knox, Beau Paxton, and Carter Hewitt. We already know Bates is Paxton's nephew, Waylon and Hart were brothers-in-law, and Knox is your cousin, but I get the sense the connections run deeper than that."

Roussanne's squinted at me. "Why are you asking?"

"Because I'm beginning to think something that occurred in the past precipitated everything that's happened around here the last few days."

"Everything?" asked Roussanne. "Even Waylon's murder?"

"That's when it started, right? Unless you've been dealing with an ongoing crime spree prior to Waylon's death."

Her eyes widened. "No, of course not."

The sheriff drained his wine glass before explaining. "We all went to school together. Except Bates. He was still a kid when we graduated high school. His mama is much younger than her brother, and Lyle's the baby of the family."

"Spoiled rotten from Day One," said Constantia. "Which most likely explains the way he turned out."

"What's Knox's connection to Bates and Paxton?" asked Zack.

"Knox and Representative Paxton were both on the football

team," said Granger. "Along with Hart and Hewitt. Hart played quarterback. He won a spot at UT. Knox was the second-string quarterback but dropped out and ran off before graduation."

"As for a connection to Bates?" He frowned. "Lyle was a starry-eyed football groupie. He hung around the team so much that the coach put him to work as a junior ball boy."

"What about Waylon?" I asked. "Was he on the football team?"

Roussanne shook her head. "Waylon never played sports, but he did have a..." She hesitated, chewing on her lower lip. "...a major...altercation with Lonnie right before Lonnie disappeared."

TWENTY

Now we were getting somewhere. "What sort of altercation?

Roussanne stared into the wine glass she clutched with both hands and continued to worry her lip. "Waylon was always a champion of the underdog. We all suspected Lonnie of mistreating Bethany, but Bethany was too scared of him to do or say anything. Waylon confronted him. He gave Lonnie an ultimatum—leave Bethany alone, or he'd report him. Lonnie laughed in his face and told Waylon to mind his own business."

"And did he?" asked Zack.

She looked up, eyeing each one of us in turn. "A day later, Waylon and I were walking along the creek and found Bethany. Lonnie had..." Her voice caught. "...had taken advantage of her, but she refused to go to the hospital or report the attack. Waylon blamed himself, that his confronting Lonnie had resulted in retaliation against Bethany."

Constantia gasped. "Why didn't you ever tell me?"

"Bethany swore us to secrecy. She was too afraid of both

Lonnie and her father." She turned to Zack and me to explain. "Bethany's father was abusive in his own right. She feared he'd blame her for leading Lonnie on."

I bit back the comment on the tip of my tongue and allowed Roussanne to continue. "But Waylon had another idea, something he believed would permanently put an end to Lonnie's reign of terror, not just against Bethany but everyone he bullied."

"What did Waylon do?" I asked.

"He hid Bethany, then led Lonnie to believe he was about to be arrested for statutory rape. He knew Lonnie would run, and Bethany and everyone else would be rid of him for good. The plan worked great except for one huge problem."

Constantia frowned. "Lonnie left Bethany with a permanent reminder of him."

Roussanne muttered into her wine glass. "No good deed goes unpunished."

"Waylon wasn't responsible for Bethany getting pregnant," said Sheriff Granger. "And chances are, Lonnie had been taking advantage of her for some time. We all suspected something was going on. No one knows when she became pregnant."

"I tried to tell Waylon that," said Roussanne, "but he stilled blamed himself."

"And to Bethany's credit," added Constantia, "she loved that baby."

While an awkward silence settled over the kitchen, my mind whirled as I connected various dangling threads. "As sad as this story is, I believe it may be the key to both murders and the attack on the sisters."

The sheriff eyed me. "What makes you think so, Miss Anastasia?"

"Lonnie Knox gets out of prison after twenty years, and what's the first thing he does? He heads home to settle a score with Waylon."

"Why?" asked Roussanne.

"Because in his mind, he's convinced himself that if not for Waylon, he would have graduated and secured a walk-on spot to play football somewhere. Thanks to Waylon, he never got the opportunity."

"His own actions were responsible for what happened to him, not Waylon," said Roussanne.

"But bullies never accept responsibility for their actions," said Zack. "They always have to blame someone else."

"Do you think he also killed Hart?" asked Constantia.

I nodded. "Quite possibly. Hart went on to have a stellar college football career, even if he never made it in the NFL. Knox had twenty-years to grow his resentment toward both Waylon and Hart. Maybe he figured, if not for Hart, the starting quarterback position—and a spot on the UT team—would have gone to him. And since he probably believed he was really the better quarterback, Hart robbed him of becoming a superstar."

"How does that tie into what happened to me yesterday and the three of us today?" asked Constantia.

"If I'm correct, Lonnie Knox is on a Revenge Tour. You and your sisters inherited your grandmother's estate. He got nothing."

"He tried to kill us over something we had nothing to do with," said Roussanne.

"It doesn't matter," said Zack. "Not in Knox's twisted mind. You got his share of the estate. He wanted payback. He blamed all of you for everything that has happened in his life." He nodded toward me. "Even the attack on my wife and me fits into

Anastasia's theory. We saved Constantia last night after he left her to die."

"We didn't force him to hold up a liquor store," said Constantia.

Granger scrubbed at his jaw as he chewed on an olive. "He's likely convinced himself otherwise." He then turned to me and Zack. "It all makes sense, but how do we prove any of it? Right now, all we have are theories and speculation. Any suggestions?"

"As a matter of fact, I do have one." I frowned at the thought before adding a disclaimer. "I'm just not sure how I feel about it. Or how anyone else will feel about it."

Four sets of eyes stared at me. I took a deep breath. "We need Lyle Paxton Bates to testify against Lonnie Knox."

"Why would he do that?" asked Roussanne.

"To save his own skin," said Sheriff Granger. "But the D.A. would need to cut a deal with him."

Constantia narrowed her eyes at him. "What sort of deal, Buck?"

"Probably dropping all charges against him."

"Are you out of your mind? Lonnie didn't act alone. Lyle helped him."

"He's going to lawyer up," explained the Sheriff. "Probably already has. Any lawyer worth his salt is going to want jail time off the table. But this is all in the D.A.'s hands, not mine. And it would be best if the five of you signed off on it."

"You mean, the D.A. could offer Lyle a deal even if we didn't want him to?" asked Roussanne.

"Yes, ma'am."

"That doesn't seem right. He should pay for what he did to us."

"He'll pay," said the sheriff. "In other ways."

"Like?" asked Constantia.

"You'll have to leave that to the D.A., but I'll give him my input. Trust me, Bates won't come out of this smelling like a rose. More like one of those corpse flowers they have over at UT in Knoxville."

After we finished dinner, Zack and I walked out with the sheriff. I had one more question for Granger before we bid him goodnight and headed to our cottage. "Do you know why Lonnie Knox received early release?"

"Overcrowding. Why?"

"I wondered if your local state representative might have pulled a few strings," I said.

He thought about that for a moment. "I'll look into it."

"While you're at it," said Zack, "it might prove interesting to learn who Knox regularly communicated with while in prison."

"It sure would, and I know just the person to ask."

~*~

Zack and I arrived at the main house bright and early the next morning. Even given the early hour, guests already filled several of the tables. The true crime busybody ladies were either sleeping in or had departed after their ringleader stumbled into Constantia's kidnapping.

Marsala arrived with the breakfast cart as soon as we settled into a table along the window wall. "Everything okay this morning?" I asked.

She flashed me a smile as she poured orange juice and coffee for us. "Thanks to you. Constantia and Roussanne told me about your conversation last night after Fisk and I went home."

"And?"

"And I hope Lonnie Knox is locked up for the remainder of his miserable life, but Lyle Bates shouldn't get away with what he did. He's an accessory to several crimes."

"I think we're all in agreement on that," said Zack, "but it's in the D.A.'s hands."

Marsala frowned before changing the subject. "Where are you off to today?"

"Grape Expectations. Then I still need to photograph Three Sisters before our flight home tomorrow."

"Saving the best for last?" asked Roussanne.

He flashed her one of his own twinkle-eyed smiles. "Absolutely."

~*~

Walking around Grape Expectations was like strolling through a crafts and fine arts fair. Every conceivable craft was represented by at least one craftsperson, and their exceptional work made me wish I had unlimited discretionary funds. I wanted to buy at least one of everything I saw.

Thanks to Dead Louse of a Spouse, though, my crafts splurging days had gone the way of the dodo bird. However, I could do the next best thing—write about them in *American Woman*.

While the owner led Zack through the vineyards and winemaking facilities, I interviewed many of the crafters, including the woman responsible for the wine label collage hanging above the bed in our Three Sisters cottage. Afterwards, when Zack and I met up, I asked him to take photos of some of the crafters and their wares specifically for my use and not for the *Vine* advertorial.

We were on our way back to Three Sisters when Sheriff Granger called. "Miss Anastasia, any chance I can convince you to relocate to the great state of Tennessee?"

"Probably not, Sheriff, but why are you asking?"

"You know I'm down a deputy, and you'd sure make the perfect replacement."

"Why is that?"

"You not only solved both murders, but you helped solve the cryptocurrency fraud."

Zack and I exchanged a quick look before he returned his concentration to the road. "How did I do that?"

"Will you be returning to Three Sisters anytime soon?"

"We're on our way back now."

"Good. I'll meet you there. Might as well tell all of you at once. And maybe I can get the sisters to help me pressure you into staying."

When he disconnected the call, Zack and I exchanged another look before we both burst out laughing. "Not a chance in Hades," I said. "The people are nice—at least most of those we've met— and the scenery is gorgeous, but the commute to work would be horrendous."

Zack quirked an eyebrow. "That's the only reason?"

"Well, that and there's no way Tennessee is ready for the likes of Lucille Pollack."

~*~

We arrived back at Three Sisters to find the kitchen island set for six and Sheriff Granger already planted on a stool and enjoying a cup of coffee. Constantia stood at the stove, frying up green tomatoes while Marsala arranged a platter of assorted cheeses and Roussanne sliced a loaf of freshly baked bread.

Once Zack and I washed up and Constantia placed a platter of fried green tomatoes in the center of the island, we all joined the sheriff. He seemed in no rush to impart any information, though, first piling food on his plate, then shoveling forkfuls into his mouth.

Across the island I watched Constantia develop a slow seethe. Her plate remained empty as she stared at the oblivious sheriff, her arms crossed over her chest. Finally, she uncrossed her arms and slammed her palms on the island, rattling the dishes. "Out with it, Buck. The suspense is killing us."

Sheriff Granger, placed his knife and fork on his plate, picked up his napkin, and wiped his mouth. "Now, Miss Constantia, I thought you'd at least let us enjoy your excellent fried green tomatoes before they got cold."

My Grandma Periwinkle used to say that honeyed words conquered waspish dispositions. Granger had that lesson down pat. Constantia locked eyes with him. "Fine. But you'll get no dessert until you tell us what happened." She paused for a moment before adding. "Homemade peach cobbler."

"With whipped cream?"

She raised an eyebrow. "Would I serve it any other way?"

Once we finished lunch, Marsala and Roussanne cleared the island, and Constantia made a fresh pot of coffee. While it brewed, she retook her seat at the island, folded her hands in front of her, and eyed Granger. "The floor is yours, Buck."

I caught him glancing toward the stove where the cobbler sat cooling. He pulled his eyes away, cleared his throat, and began. "We all owe a huge debt to Miss Anastasia. As you know, we've had very few murders around here over the years. The ones we've had were cut and dry. We either caught the perpetrator red-handed or had eyewitnesses. What's gone down here this week was completely outside my wheelhouse."

He turned to Constantia. "I'll be the first to admit I bristled when you suggested I ask Miss Anastasia for help investigating Waylon's murder, but I'm also man enough to admit when I'm wrong."

When Constantia nodded her acceptance of what was tantamount to an apology, he continued. "And with Miss Anastasia, I got a two-for-one package deal. Turns out Zack here is far more than just a photographer."

I glanced at my husband. His expression suggested he had no idea what Granger was talking about, which only led me to add another mental checkmark in the Alphabet Agency column.

Granger finally got to the meat of his information. "Miss Anastasia was right about Bates. Faced with a lengthy prison term, he immediately accepted a plea deal and flipped not only on Knox but on Paxton."

"Beau Paxton?" asked Roussanne. "Are you saying our state representative was behind Waylon's murder?"

"I'll get to Paxton in a moment," said Granger. "Lonnie Knox was indeed carrying out a personal vendetta, as Miss Anastasia suggested. He killed both Waylon and Hart."

"Because he blamed them for the way his life turned out?" asked Marsala.

"Exactly. And he came after you and your sisters for the same reason. For twenty years he nursed his grievances. They festered and grew until revenge became his only goal once he got released from prison."

"But how does Beau Paxton figure into that?" asked Constantia.

"Thanks to a suggestion from Zack, I contacted the prison in Mississippi for Knox's phone and visitor records. Turns out both Bates and his uncle were in regular communication with Knox over the years. Paxton greased the wheels for the early release."

"Why?" I asked.

"Because Paxton also wanted both Waylon and Hart permanently eliminated. He knew Knox would do him that favor in exchange for finagling his release."

"I thought he was released due to overcrowding," I said.

"That's the official reason. I suspect a few palms were greased to get him on the list, given he still had five years to serve."

"I don't understand," said Roussanne. "What could Beau Paxton possibly have against my husband?"

Granger turned to me. "Have you figured it out yet, Miss Anastasia?"

I thought for a moment. "I'm guessing it might have something to do with the cryptocurrency fraud."

Granger nodded. "And more. We know that Paxton was Hart's partner in the crypto deal, but what no one realized until Bates started spilling secrets is that Paxton was also in cahoots with Carter Hewitt. They planned to defraud the crypto investors and use the money to buy up land for development. Paxton was Hewitt's silent partner."

"And that's what Hart had discovered and brought to the D.A.?" I asked.

"Yes, ma'am. Once again, you were spot on with your theories. The fund never went belly up as Paxton claimed."

Something about that made no sense to me. "It never occurred to Paxton that Hart or the other investors would want more information about the collapse of the fund?"

"Paxton banked on the fact that quite a few crypto funds were teetering on the brink of bankruptcy. He had a contingency plan consisting of forged documents if he had to provide proof. When a few of those crypto funds suddenly declared bankruptcy due to corporate corruption, Paxton decided the time was right for executing his con."

"What made him partner with Hart?" asked Constantia. "It's not like my husband knew anything about cryptocurrency, and until he started the architectural salvage business, he'd failed at everything he tried."

"Which made him the perfect patsy," said Zack.

"Exactly," said Granger. "Paxton knew Hart would jump at the chance to partner with him, and he'd be the perfect person to convince the other winery owners to invest."

"Because they all wanted to keep Hewitt from buying up land," said Marsala. "They bonded in a common cause."

Granger nodded. "Paxton figured Hart didn't have the smarts to figure out the con until it was too late, but Hart grew suspicious and began digging, even before Paxton announced the fund had gone bust."

"If the fund didn't dissolve," said Zack. "Paxton and Hewitt still have all the investors' money."

"Only Paxton," said Granger. "Looks like he was trying to pull a fast one over on Hewitt. Instead of transferring the funds into the offshore shell company Hewitt had set up, Paxton deposited everything into more than a dozen personal accounts at various banks."

"Rookie mistake," said Zack. "He obviously didn't bother to read *Embezzling for Dummies*."

Granger laughed. "And one that's sealed the deal on his indictment. He has no way to explain away his sudden windfall."

"Does that mean all the investors will recover their investments?" asked Roussanne.

"Plus, what they earned while the money was in the crypto fund," said Granger. "They can still go ahead with buying land to keep the area from turning into one huge megamall."

I thought about our last encounter with Shasta and Nash Summers, how they appeared on the brink of divorce over the possible loss of their winery. This news might save their marriage.

"So that's that," said Granger, clapping his hands together, "the D.A. intends to throw the book at Paxton, Knox, and Hewitt. Now, Miss Constantia, how about that peach cobbler?"

Constantia scowled at him. "But Bates walks free?"

Sheriff Granger shook his head. "Guess I forgot to mention that. Turns out the D.A. wasn't willing to let Bates walk, not given the severity of his crimes. He'll do eighteen months for his involvement."

"Doesn't seem like much for what he did," said Roussanne. "How much time would he have gotten had he not talked?"

"Upwards of fifteen years for each count of attempted murder, but keep in mind, had the D.A. not cut a deal with Bates, we wouldn't have gotten Paxton and Hewitt." Granger turned back to Constantia. "Now, how about that peach cobbler?"

I smiled as I watched the sisters busy themselves serving the cobbler. Zack and I would leave Tennessee knowing we'd helped bring them a bittersweet closure.

We couldn't have prevented what happened. Had we never stepped foot in Tennessee, Lonnie Knox still would have killed Waylon Oakley and Hart Kingston. With the help of Lyle Paxton Bates, he would have also killed Constantia, Roussanne, and Marsala. As for the cryptocurrency fraud, state representative Beau Paxton and developer Carter Hewitt still would have conned the winery owners out of their investments.

Would Sheriff Granger have solved the cases without our help? He freely admitted he didn't think so. Before we parted ways, he tried once more to entice me to give up New Jersey for Tennessee, this time dangling the enticement of a balmier climate. "We never get blizzards."

"Tempting, but you do get tornadoes." Personally, I'd much rather dig out of a Nor'easter that drops two feet of snow than cower in a bathtub as hundred mile an hour winds rip my home apart around me.

"True," he admitted.

"Besides, Sheriff, I like you too much to subject you or anyone else around here to my communist mother-in-law."

Both his eyebrows shot up under the brim of his hat as he zeroed in on Zack. "You're mother's a commie?"

Zack held up both hands. "Not mine."

Apparently, Detective Spader hadn't divulged anything about Lucille when Granger called him to ask about me. "Lucille is my deceased first husband's mother. For reasons beyond my control, I'm stuck with her."

"Sounds like a horror story."

"You've got that right. I'd tell you all about her, but we've got a plane to catch."

"Another time then." He hesitated, scrubbing at his jaw for a moment, then asked, "Miss Anastasia, would you mind if I pick your brain now and then?"

"I'm always happy to chat with you, Sheriff, but let's hope it's a long time before you experience another crime wave."

~*~

One mystery had gone unsolved, though, and as we boarded the plane back to Newark Liberty, I made up my mind to finish listening to the Sleuth Sayer podcasts. Someone was profiting off my life. I wanted to know who and why. And who was supplying her with all that information about me.

By the time the plane landed, I was no closer to uncovering the identity of the Sleuth Sayer. However, as I had listened to the other episodes, I realized who had supplied her with much of the information about my first foray as a reluctant amateur sleuth.

EPILOGUE

Four days from now, my oldest son would graduate from high school. By the end of the summer, Alex would head off to Cambridge, Massachusetts, thanks to a generous scholarship from Shane Lambert. I had little time to stew about the Sleuth Sayer and even less time to do anything about the podcasts, but I obsessed anyway.

We arrived home to a quiet house. Nick, Leonard (the dog formerly known as Mephisto the Devil Dog), and Ralph were still camped across town at Shane Lambert's home. Alex and his classmates had departed Thursday for their senior class trip to a resort in the Pocono Mountains and wouldn't return until tomorrow. Lucille was nowhere in sight.

"She's spending more and more time at Harriet Kleinhample's apartment," I said. "Maybe we can bribe her into moving there permanently."

Zack laughed. "Good luck with that. Knowing Lucille, she'd spite you by not only refusing to leave but making sure Harriet becomes a permanent fixture here."

"Point taken." We dropped our suitcases in the bedroom and headed out for a quiet dinner.

We had finished our main course and were waiting for our dessert to arrive when Zack said, "You've been extremely pensive since we arrived home. You aren't regretting turning Granger down, are you?"

"Hardly. I finished listening to the Sleuth Sayer podcasts on the plane."

"I figured as much. Your expression was too serious. I knew you weren't listening to any of your favorite show tunes."

"I still don't know the identity of the Sleuth Sayer, but I've got a pretty good idea who supplied her with the information."

"So do I."

"Why didn't you tell me?"

"I was hoping I was wrong, but the more I thought about it, I realized I wasn't. The question now becomes, what do you plan to do about it?"

I sighed. "I haven't a clue. I suppose I could still be wrong."

"You're not."

"But why? What was the motivation to blab about me like that? Certainly not spite or malice."

"There's only one way to find out."

"I know, but not now."

"Agreed."

~*~

Late Wednesday afternoon, Zack, Mama, Nick, and I arrived at the Westfield High School football field. Risers had been erected at the fifty-yard line for the graduates and speakers. Several hundred white folding chairs formed even rows below for family and friends. Zack, Mama, Nick, Shane Lambert, and I settled into our reserved first row seats. The high school band began to play, and we rose to our feet to watch the graduating class march across the field to the strains of Elgar's *Pomp and Circumstance.*

As the student with the second highest GPA, Sophie Lambert gave the salutatory address, welcoming family and friends. She was followed by remarks from the principal and president of the school board. Awards were then handed out, with both Alex and Sophie winning several. After the presentation of diplomas, Alex was introduced as the class valedictorian.

I had no idea what my son planned to say. He hadn't shared his speech with me ahead of time. A typical valedictorian speech is inspirational and uplifting. It highlights the shared experiences of the graduating class, talks about lessons learned, and friendships formed over the years. Alex's speech did all that, but then he veered from the tradition of naming the various teachers who had inspired him.

"My high school years were impacted by many great educators. You know who you are and how grateful I am for the honor of learning from you. However, as I stand here today, I want to thank the person who has inspired me more than anyone else in my life. My mother is the most amazing person I've ever met and will probably ever meet."

Tears filled my eyes and choked my throat. Zack reached for my hand and held fast as Alex continued. "Over the last year and a half, my mother has faced and survived adversities that most people will never encounter in an entire lifetime. Her strength of character and refusal to cower in the face of such overwhelming odds has been both an inspiration and a life lesson to my brother and me, as she met each new challenge with ingenuity, creativity, and integrity. She never once lost either her wits or her sense of humor, even at the darkest moments. She never gave up, and she refused to let us give up."

Alex then stared directly at me and finished by saying, "Thank you, Mom. I love you."

I completely lost it. Tears spilled down my cheeks. I placed a hand over my mouth to keep from bawling. Mama pulled a package of tissues from her purse and thrust them at me.

Zack helped me to my feet and wrapped an arm around my shoulders, drawing me close to his side as the band struck up the recessional music, and the graduates filed off the risers. I heaved a series of deep breaths to impede the continuing flow of tears but had minimal success. The next thing I knew, Alex was gripping me in a bear hug, precipitating a fresh flood that soaked the shoulder of his graduation gown.

After what seemed like an eternity, the tears finally stopped. I took a deep breath, and he released me. "You okay, Mom?"

I dried my eyes, blew my nose, and smiled. "Never better."

"Good," said Nick. He yanked at his brother's sleeve. "Let's go. I'm hungry."

We had planned a celebratory dinner with Shane and Sophie. Once we had all arrived at the restaurant and ordered, Alex said, "Anyone know a good lawyer?"

I stared at my son. "Why do you need a lawyer?"

Sophie grinned at us. "Actually, we all do."

"All three of you?" asked Zack.

"All four of us," said Alex. "Sophie, Nick, me, and Mom."

My jaw dropped open. "What's going on?" The three of them certainly didn't look like they'd gotten into any sort of trouble. On the contrary, they appeared ready to burst with excitement.

"Maybe we should start from the beginning," said Sophie. "For our Honors English project this year we created a podcast."

Zack and I exchanged a quick look as he placed a calming hand on my thigh. As much as I had hoped otherwise, there was no longer any doubt as to who had supplied the details of my life to the Sleuth Sayer. But why?

"And it's sort of taken off," said Alex.

All the way to Tennessee and beyond.

"Big time," added Nick.

"What was your role in this?" I asked him. "You're not a senior."

He puffed out his chest. "I handled the technical stuff for them. We used the school's recording studio."

I eyed all three of them across the table. Every true crime junkie in the country now knew about me. How much worse was it about to get? "Define *taken off*."

Alex reached into the pocket of his suit jacket. He withdrew an envelope and handed it to me. I pulled out the single sheet of paper and held it so that both Zack and I could read at the same time. "Is this legitimate?" I asked, recognizing the name of the company.

"It is," said Shane. "I called to verify when Sophie showed me her letter."

"We were hoping the podcast would generate enough in ad revenues to help pay down some of the debt Dad saddled you with," said Alex. "But this..." He pointed to the letter. "If the podcast becomes a TV series, you'll be able to pay off all the remaining bills."

And then some. The option alone would take care of most of what remained. "And that's why you created a podcast about me?

To help me?"

Alex grinned sheepishly. "That and to get an A."

"It worked," said Sophie. "Beyond our wildest dreams."

How could I possibly fault them when they'd had such a pure and unselfish motive? Not only that, but because of the podcast, I had helped bring a killer to justice, prevent three additional murders, and solve a fraud case.

One mystery still needed solving, though. "But who's the Sleuth Sayer?" I asked.

"Oh, that would be me," said Sophie, deepening her voice and assuming a sultry English accent.

ANASTASIA'S COLLAGE CRAFTS

Collage, which comes from the French *coller* and means to stick or glue, is the technique of gluing various two-dimensional materials to a surface to create a unique work of art. Paper, fabric, photographs, wallpaper, gift wrap, magazine pages, and newspaper clippings are some of the materials used in collage. The collage is then often embellished with text and paint and sometimes various 3-dimensional objects. In *A Crafty Collage of Crime*, a framed collage of wine labels hangs in the cottage where Anastasia and Zack are staying.

Collage has been around since the invention of paper in China around 200 BC. It was used by Japanese calligraphers in the 10th century and in medieval Europe as early as the 13th century. Victorians practiced the art of collage to create memorabilia. In the early 1900s cubist painters Pablo Picasso and George Braque coined the word "collage" when they began experimenting with the technique and incorporating it into their drawings and paintings.

The beauty of collage is that you don't have to be skilled in drawing or painting to create visually interesting works of art. All you need is a bit of imagination.

Collage is also an inexpensive craft. All it really requires are paper, scissors, and glue. Three-dimensional collages might also include beads, buttons, shells, ribbon, lace, feathers, wood, pottery shards, costume jewelry or various other found objects.

To create a collage, it's often best to start out with a theme. For instance, if you like flowers, you might want to create a floral collage, cutting out the simple shape of a vase from a patterned piece of paper and a variety of flowers in different sizes and colors from magazines. Arrange the images on a larger piece of solid color or patterned paper.

However, your theme doesn't have to be so literal. For instance, you can make an abstract collage by choosing a specific color or color palette as your theme and creating a composition of only elements of those colors.

Or choose a broader theme, such as birds, sunsets, or even food for a collage you'd hang in your kitchen.

You can also create visual texture by tearing the edges of some of your elements instead of cutting out all of them.

Once you're happy with the arrangement of the elements you've chosen, glue the images in place. Choose glue specifically made for paper. Such glues won't warp or buckle your paper or cause the inks to bleed.

After the glue is dry, you might want to embellish your design further. Using the flower vase collage as an example, with gem glue attach beads or buttons to the center of some of the flowers, decorate the vase with ribbon, highlight specific areas of the design with paint, or add a quote or inspirational saying using calligraphy or a rubber stamp alphabet.

The beauty of collage is that there's no right way or wrong way to create a collage. It's all about letting your imagination run wild and having fun.

A NOTE FROM THE AUTHOR

Dear Readers,

As you all know, Anastasia is a quintessential Jersey girl. However, ever since my husband and I moved to Tennessee two years ago, people have been asking me when Anastasia would be following her author to Music City. My answer? Never! As Anastasia herself said in *A Collage of Crafty Crime*, Tennessee isn't ready for the likes of her communist mother-in-law. Besides, after experiencing my first tornado warning, I couldn't subject Anastasia to anything that harrowing on top of everything else I've dumped on her over the years.

However, to appease my Southern fans who have requested the change of venue, I decided Anastasia and Zack deserved a trip to Tennessee. I hope you liked their adventure. Maybe they'll make a return visit at some point. Meanwhile, if you enjoyed *A Collage of Crafty Crime*, please consider leaving a review at your favorite review site.

Happy reading!

Lois Winston

ABOUT THE AUTHOR

USA Today and Amazon bestselling author Lois Winston began her award-winning writing career with *Talk Gertie to Me*, a humorous fish-out-of-water novel about a small-town girl going off to the big city and the mother who had other ideas. That was followed by the romantic suspense *Love, Lies and a Double Shot of Deception*.

Then Lois's writing segued unexpectedly into the world of humorous amateur sleuth mysteries, thanks to a conversation her agent had with an editor looking for craft-themed mysteries. In her day job Lois was an award-winning craft and needlework designer, and although she'd never written a mystery—or had even thought about writing a mystery—her agent decided she was the perfect person to pen a series for this editor. Thus was born the Anastasia Pollack Crafting Mysteries, which *Kirkus Reviews* dubbed "North Jersey's more mature answer to Stephanie Plum." The series now includes twelve novels and three novellas. Lois also writes the Empty Nest Mysteries, currently at two novels, and one book so far in her Mom Squad Capers series.

To date, Lois has published twenty-one novels, five novellas, several short stories, one children's chapter book, and one nonfiction book on writing, inspired by her twelve years working as an associate at a literary agency.

To learn more about Lois and her books, visit her at www.loiswinston.com where you can sign up for her newsletter and follow her on various social media sites.

Made in the USA
Middletown, DE
16 June 2023